Praise for the novels
of Jessica Barksdale Inclán

When You Go Away

"This is by far Inclán's most daring novel and evidence of a rapidly developing talent that nimbly manipulates the tragic aspects of human nature to produce a book that is true to life in its heartbreaking quest for hope." —*Booklist*

"Muted, poignant drama with an immensely appealing depth, plain grace—and echoes of Inclán's *Her Daughter's Eyes*." —*Kirkus Reviews*

"A story that every beleaguered mother will take comfort from. And comfort is good." —Ann LaFarge, *The Village Ledger* (New York)

"Inclán is courageous in confronting family tragedy and in trying to put a human face on it."—Dan Barnett, *Chico Enterprise-Record* (CA)

"Jessica Inclán immediately brings her readers into the emotional environment of a family in danger of falling apart. . . . A truly gifted writer who has a profound understanding of the characters she creates . . . Inclán has written a powerful novel, filled with the emotional ups and downs of real people in rocky relationships." —Barbara Sloan, *Contra Costa Times*

continued . . .

Written by today's freshest new talents and selected by New American Library, NAL Accent novels touch on subjects close to a woman's heart, from friendship to family to finding our place in the world. The Conversation Guides included in each book are intended to enrich the individual reading experience, as well as encourage us to explore these topics together—because books, and life, are meant for sharing.

Visit us on-line at www.penguin.com.

The Matter of Grace

"[An] engaging, down-to-earth second novel. . . . Inclán has a sharp, compassionate feel for how women look at relationships, sex, and marital issues; her female characters are strong and well-drawn. . . . The twists and turns of Grace's story will keep readers guessing until the final chapters."　　　*—Publishers Weekly*

Her Daughter's Eyes

"A debut novel as gutsy [and] appealing . . . as its heroines. But it is the plight of the teenage sisters, in all their clever foolishness, that strikes at the heart."　　　*—Publishers Weekly*

"A modern-day depiction of familial disintegration with offbeat twists and luminous sparks of hope."　　　*—Booklist*

"Well-written, thoughtful. . . . Inclán never condescends and never judges, preferring to let her subtly drawn people speak for themselves. . . . The understanding portrayal of her teenage heroines—stubborn, careless, and fiercely honest—is remarkably astute."　　　*—Kirkus Reviews*

"An exquisitely poignant look into the heart of a troubled family."
　　　—New York Times bestselling author Deborah Smith

"Poignant, sharply introspective, and thought-provoking. Every parent of a teenager and, indeed, every teenager should read this work with care."　　　*—New York Times* bestselling author
Dorothea Benton Frank

"Haunting, compelling . . . takes the reader on an emotional roller-coaster ride."　　　*—New York Times* bestselling author
Kristin Hannah

JESSICA BARKSDALE INCLÁN

One Small Thing

FICTION FOR THE WAY WE LIVE

NAL Accent
Published by New American Library, a division of
Penguin Group (USA) Inc., 375 Hudson Street,
New York, New York 10014, U.S.A.
Penguin Books Ltd, 80 Strand, London WC2R 0RL, England
Penguin Books Australia Ltd, 250 Camberwell Road, Camberwell, Victoria 3124, Australia
Penguin Books Canada Ltd, 10 Alcorn Avenue, Toronto, Ontario, Canada M4V 3B2
Penguin Books (N.Z.) Ltd, Cnr Rosedale and Airborne Roads,
Albany, Auckland 1310, New Zealand

Penguin Books Ltd, Registered Offices: 80 Strand, London WC2R 0RL, England

First published by New American Library, a division of Penguin Group (USA) Inc.

First Printing, April 2004
10 9 8 7 6 5 4 3 2 1

FICTION FOR THE WAY WE LIVE
REGISTERED TRADEMARK—MARCA REGISTRADA

LIBRARY OF CONGRESS CATALOGING-IN-PUBLICATION DATA:

Inclan, Jessica Barksdale.
  One small thing / Jessica Barksdale Inclan.
    p. cm.
  ISBN 0-451-21119-7
  1. Illegitimate children—Fiction. 2. Married women—Fiction. 3. Suburban life—
Fiction. 4. Childlessness—Fiction. 5. Stepmothers—Fiction. 6. California—
Fiction. 7. Boys—Fiction. I. Title.
  PS3559.N332O54 2004
  813'.6—dc22   2003020304

Set in Simoncini Garamond

Printed in the United States of America

For Mitchell and Julien

It's not having what you want,
It's wanting what you've got.

—Sheryl Crow

ONE

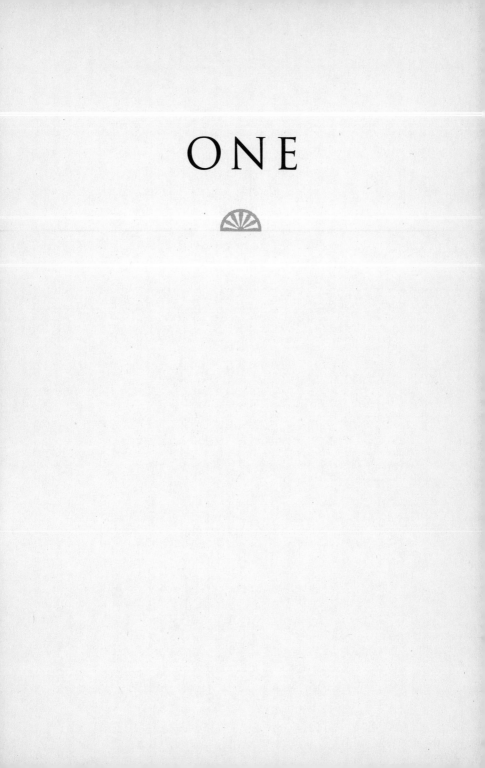

One

Because it was almost a hundred degrees outside, the sky a thin pale blue, the grass on the hills almost waist high, dry, and blowing wild in the hot breeze, Dr. Browne's office was freezing, the nurses cranking up the air conditioner enough that Avery Tacconi's toes were a deep red, almost purple. Under her cotton gown, she shivered, rubbing her thighs together for warmth, wishing Dr. Browne would come in and get this over with. She already knew the answer, anyway. It didn't take an MD to tell her she wasn't pregnant, again. Anyone with an eighth-grade education or an IQ over one hundred could do that. So why, she wondered, was her heart thrumming?

Earlier, in the waiting room with the other women, she'd smiled as she listened to their conversation, nodded when one woman said, "I won't shop anywhere but I Bambini. I just love their furniture. And the clothes! All from Europe. I've gone crazy there in the last weeks." The woman rubbed her nine-month stomach with satisfaction. Avery could see the beak of the woman's distended belly button through her expensive Pea in the Pod maternity outfit. She wondered about the wisdom of having an infertility specialist sharing office space with traditional OB-GYNs, but she knew that a very rounded, full, awkward body was exactly what she wanted. In fact, that was precisely what Avery had written out for herself way back in high school, the schedule like this: finish college at age twenty-two (at the same time deciding upon the man she would marry), find a great job by twenty-two and a half, get married by twenty-five, establish her reputation at her job, get pregnant at twenty-seven, quit said fabulous career, have baby. A perfect, healthy baby, preferably a boy first, then at the end of her twenty-eighth year, a girl for the second baby.

The only things now missing from her careful timeline were the pregnancy and the baby, the order all messed up because even though she was twenty-eight and Dan's count was high, his sperm motile and perfectly shaped—those tiny tadpoles swinging their tails and scurrying around just as they should—she hadn't conceived, not once in two years, not even with the new treatment, the intrauterine insemination, IUI, something she'd never believed she'd have to do.

Everything was off, ruined, because here she was at twenty-eight, no career anymore, no baby one or baby two, her whole future jumbled into a mess she couldn't even begin to forecast.

Sometimes, before she could stop herself, Avery let herself slip into a mother daydream, feeling the soft weight of her baby in her arms, the lovely baby-skin smells of lotions and ointment in her nose, the sounds of her baby's soft breath in her ears. In her dream, she sat in her rocker, with Dan, her mother, and her sister around her, all of them reaching to touch this bundle of wonder. As she thought, her heart would slow, her face would grow slack with joy, and then she'd snap herself out of it, hitting her fist on her thigh, determined not to fall into reverie, into hope, because it was bad luck. Terrible luck. She needed to keep focused on reality.

So here she was, trying to be real. Sitting on the table, shivering, she wished Dr. Browne would come in and tell her the home pregnancy kit had been wrong. It was a miracle! Here was the real, true result right now. He would wave a paper in front of her, and then find the heartbeat for her, the crackly echo loud in the small room. Avery knew this is what would happen, because she'd watched every episode of *Labor and Delivery, Maternity Ward,* and *A Baby Story* on the Learning Channel. Her eyes widened and watered when she heard other women's babies' heartbeats and saw with them the first sonograms, the babies all black fish eyes and veins swimming in the dark uterine sack. Sometimes at night when she lay awake next to her husband, Dan, listening to him sleep, she imagined she felt a flash, the flip of life in her womb. But it always turned out to be gas or bloating or the flu. Still, Avery could imagine it; she knew what it would be like.

"Avery," Dr. Browne said, knocking on the slightly open door and then pushing in. "Here you are?"

"Back again." She felt her fake smile spread across her face. Where else would she be? Running down the street in her gown? Breathing in quickly, she resisted the urge to jump down onto the freezing floor and grab him by the shoulders, demanding, "When? When is it my turn? I did everything I was supposed to do. I've waited. I've done everything right. I've taken the Clomid. I've come in for all the blood tests. I've made sure Dan gave a great sperm specimen, four full days of sperm every single time. Just like you said."

Dr. Browne smiled back at her, putting the already thick file on the counter, looking at the last page. "Okay. Let's just take a quick look. Mary?" he called out to the hall. Mary, Dr. Browne's nurse, walked in, nodded, put on a pair of rubber gloves.

Avery assumed the position she'd taken for more than two years, the familiar leg spread, putting her feet on stirrups that were covered in cute, hand-knit purple socks. Her cold toes almost matched the socks, and she found it hard to relax against Dr. Browne's gloved fingers and then the warmed speculum. *Crank, crank, crank,* and she closed her eyes, wishing he could feel that she'd changed, that her uterus was somehow full with a baby. But he found nothing because *crank, crank, crank,* and he pulled out the speculum, dumped it in the sink, slipped off his gloves.

"Well, you aren't pregnant. And, Mary, we don't need to do the ultrasound today."

You are a real rocket scientist, she thought, taking back the thought right away. She liked him. She wanted to become the kind of woman who wouldn't want to snap back, a woman who could relax into his open smile without sarcasm and impatience. Avery wanted his good humor and his pleasant expression to infect her, make her body ripe for a baby. Before she and Dan had even begun trying to get pregnant, she'd listened carefully to the women at the Oakmont Fitness Club locker room, one saying, "One visit to Dr. Browne, and I was pregnant. He's amazing. Got that magic touch. He says the exact right thing every time."

Avery scooted up, as if the magic words would fall from his lips and slip up inside her. The paper below her crackled, and she pulled the gown down to her knees. "I know. I thought maybe. I was a couple days late."

"Thanks, Mary," he said, and Mary walked out of the office, closing the door behind her.

He wrote something on Avery's file and then looked at her, his brown eyes understanding, as only someone with four children could be. Brandon, Austin, Haley, and Madison Browne decorated every exam room, with photos of birthdays, soccer matches, first days of school in the hand-decorated frames (shells, buttons, cracked marbles, dried pasta) that Mrs. Browne made for the office.

When Avery had told her best friend and neighbor, Valerie, about the kids and the photos, Valerie had shaken her head and said, "One of the reasons people have children in the first place is just to name them." Avery had laughed, but didn't bring it up later when Valerie read every baby name book on the bookstore shelf before picking out the name Tomás Victor, after Luís's father and uncle.

"We've talked about this before, Avery," Dr. Browne said. "You are so young. I know it seems like a long time, but two years isn't out of the ballpark. We've done seven rounds of the IUI because you've been very persistent. If it were totally up to me, I'd have had you do it the old-fashioned way for a bit longer. Recent research has shown that those who don't conceive in the first year of trying will conceive in the second. I'm not saying we should stop. In fact, we'll do one more month of the IUI, and if we don't have the result we want, I'll suggest moving forward."

Avery nodded. That was what she wanted, in vitro. The real thing, not IUI. Dan called IUI "spin and shoot." The day after Avery injected herself with the hormone HCG to induce ovulation, she and Dan would drive down to the clinic in the afternoon, Dan taking a magazine into the small "collection" room. After handing over his sample to the nurse, his sperm was spun in a centrifuge to wash and concentrate it, and then it was injected directly into Avery's uterus through a catheter, toward her pumped-up eggs, enhanced and activated and sailing down the fallopian tube. At three thousand dollars a round, it wasn't even half as expensive as in vitro fertilization, but she didn't know how many more rounds she could handle; her PMS was so intense, she found herself weeping on the couch while watching *Desires* because Pedro left Alma due to the affair he thought she'd had but hadn't. And usually Avery didn't even watch soap operas.

"I want to keep trying. I think it will work," she said. "I want it to work. It has to."

"Avery. You're a young woman. My wife had Madison when she was forty-two. Anyway, talk to Mary on your way out, and we will get you scheduled for the next round. Take care. And think about that acupuncture clinic I told you about. Some of my patients swear by it."

He smiled and left the exam room. Avery stood up and took off her gown, folding it into a neat square and laying it on the table. So what if his wife had a baby at forty-two. She wasn't forty-two when she'd begun popping out those four kids.

As Avery slipped on her blouse, she looked in the mirror next to Dr. Browne's desk. He was absolutely right. She was a young woman, her breasts firm, her stomach flat, her thighs so cold in this freezing room because they didn't touch, hadn't since she was thirteen and had gone on her first and only diet. Compared with the women in the waiting room, with their huge breasts strapped in milk-soaked nursing bras, their hair straight and dark from coursing hormones, she was perfect. A size six, sometimes four. She could walk into Nordstrom and put on anything, and it would look good. Sometimes, the saleswomen actually waited for Avery to come out and show them how a dress or skirt looked. She had her hair cut every five weeks to the day by Richard at Anthony's, her feet and nails done every two weeks by Nanette, her skin massaged and buffed by Laura once a month at Oakmont.

But as she zipped her jeans and slipped on her loafers, she thought, *So what?* What did all that matter when her body wouldn't do what she most wanted it to do? So what if she could make every limb lean and tan and firm? So what if she could work out on the StairMaster for fifty minutes and then do her weight reps? What did any of that matter when it took Clomid or gonadotropin injections to push perfect eggs down her fallopian tubes right on time? When her egg wouldn't take in the one thing that would make her life just right?

Avery's body felt like an engine that had never been jump-started, no gears lubed, nothing moving, not even when the hormones were pumping through her system. And after Dan's sperm passed the semen analysis with flying colors, she had no one to blame but herself. Her body just didn't work.

Out by the nurses' station, Mary patted her hand. "Honey, you don't know what I've seen in this office."

Avery leaned on the counter, her breath in her throat. "Yeah?"

"Oh, yeah. People try for years and years. We're talking cycles and cycles of IVF. We're talking they finally give up and go to China and adopt a baby girl. You, honey, have so much time."

Avery pushed back and pressed her lips together, not wanting to say what she knew about time. Whatever she'd wanted before—a degree, a husband, a house, a job—had been hers to get. If she needed to ace a test, she studied all night; if she wanted Dan, she smiled and then ignored him until he came over and sat by her at Peet's Coffee, buying her a double latte, walking her home to her dorm room. After graduating summa cum laude from Haas School of Business, she'd networked and honed her résumé until Pathway Solutions hired her first as an assistant to Brody, her current boss. And then, within a year, he'd asked her to help oversee their sales division, a group of almost fifty people. For the next two years, they sold computer systems to businesses all over the country, Avery traveling to St. Louis and Dallas and Chicago almost every month. Coming home to Dan was almost like a vacation, their entire marriage more of a honeymoon than a real life.

But when she realized the baby thing wasn't going to happen if she missed sex nights because she was at the Hilton in Newark or the Ritz-Carlton in Manhattan, she quit. The moment of her realization, she called Brody and said, "I'll give you two weeks' notice, but I really want to quit now. Tomorrow. I'm going to have this baby or else." She didn't go further, didn't tell him she wanted to stay at home to focus on ovulation and mucus, taking her temperature and checking her discharge for egg-white consistency. Whatever it was, Avery did what she needed to do to get things to happen, to be right. To be perfect. And this wasn't perfect. Not in the least.

"I know," she said, wanting Mary to like her, too. "I do have a lot of time."

"I'll let you know when it's time to start worrying. I promise." Mary nodded. "I never lie."

Avery smiled and nodded. "Thanks."

"So here's your next appointment. You know the drill. Remind your husband of the rules. No hanky-panky for at least a couple of days before. The more the merrier!"

Taking the sheet and thanking Mary, she left the office, trying not to notice the women in the waiting room, ripe and round and ready to pop. First it was her sister Loren who'd had a difficult time getting pregnant, but then she'd had three! And so close together? So adorable? Then, it was babies everywhere she looked. At the Oakmont Café. At Safeway and Andronico's in the produce aisles. In her neighborhood in strollers. And three months ago, Valerie had had Tomás. One month of trying, and boom, Valerie was pregnant. Just like that. Nine months to the date, Tomás was born at home with a midwife, Avery holding Valerie's hand. Tomás was her godchild— both she and Dan had held him as the priest dotted his head with water—and she knew she should be happier. But sometimes, all the time really, she swallowed down her jealousy, a lumpy green lozenge.

In the parking lot, Avery put on her sunglasses and kept her eyes on her black Land Rover, wanting nothing except the blast of cold air, the radio, the ride home to help her forget she wasn't pregnant.

The Monte Veda sewer system never seemed to be in the right state of repair, and each summer, the drives on city streets became a series of stops and starts, orange cones, and hot, bored flag people. Irritated, Avery idled behind a cement truck. Tiny pellets of cement hit her windshield, and every so often she turned on the windshield wipers and flicked them off, a fan of white dust floating heavily past the driver's side window.

An au pair—Swedish probably, tall, blond, blue eyes, a tattoo around her ankle and one on her shoulder—pushed a stroller down an intersecting street, and Avery sighed. She knew what it would be like to have a baby, maybe two. She could almost feel herself grow rounder and softer, her breasts heavy with milk, her thighs and stomach fleshy from pregnancy. The babies would curl in her arms as they all lay on the bed, Dan in the kitchen cleaning up or making something for dinner. The bedroom would be awash with light, and so would Avery's heart.

The nursery would be filled with plush toys and blankets and presents from all the grandparents, everyone finally brought together because of the children. Avery wouldn't care if the house was dirty or if she might never lose the twenty pounds around her middle. She wouldn't care that she'd drifted away from technology and business and her now too-small St. John's suits. In the days and months that would follow, her hours would be filled with walks with Valerie and Tomás, playdates at Monte Veda Park, Mommy & Me classes at the community center. She would call her sister Loren and commiserate about childhood illness and diapers and fatigue. Each night, she would sit around a table with her husband and children, everything conspiring to keep them together and happy, exactly as she had planned on a piece of binder paper when she was a freshman, positive she could make her child's life happier than her own.

This was the family she was meant to have, the real family she would remember.

Everything had been fine in her own family before her father died, but those early years seemed underwater, murky, like a dream she'd almost forgotten. What came next was what stayed. Isabel sank into depression, reading all day, stumbling out in the afternoon to defrost a frozen Stouffer's meat lasagna and to toss an iceberg lettuce salad.

It would be different for Avery's babies. They would never have to worry that the bills weren't paid or wonder if someone had called about the broken furnace. They would never have to empty buckets collected from the living room during a winter storm because someone forgot to call the roofer. Her babies, her children, would never sit around a dining room table as she, Loren, and Mara had, wondering if their mother had bought any Christmas presents. Grief had sunk the house, dragging them through dark waters.

Yes, her mother had snapped out of it, slowly but completely, humming back into life four years after her husband died from stomach cancer. During all of Avery's high school years, especially the three when both Mara and Loren were out of the house, she learned to watch for clues, to check the air every day when she woke up, sniffing for signs of her mother's depression. Would today be a good day, her mother sitting at the kitchen counter in her robe, a cup of tea in her hands, asking Avery about English and math? Or would it be one of those days or weeks when she didn't emerge from her room until evening? Or worse, a day when Avery would have to gently pull her mother out of bed for a shower? Each morning when the alarm went off, Avery wondered whom she'd have to talk to—the Visa representative, the PG&E repairman, her mother's old bridge friends. "She's good," Avery learned to say, her voice crisp. "Just tired."

One morning in the middle of Avery's senior year, Isabel was making eggs at the range when Avery walked into the kitchen. "Scrambled's okay, right?" Isabel said, pushing down the toast.

Avery nodded, sat down at the counter, saw her other mother, the one from the time before, the one who'd loved her children and husband. What a change from the bedraggled woman who crawled out of her room at dusk to discover that she was left with only one daughter at home. In an effort to keep her mother from hearing the silence of their house, Avery learned to talk about everything except her father, feeling that one wrong word would capsize them both. She knew neither she nor her mother could live through more years like the ones they'd just endured.

Finally, there was movement. The truck lurched, backed up a bit, and then pulled forward. Avery started the car and followed the cement truck slowly down the street, passing the sweating flagwoman, who stared at her watch, a staticky walkie-talkie blaring from her work belt. From habit, Avery began to think, *That's what happens when you don't go to college,* but she cut herself off. She'd read the books on mindfulness and forgiveness and karma. Even if she didn't really believe any of the theories, she needed to practice being a person who could actually become pregnant. A person who deserved it.

Avery took off her sunglasses and put her Prada purse on the granite kitchen counter. She'd barely stepped into the house when she heard the phone ringing. "Mom. Mom! I told you I'd call you."

"But you're so late. I thought maybe something had happened at the doctor's."

"There's construction going on everywhere. I was stuck in traffic."

"So? What's the news? Is it good? I had to know. I figured that your appointment was over at two thirty, so even with the traffic, I timed it just right, didn't I?"

"Yes, Mom." Avery opened the fridge and took out Calistoga water, cradling the phone between her cheek and shoulder as she opened it. The day was so hot. She wanted nothing more than to hang up the phone, go outside to the pool, and sit in the shallow end until she needed to get dinner ready. Had she even been in the pool at all this summer? She couldn't remember. At one time in her life, water had been as familiar to her as air. She'd loved all the laps, the distance, the way the world was shimmery through her goggles, the strength in her body as she pulled across the pool. But she'd stopped feeling that way after her father died, the tightness of water around her head claustrophobic, keeping her stuck in her thoughts, all of them about those last minutes in the hospital. She'd quit the team and never competed again, jumping in pools only to cool off, as she wanted to do today.

"So?"

"I told you it wouldn't be good news. I already knew."

"But I thought maybe . . ." Even though Avery herself had hoped for the same thing, she was irritated, grinding her teeth as she listened to her mother go on. "You've just been through so much, sweetie. All those shots and blood tests and ultrasounds. I just want you to get the news you need."

"Listen, I would have called you from Dr. Browne's if I had something worth telling. You know that. I'm sorry."

Isabel gasped. "Don't be sorry. I'm not sorry. I know you'll get pregnant. Look how long it took your sister!"

"Oh, Jesus, Mom! Do you have to bring up Loren every time?" Even as she said it, Avery knew that Loren and she would always be placed side by side. Loren lived close by, in Walnut Creek, and often came over to Avery's with first one, then two, and now three children. Isabel baby-sat frequently, calling Avery with updates: "Sammy's learned to read!" and "Jaden's walking!" and "Dakota rolled over!"

Her mother was silent, and Avery could almost hear Isabel biting on her lower lip to keep more words from spilling out. "I'm sorry, Mom. I didn't mean that. It's just that Loren is so lucky to have her children. I don't really want to hear about her all the time. You're always comparing us."

Isabel sighed. "Sweetie, I'm sorry. But we're women in the same family. You have to remember how hard it was for her."

Avery nodded. Loren had tried for almost three years before conceiving Sammy. And then in three more years she'd had Jaden and Dakota. But now Avery was as old as Loren had been with Jaden. It was time. It was her time.

"I don't think Mara will ever have children, so you're next." Mara lived in Philadelphia in a nine-thousand-square-foot house with her architect husband, both of them so busy they rarely came to California on visits. She was a pathologist, cutting up who knew what for a living. Once when Mara was in medical school, she brought home a book about sliced-up body parts, even a brain and a penis. Avery couldn't sleep the night after she'd flipped through the entire book, unable to tear her eyes away from the glossy, cross-sectioned flesh. For days, the pictures popped up in her mind, the red-and-tan pieces of a human body. Mara had just laughed, saying, "God. Don't think about it. Let it go." Even now, Avery shivered, thankful that Mara's visits were few. Each time she did show up at a holiday dinner, she brought work stories about hearts in pans, cancer on skin, lungs with loops of disease. After what Avery had been through the past months, she didn't need any more woeful tales about the body.

"I know, Mom. But you're not . . . It doesn't help when you call me all the time. I'm worried enough. This whole thing is driving me crazy. It's like—it's like this is all I am. All I've become. An egg. A broken egg."

"You're not broken. You're the most put-together girl I've ever known. Look how well you did in school! How quickly you proved yourself at Pathway Solutions! This is just a minor setback for you, sweetie. I know about those."

For a moment, the quiet dark years pressed against Avery's throat, and she wanted to ask, "Do you miss him?" She wanted to know what it was that had flicked Isabel into action again, brought her out of her room and back to her life of bridge games and gardening and

Russian and history and art classes at the community center. But Avery didn't ask, couldn't, the rules still in place.

"Listen, Mom, Valerie, Luís, and Tomás are coming over for dinner, so I've got to get things ready. I'll see you on the Fourth."

"Should I bring anything?"

Every Fourth of July, the entire neighborhood closed off the cul-de-sac, hauled out their gas grills, and then lit illegal fireworks in the center of the court, while they waited for the sanctioned Monte Veda Fire Department's yearly fireworks display. The women made pesto and grilled eggplant and fixed lentil-and-walnut salads. The men stood over the barbecues and grilled salmon and chicken breasts and sometimes abalone or oysters. One grill continuously spun out hot dogs and hamburgers for the kids, who in the gathering of adults, felt safe to eat everything and run over everyone's perennials and feed the pets Fritos and watermelon. Each year they'd lived there, Avery always warded off her mother's gross green Jell-O salad with cottage cheese by saying, as she did now, "Oh, Mom. We've got so much. Just come and we'll have a good time."

"That's what you say every year. One year, I'm just going to bring my salad. You know, the one your father loved so much?"

Avery smiled, knowing that her father had hated the salad, but he'd loved Isabel, so with each bite, he'd said, "Delicious. This is my favorite."

"You are our guest, Mom. Just come."

Isabel sighed. Avery imagined her curling the cord of her old rotary phone around her finger. "All right. But you call me before if anything happens. You know."

"Yes, Mom. I'll call. Got to go." Avery hung up, knowing that nothing was going to happen. Not this month. Not for a while.

Tomás was asleep in Avery's arms, Valerie eating as if it were her last meal. In fact, her best friend's face looked too thin, Tomás sucking every last bit of fat out of her. "I had my cholesterol checked," Valerie had told her last week. "One eighteen. One eighteen! My doctor wondered how I was still alive."

Avery looked down at Tomás, the milk drinker, her godchild, his beautiful brown face so sweet in sleep, his eyelashes long and black, his hair a fuzz of darkness.

"I am so hungry," Valerie said, scooping up the last of the lasagna on her plate and then serving herself another square.

"I can see that, *amor*," Luís said. "Hey, why don't I just slide the casserole in front of you?"

"Watch it, Luís," Dan said, winking at Avery. "You're on dangerous ground." Dan smiled, his eyes dark with laughter. When she and Dan were first going out, back at Cal, she had warned him, "Don't ever say the word *fine*. Don't say, 'It's all right.' Women know what *fine* and *all right* mean. And to be on the safe side, don't talk about thighs or weight or hair. On a bad day, I won't be able to take it."

Luís nodded. "I know it, man." But Valerie didn't blink, cutting into the lasagna, flipping her long red hair behind her shoulder when it got in the way of her fork. Avery knew Luís wouldn't care what size Valerie was; he loved her so completely, his eyes always on her, appreciative, glowing. After Tomás was born, he sobbed as he cut the umbilical cord, saying, *"Dios mio,"* and other Catholic Spanish sayings Avery and Dan couldn't catch. To Luís, Valerie was a queen, *La Reyna,* as he called her.

In a different way, Avery knew how he felt, because she looked at Dan with those same appreciative eyes. While she picked on him and teased him and felt he was her equal, she knew that he would protect her, care for her, love her. Sometimes at night, she wondered what she gave him, what he truly loved about her. Was it that she was beautiful? That she could earn a living? That she could cook? Then he would throw a heavy, sleepy arm across her and pull her close, and she would forget to question what their marriage was all about, safe in the warmth of her husband's flesh.

Tomás made a small cry and stretched out an arm, turning a bit in Avery's arms. She bent her head down and breathed him in. She knew her own baby would be as sweet and wonderful as he was. Sometimes, when she watched Tomás, while Valerie took a long, soaking bath or went to the grocery store, she imagined that he was hers. When Valerie walked back into the house, Avery almost had to shake herself into the real world.

"So what did the doctor say? Did you ask him about the herbs?" Valerie asked, finally pushing her plate away. "Luís's cousin Rosalinda swears by them."

"I didn't ask. I forgot. But he wants me to do acupuncture."

"That's crazy stuff, man," Luís said. "The Chinese say our body is all connected by electrical currents, which is true. But to stick in needles to activate them . . . What is it? The *chi?* And a teacher at my school, she told me about cupping. They light a match in a cup and extinguish all the air and stick them on your back. To pull out the 'bad humors' or something. It's superstition."

Luís taught high school science at Las Palomas High School, and whether it was a cow's eye or a frog or a twenty-five-pound feral cat that his students had to dissect, it was straightforward and clear, muscles and nerves and flesh in clear understandable systems. In some ways, he sounded just like Mara, though he talked less about his work.

"Don't get me started on superstition," Valerie said. "Every time we leave on a trip, you're genuflecting all over the place. Kissing your Saint Christopher and whatnot. How can that be scientific?" Valerie smiled and patted Luís's shoulder. "There are things we just don't know about, and getting pregnant is sometimes one of them."

Dan nodded. "I know. One of the administrative assistants at work adopted a baby, not knowing that she was actually four months pregnant. She'd been trying for years, and then she and her husband decided to adopt. The night they brought the baby home, she realized what was going on. She thought she wasn't having a period because of all the hormone treatments."

Avery leaned in closer, hovering over the happy story that floated in the middle of the table. She loved these tales where the miracles happened. Sometimes, with the right crowd in Dr. Browne's office, the women would begin to recount the unbelievable—the twins after five years of hormones, IUI, and then in vitro. The adopted baby who was now in the same grade with the baby the couple conceived after the adoption went through. The triplets, identical, no fertility drugs at all. The quads that weighed four pounds each and were now thriving. The sister of a friend of a women's husband who didn't even know she was pregnant and went to the hospital for indigestion. All these stories had to be true, and one of them just might end up being Avery's. She didn't care which, because all of them ended happily with a child.

"Unbelievable, man," Luís said, standing up and clearing dishes from the table. "God was sure good to us."

"Superstition," Valerie whispered as he and then Dan left the room, loaded down with plates.

"No, maybe he's right," Avery said, pressing Tomás just a bit closer. "You guys are so lucky. Tomás is beautiful. Look at him!"

Valerie reached a hand over and rubbed Avery's arm. "Hon, you'll have a baby. I know it. Some people just take longer."

"Yeah. So I've been told." These were the stories that were harder to listen to—the couple who tried homepathetic treatments, psychotherapy, weeklong infertility retreats, acupuncture, IUI, and IVF for twelve years before giving up, having spent almost all their retirement money. The coworker's daughter who had fibroids removed, tubes blown clean, a dye study, and a uterus scraped—all for nothing. The woman who went to England for a new procedure that cost twenty thousand dollars and still had failed. Even afterward, she kept trying and was still at it ten years later.

"Look, it's summer," Valerie said. "We're going to hang out by your pool and relax. Your body is going to be so rested, you'll be pregnant by fall. You're ripe, girl. Don't get down."

Avery smiled. "I am like a melon, a tomato, a plum."

"Damn right," Valerie said. "A veritable garden. You've just got to get seeded."

"What?" Dan said, walking into the dining room, Luís behind him.

"Don't ask," Avery said, laughing. "I'll explain it all to you later. I promise."

Avery lay behind Dan, his body a strong silhouette in the bed. She pressed closer, wrapping an arm around him.

"What?" he asked, turning his head toward her. "Are you a little anxious?"

That was their term for needing each other—anxious. They would be at a party dancing to music in the middle of a room, arms tight around each other, and Dan would lean into her ear and whisper, "I'm feeling a little anxious," rubbing the silk covering her back.

Now, while she would welcome the forgetfulness of sex, the

familiar and comforting ways their bodies moved together, the skin she knew so well, she was actually anxious. Worried. Frightened. Even though Dr. Browne, Valerie, her mother, Loren, and all the women in the waiting room had declared that anxiety and stress of any kind would ruin her chances. That's why she'd quit her job, despite how hard she'd worked for years. She couldn't help it, though, still feeling Tomás's warm weight against her body, the empty space after Valerie had taken him from her.

"I'm . . . I'm scared it's not going to happen. Another cycle, Dan, and nothing."

Without saying anything, he turned to her, pulling her across his chest. He was always so warm, she often thought of buttered toast or anything brown and hot when she was near him. He was so alive, she'd always known that it was her fault they couldn't get pregnant—her body so still and slim and cold.

"Don't do this to yourself, Aves. You've been so good about just going forward. You know it's going to happen. It's just a matter of when." He held her tight, spoke in his confident sales voice, the one he used every day at VentureOut, a telecommunications company. While most salespeople's overeager tones would convince her the worst was around the corner, Dan's voice was as sure as her father's had been. He sold promise and hope, as he always had. Everything he'd told her since his first hello had been the truth.

"I know. I want it so bad. I look at Tomás and Loren's kids, and I know I'd be a good mom."

"Of course you'll be a good mom. That's not the point. The point is you need to do what Dr. Browne says, go to this acupuncture place, and rest. We have to follow the program, and it will happen."

Avery nodded against her husband's skin. Dan had always followed the program, and look how well things had turned out for him. Maybe he'd spent a couple of vague years working after high school instead of going right to college, but in short order he'd been admitted to Cal, earned his degrees, and been hired right out of business school. He worked long hours, putting out fires with testy clients, traveling all over the state for meetings, taking calls from his boss, Steve, well into the night. But look how well it had all worked out. They were married, had bought the house, and eventually, they would have children. Two or three. A boy and a girl for sure, as Avery had always planned. The boy old enough to protect the girl. That's the way she saw it, and she wanted to believe Dan. She had to. There was no reason not to.

"All right," she said. "I'm sorry. I can't stop thinking about it. You know me. It's the way I was in school and at work. I think that because it's possible, I can do it. If I can't for some strange reason, I just cut bait and move on. But I just don't have much of a say here. I can't go in and pluck the egg myself and slap a sperm in it and watch it grow in a petri dish on the kitchen windowsill. I can't do anything but lie back and let people do things to me. I hate it."

"That's why you'll be a good mother. Our kids won't have anything to worry about, not with you around. You'll be the president of the PTA. In charge of all the fund-raisers. I wouldn't be surprised if you ended up running the school."

Avery pressed into him again, wondering how she had found this man who knew her and still wanted her close. This close, rubbing her body, kissing her hair.

"I'm actually feeling a little anxious myself right now," Dan said, touching her breasts, kissing her neck. "And I happen to know the perfect cure."

Avery closed her eyes, let herself forget about the day. She stopped thinking about her insides as if they were charts in the exam room—the red curve of uterus and fallopian tubes, the small, potent egg falling down to swimming sperm. She blinked away the vision of her own body through the laparoscope lens, the slick, shiny organs that didn't work right. She forgot to be jealous of her sister's fertile reproductive fortune. She even let go of the sweet smell of Tomás, his baby hands, his rosebud mouth, his caramel skin. Her husband's warm palms, his mouth, his dark hair against her cheek, neck, breasts brought her to a place where it had all started, this solid attraction between them. Avery pulled Dan close, let go of all her anxiety, the real and the imagined.

Two

Luís leaned in and laughed. "Tom thinks his oysters have it all over us, man. But he hasn't tasted my mother's *carne asada*. And she also brought over some homemade chorizo. I'll bring that out later. Wait until you taste that!"

Smoke rose from the old Weber, Luís insisting on using charcoal. "The flavor, man. You can't get that from gas!"

Dan looked at the thin, tender strips of beef on Luís's grill, knowing that with the salsa and the fresh corn tortillas Luís's mother, Dolores, had brought over earlier in the day, the oysters would be just appetizers. "I think you're right. Happy Fourth." He brought up his Corona bottle and clinked it against Luís's.

"Damn straight. Fourth of July. I'm just so glad school is out. Now I can spend all my time with Valerie and Tomás. But probably she'll make me do all the laundry."

Dan nodded and swallowed his beer. Out in Dias Dorados Court, the neighbors were busy preparing for the long afternoon and evening, grills fired up, the air full of cooking meat and smoke. Earlier, Dan had helped set up about ten tables in the middle of the court, and now Frank Chow and Tim Mueller were bringing out large, green canvas umbrellas they'd all chipped in for after last year's epic sunburn, when every other person spent all night tossing on painful sheets. Kids were sitting on the curbs, wishing the day away, holding boxes of fireworks Ralph Chatagnier had bought in Livermore—Lotus Bloom, Flame Tower, Go Forever, Night Parade. Dan had already filled three water buckets so they could put out the blaze if a rare Monte Veda policeman were to drive by. They'd held the line at bottle rockets, knowing that even one spark could set a roof or a dry, blond hill ablaze. In fact, even though it was only ten a.m., it was already eighty-five degrees, as hot as it had been for weeks. By two o'clock, they'd all be huddled under the umbrellas, taking turns bringing the kids to either Dan and Avery's or the Chows' pool. When the sun finally set sometime after eight, they'd relax, take in the night, wait for the big guns to come out, the sky to alight with color.

"Yeah," Luís was saying. "It's great being able to watch him just sleep. I'm usually at the high school by seven."

Dan nodded again, feeling the muscles in his neck tense. "Summer will be great for all of you. Hey, I'd better go see what Avery wants me to do next."

"Okay, man. But don't leave me out here too long. I'll end up having to listen to Frank tell me about his new foundation."

Dan patted Luís's shoulder, leaving his hand on his friend for a second. If someone had told him three months ago that he'd be jealous of Luís and Valerie, Dan would have laughed, saying, "They're my best friends!" But in truth, he *was* jealous. Or maybe it was more. Maybe he was beginning to feel that he didn't deserve a baby. Maybe he thought that it wasn't about Avery's body at all—it was about him. Not his sperm. That he knew. Motility and morphology had checked out, A-okay, sperm 100 percent active and overpopulated, just as they should be. It was what he'd left behind that was the problem.

"Dan! God, where have you been?" Avery pulled open the garage door. "I need you!"

Dan dumped the Corona bottle in the maroon recycling bin and walked toward his wife. Avery's hair was up in a ponytail, her neck shiny with sweat. He wondered why she'd felt it was necessary to wake up at six thirty and take the kickboxing class at Oakmont, when the preparations for the long day were obviously exercise enough. As he followed her inside the house, focusing on her tight, muscled calves, he knew she would never like the changes in her body when she finally got pregnant. Avery had organized all the changes in their life, but extra fluid and flesh were something she'd be unable to stop.

"What is it?"

"The damn pool cover. I swear it's absorbing water. I can't roll it up. You know how that thing worries me. If we turn our backs for a second, some kid is going to get sucked up by it."

"Let's go figure it out," he said, holding the kitchen door open for her. She didn't look at him. She was in one of her "let's finish this" moods. If he didn't do as she said, or if he teased her about her worries or the fact that her pasta wasn't done yet or said that Isabel had called three times and was, in fact, bringing over the dreaded green Jell-O salad, they'd have a fight. Sometimes, when he was tired after working for fourteen hours, he couldn't stop himself, the tickle of the irritating sentence too much to contain. Those nights, she slept on the edge of the bed, forgiving him only when he kissed her shoulder, neck, cheek, only when he held her close and said, "I'm sorry."

Then, she would turn to him, pull his face to hers, whisper, "Don't leave me," and he'd wonder what they had really been fighting about after all.

But Dan didn't want an argument today. He was rested for the first time in weeks. He had the next three days off. He was going to work in the yard, swim, take Avery on a drive up the Sonoma Coast on Sunday. For at least one day, they weren't going to think about the pregnancy. They weren't going to mention the phrases "uterine body" or "blood levels" or "prostaglandin removal."

No. This weekend, they were going to be married, a couple, like they used to be, when it was simpler, when they could try to have a baby by turning out the lights and touching each other, back in the time when Dan was still ignorant of little rooms and girlie magazines, when he'd never had to hand his spunk in a little plastic container over to a nurse.

They stood by the edge of the pool, looking at the cover, and Dan could see that somehow, Avery had lumped a section of cover on the roll. He knew he'd have to unroll it and start over. "Listen, I can do this. Go ahead and finish your pasta. Don't worry about the cover."

Avery wiped her forehead and then heard what he said, looking up and smiling. There she was. There was his girl, the one he had met at Peet's six years ago, her hair the color of the summer foothills by his childhood Sacramento home. Her eyes were blue, sometimes gray, always full of light. He had imagined then and still imagined now that the light came from within her, her electricity, her drive, her current too strong to contain. If he had the right eyes, he knew he would see streaks of white shooting from her body like the flurries on the sun. She was that full of energy, electricity. She was that strong. As he'd waited long ago for the Rastafarian dude behind the counter to pour his coffee, Dan knew he'd found the woman who would make all the difference. The one who would burn away the past, leaving nothing but a space of time to be forgotten and then rewritten.

"Thanks, honey." Avery looked up at the sky. "It's going to be hotter than all of last week."

"Yeah," he said, bending over the cover, breathing in chlorine. "Go on. Get your work done."

She smiled again and turned away. He pulled on the wet plastic fabric, feeling the trail of her strong, hot light flick at his legs and then curl into their house, exactly where Dan wanted it.

"I couldn't help myself," Isabel was saying, opening the fridge, where she carefully placed the plate that held her wobbly green Jell-O salad. "I know you said you didn't need it. But honestly, sweetie, I saw all the people out there getting ready. Another salad never hurts, believe you me."

Dan turned to Avery, who was biting the inside of her cheek. She'd finished the pasta; filled the cooler with Coronas, Calistoga waters, and soft drinks; taken a shower; and dressed, her white shorts and red top clearly Fourth of July, but not the spangled red, white, and blue Isabel wore. Dan stared at his mother-in-law's sequined baseball cap, the kitchen light reflecting off her entire head. She even had on red Keds with blue shoelaces and little white socks with lace. Her fingernails were painted red, and she wore a blue bandana twisted around her neck. A vein in Avery's tight, smooth throat pulsed—one, two, one, two.

"Great!" Avery said. "You're right."

"The more the merrier," Dan said, wishing he hadn't. That was the phrase Mary, the nurse at Dr. Browne's, always used just before he went into the little room, clutching the latest copy of *Playboy*.

Isabel smiled at him. "Loren and her family will be here soon. She's got a terrific surprise! That whipped strawberry pie you girls used to love. You know, your grandmother's recipe? What was it called? Sky Pie?"

"Spy Pie." Avery was biting her cheek again. "She called me."

"How about a soda, Isabel?" Dan said, leading her into the family room. "Or why don't we go over and say hi to Valerie and Luís. You haven't seen Tomás in a while, have you?"

As he pulled her along, he turned back, and Avery sighed and shook her head. He and Isabel walked through the house, into the garage, and out into the bright late morning light of the Fourth of July, her arm through his. Isabel was irritating, that was for sure. She'd lived alone for too long, coming over to their house with a flurry of words she must have saved up at night, the desperate sentences coming out all at once. When they went to the movies, she sat by Dan and asked, "Is that actress someone I should know? What film was she in before?" Before she read a novel, she made Avery tell her the end of the story, not wanting, she said, "anything too ugly."

But he squeezed her arm, knowing that what he would like more than anything was to be able to squeeze his own mother in this way, walk her over to Luís and Valerie's, sit her down at one of the party tables festooned with red, white, and blue crepe streamers. But when his mother, Marian, and his father, Bill, drove down to the Bay Area, it was first to see Dan's brother, Jared. And then, if he was lucky, he'd get a phone call. "We're just headed home, but we wanted to say hi. How's Avery?"

Because Jared was coming to the cul-de-sac this year to eat and watch fireworks, Dan had hoped that his parents would come, too, sit with him, and enjoy the life he'd made for himself and Avery. But they'd called at the last minute, saying, "Oh, Dan, it's too hot to drive. We'll stay here and watch the fireworks with the Davidsons."

"You do have air-conditioning in the Oldsmobile, don't you?" Dan had asked.

"Yes, of course. I meant at your house," his mother said. He could hear her tap something—a pen, a pencil, her glasses—on the counter.

"Mom, we have the pool. And air-conditioning. It won't be bad. And you can see Jared." He dangled the good-son carrot.

"Not this year. Say hi to Avery." His mom hung up, and Dan had put down the phone, wondering how long it would take before they trusted him again.

"Oh, my," said Isabel. "This is so charming. How festive! What a wonderful day. You two are so lucky to live here. You can't pay for this kind of neighborhood bonding!"

Dan reached for Isabel's hand, and she turned to him, surprised, but let her small, soft, wrinkled hand stay in his. Is this how his mother's felt? If he grabbed Marian's hand, would she snatch it away?

Together, Isabel's Keds tap-tapping on the sidewalk, his own steps slow and patient, they walked to the Delgados'. Valerie pulled open the door, Tomás on her shoulder.

"Oh, Isabel. I am so glad to see you. Could you hold Tomás? Luís is having some kind of salsa incident in the kitchen. He and his mother are on the floor, scrubbing."

Isabel carefully took the sleeping Tomás from Valerie, who then rushed back inside. Dan walked behind Isabel as they moved into the cool air of the house, and he swallowed. Soon, she would be carrying her own grandchild. His and Avery's. Soon, he might be able to forget the past.

"Do you remember when we accidentally exploded the Davidsons' mailbox?" Jared asked, leaning back in his chair, watching the kids light Flame Tower after Flame Tower, the air hanging thick with sulfur and smoke.

"An accident?" Dan said, and then looked behind him. Avery— with Tomás in her lap—was sitting next to Valerie, Valerie's sister, Yvette, and Loren. "I hardly think we can call that accidental."

Jared sipped his beer. "You're right. But that the whole thing exploded *was* an accident."

Dan nodded, picturing the steel grimace of the torn mailbox, his parents' disappointed faces. He'd only been ten then, Jared eight.

"Uncle Dan! Uncle Dan!" Sammy, Loren's oldest, called, breathing hard, leaning on his knee. "Did you see that one? Did you see how high the flames went?"

"I did, Sammy. Are you having fun?" Sammy nodded, grabbed a Coke on the table, and drank it down, two thin streams of soda sliding down his chin. He put down the can and wiped his mouth. "I'm going back."

He ran into the swirl of kids, their giggles and whoops twirling up with the smoke. Dan looked down at the extra bucket of water he'd just filled. He was prepared for all emergencies.

Luís and his mother, Dolores, came back to the table with a layer cake Valerie had picked up at Andronico's. The piped red frosting read HAPPY FOURTH.

"*Ay,* this party, it goes on forever," Dolores said. "The baby should be in bed."

Tomás slept in the boat of Avery's arms. Avery and Loren listened to Valerie, all three of their heads close together. Loren's husband, Russell, sat next to Ralph Chatagnier, words like *distribution* and *market value* mixed in with the children's yelps.

"He's fine, Mrs. Delgado," Dan said. "Look at him. Like they say, 'Sleeping like a baby.' "

Just then, a Flame Tower erupted in the middle of the court, the parents oohing and aahing as their children put on the show.

"And then that time in high school," Jared said. "Before . . . that time at Larch Bank Pool? Do you remember that?"

Dan closed his eyes, feeling the smooth pool water on his waist, the noise from the bottle rockets whizzing above him. What year was that? It must have been before he'd slipped out of his parents' house for good, before he'd unlocked his father's coin case, plopping the meaty coins in his Adidas bag like magic plums. Before he'd taken their credit card and racked up charges at the hotel in Las Vegas. She'd said she'd marry him that weekend at the Chapel of Love, but all they'd done was drink and smoke in the room, ordering room service, snorting line after line.

"Yeah," he said, standing up, his legs stiff from sitting. "Do you want another beer?"

"I'm good. Look at that one." Jared pointed to a Lotus Bloom, white and furious and burning hot.

"I'll be back." Dan walked over to the cooler, patting Avery's shoulder as he passed by. She didn't seem to notice him, listening to a long story Loren was telling about Dakota's birth.

"Great party this year," Frank Chow said, manning the hamburger grill, children still eating, their smudged hands holding out plates, waiting for Frank to slip a half-burned patty on their buns.

Dan dug in the cooler and found the last Corona. He wondered if he should put it back for Frank or Tim or Ralph, but then he wiped the water off the bottle with the flat of his hand. It was the only alcohol he allowed himself now. "Sure is," he said, putting down the bottle opener and taking a sip. "The fire department should be getting their show going soon."

"Usually, it's what? Nine fifteen? Nine thirty? Better be good what with the fund-raising drive they go through."

"Yes, it always is." Dan nodded and walked toward his table but then moved close to the circle of children, standing back just enough so that Sammy, Jaden, or Dakota didn't see him. The sky was falling light gray, darker, darker, until only a tiny white slip of light hung over the Berkeley hills, the triangles, ellipses, rectangles, and squares of neighboring lawns rich and emerald in the twilight. Gray bunches of indistinguishable perennials—sage, penstemon, lamb's ears—were artfully positioned around the lawns and professionally designed slate, concrete, or brick paths.

Back in Sacramento when he was growing up, Dan knew every yard. From the time he was eight until he was a teenager he, Jared, and his father had helped pour patios, build retaining walls and fences, and plant sod for neighbors. He could look at someone's fence, and think, *I did that*. He would find the corner of the Addonizios' patio and see his and Jared's thin initials, D.T. and J.T. Later he'd answer his father's requests for help with ridicule and a curled lip, adolescent disdain.

Here, none of the guys did any of their own work, even though, like Ralph Chatagnier, they talked about it enough. In the mornings, trucks full of plumbers, masons, gardeners, and pool men would roar into the cul-de-sac. Workers would stream out, grab tools, slip into the backyards. In a few weeks, Dan and Avery would be invited over for a barbecue and see, amazingly, a new gazebo or a series of retaining walls and a new lawn. Sometimes on the weekends, neighbors would knock on Luís's door, embarrassed, and say, "I was wondering if you'd be able to, um, talk to these fellows I have here to cut down the sycamore or rototill the vegetable garden or tear down the fence." Luís would nod, walk over, slap the guys on the shoulders, and listen. Dan never asked him how it felt to translate his neighbors' demands, but he'd watch Luís walk home across the cul-de-sac, his hands in his pockets, his lips pressed together.

Dan never asked if Luís liked it here at all. His friend had moved to Monte Veda from Oakland only because of the schools, the safe, quiet streets, the farmer's market on spring and summer Sunday mornings, the new library and community center. Because of the set of Luís's face as he walked home from Frank's or Ralph's, the stories of Guatemalan, Salvadorean, Mexican immigrants in his head, men who stood to the side of the Home Store parking lots in the mornings, looking for a contractor to pick them to work for a day, Dan never brought up anything related to Luís's being Latino in a mostly white neighborhood. He knew that Valerie's mother had helped them buy the house, and he knew that they loved the spacious four-bedroom rancher, the Tacconis as neighbors, and the cul-de-sac in general. But he wondered what Luís thought as he walked home.

The children screamed and backed away as a Go Forever spun its red light in a whooshing circle. Dan sighed, ready to go inside, his lungs full of sulfur and memory. He'd had enough of talking to his brother. Jared recounted their childhood like it was some kind of fantasy adventure. "Oh, remember this?" and "Oh, remember that?" Every time he visited, Jared, a history professor at Contra Loma Community College, became a living example of the historical dictum, "Those who forget history are doomed to repeat it." He couldn't stop bringing up their childhood, Dan's past, the stories that Dan needed to forget, not that he had the chance to do so when Jared was around.

However, Jared was a revisionist, ignoring the part of the story that involved their father's bullying and teasing, their mother's passivity. He'd been able to forget some things, mercifully. But when Dan wanted to forget, Jared was there on his shoulder like a drunken parrot, forcing him to remember. Did Dan bring up Jared's past, his failed relationships with women? All the history books in the world hadn't taught Jared how to stick out a relationship past six months, a year at most. Dan didn't say a word when Rita turned into Samantha, Samantha into Susie, Susie into Joan. He let go. Dan let his brother disremember what he wanted to.

Not Jared, though. Like tonight with the mailbox and the pool and her. Every time Dan thought he'd forgotten, there she was, smiling at him, her dark eyes, her freckles, the way she always made him do what scared him most.

"Dan?"

He almost spit out his swallow of beer, and then he relaxed. It wasn't 1984 or 1985. It was a whole new century. It was over. She wasn't here, not anymore. Only Avery. Avery. "Sorry. I was thinking."

"I can see that." Avery held his arm. "We think they're about to start."

And then, as if Avery had control of the fire department, too, the first sizzle of rocket flew up and burst into the night, a sprinkling of gold and silver and then, yes, surprise, red, white, and blue. The cul-de-sac's appreciative yes rose up high into the holiday night. And before they could even think to want another one, there it was, and then another, the sky so bright and full of light, Dan felt like it was morning.

It was late. Children were spread out on cool night lawns, talking as they looked up at the stars. Neighbors sat at tables, drinking beer, their babies asleep in laps or on shoulders, laughter erupting up and over the cul-de-sac. Avery leaned against Dan's shoulder, talking to Dolores about herbs and some cousin named Rosalinda. Luís and Valerie were listening to Russell talk about the difference between 403(b) and 401(k) plans. Jared had actually asked Ralph Chatagnier about his foundation, and was nodding as Ralph waxed on about retrofitting, bolts, shear wall, rebar.

Dan closed his eyes, shifted as Avery stood up to sit closer to Dolores. The baby they didn't have was never far away, the conversation somehow turning to how Avery should do this or that in order to conceive. At work, Dan forgot about the baby, focused instead on his clients and sales projections and how he could get ICX in the South

Bay or Alliance Insurance in Marin to commit to telecommunication packages. He would get into the office at seven thirty or eight, go from client calls to a staff meeting to a working lunch to a field visit without thinking once about hormones or ovulation cycles—or even Avery. But the moment he walked in his home, he felt he was in an empty nursery, the whole house filled with hope and a thin sliver of despair.

When Avery first quit her job at Pathway Solutions, he told her he would be working extra hours to make up for her lost income, which wasn't necessary as she had a great severance package. He really worked late because he couldn't handle the cutting edge of her incredible, needy hope that kept whacking him across the face. Each month, it was worse.

"Honey," Avery said, looking back. "Could you go bring out that carafe of coffee? I actually think it's cold enough for it."

"Sure," he said, standing up slowly, his body stiff with relaxation. "Anything else? Anyone?"

"A sleeping bag, man," Luís said. "I don't think I'll make it into the house. The heat melted me to this damn bench."

"Coming up." Dan pushed his chair back in. "Last call."

"Don't forget the cream. And the cups." Avery smiled and turned back to Dolores, Isabel now listening, too.

"No problem." Dan walked toward the house, on the way teasing the youngest Chow boy about his red candy smile. In the driveway, he picked up three Hefty bags of garbage and pushed them down into the cans.

Inside, he was picking up the carafe and the cups and the small thermos of cream Avery had neatly laid out earlier, when he noticed the phone machine had three messages. The people he cared about were right outside his house, except his parents, of course. His parents. Dan put down everything and pressed the button, not wanting to hear his mother's worried voice, the quaver of fear that ran through many of her conversations. Or the irritation. Or disgust. Maybe he should go get Jared to listen. They liked him best, anyway. Then Dan just listened.

"Hello, this is a call for Mr. Tacconi. This is Midori Nolan. Sorry for calling you on a holiday, but I need to talk to you. It's urgent. Please call me at the following number: 209-555-4972. Thank you."

Dan rubbed his forehead. Midori Nolan? And in area code 209? Aside from his parents and a couple of his old community college buddies, the only people he knew in the 209 area code worked for businesses in Modesto and Turlock and Stockton, folks from Pac-West and RealCall. But they wouldn't call him at home on the Fourth of July. He pressed for the next call. "Hello, this is Midori Nolan again. You must be out. I'm calling from the Stanislaus County Social Services Department. I don't think I mentioned that on my first call. I'm calling you about an urgent matter regarding Randi Gold. Please call me as soon as you can. Here's my cell number: 209-555-5689. Thank you."

Dan sat down on one of the stools by the kitchen counter. Randi. Again. She was in front of him as she had been when Jared had mentioned Larch Bank Pool, her skin wet and shiny from pool water. Those had been the good times, during high school, before everything went to hell. Before he changed into something he couldn't recognize in the mirror, another person inside his skin.

He looked at the phone machine. One message left. It had to be Midori Nolan again. His parents didn't need him, never would. He could erase all three messages and then try not to answer the phone for the rest of the weekend. Or, he could write these numbers down and go out and call back from his cell, tell her he didn't care. He'd given up Randi and the past like a bad paperback novel, leaving it outside to weather and decompose. "Leave me alone," he'd say. "My wife knows nothing about Randi. Do not call here ever again. I'll sue you for harassment. I'll call your boss. I don't want to hear anything. Do I make myself perfectly clear?"

But if his past had taught him one thing, it was that he could never escape it entirely. Look at tonight. Jared wanted to talk about it, even though Dan had asked him several times before to let it lie, bury the bones, forget. This baby thing brought it up, too. He knew he was being punished. He hadn't escaped after all. But he could try. He would listen to the message and then deal with this Midori Nolan.

Dan pressed the button, and there was her voice again. "This is Midori Nolan. I guess you're away for the long weekend. Here is what you need to know. Randi Gold has passed—has died. Over a month ago." He pressed the stop button, his heart pounding, unwelcome tears at the corners of his eyes. Randi? He breathed out and pressed the button again. "When we finally found out she had a child, we also found some materials that mentioned you. The boy is currently in foster care, and we need to look into this situation as soon as possible. It's for the child's sake. He had a very difficult experience. The last few months for him . . . Well, whenever you get in from the holiday, please call. If it weren't urgent, I wouldn't have called this often. Again, my cell is 209-555-5689."

Sitting back, wiping his eyes, Dan tried to breathe. She was dead. He hadn't seen her for ten years and hadn't wanted to, but she was alive still in his mind, her dark eyes, the way she flipped her curly hair away from her face, her arms akimbo as she said, laughing, "Tell me something, bonehead, that I don't know." There were the later memories, the hazy, bruised, dirty ones, but he'd cleared those away so that she was always sixteen in his mind. Larch Bank Pool memories. High school memories. Before memories.

And now she was dead and had left a son. Why did Midori Nolan want him to know that? Why had Randi left his name? He ran his hands through his hair, and then stopped. Oh, God. It couldn't be.

"Dan? Dan? What's going on? They're dying for the coffee out there."

He looked up, trying to focus. Avery stood before him, her hands on her hips. Just like Randi used to hold her hipbones, but Avery's held no baby between them. A baby? A boy.

"I . . ."

"What is it?"

He swallowed and looked at his wife, knowing he didn't have an answer that either of them wanted to hear.

Three

After Dan had disappeared into the house and Valerie and Loren had fallen silent, watching neighbor children play tag in the court, Avery stood up. "I don't know where he went. I think we all need some coffee about now. There is a definite lull in this conversation."

"Bring on the caffeine," Loren said. "I think I'll need a jolt to make my legs work. I'm so full, my stomach must be pressing down on necessary nerves or something."

"Bring out that whiskey, man," Luís said. "Who needs cream? Who needs conversation?"

Avery laughed. "That's a good way to wrap up this party. We'll just fall asleep out here."

"Dan's bringing me a sleeping bag, remember?" Luís laughed. "I'll be all set."

Avery pushed in her chair. "Valerie would just love a break from you, huh, Val?"

"No way. He's stuck in the house. He covers the two-o'clock feeding."

"My God," Dolores said, patting Luís's hand. "My husband, he never changed a diaper."

Avery felt a snippy feminist comeback slip up the back of her tongue, but it disappeared into sadness. A two-o'clock feeding. Would she ever know what that was like, even enough to hate it?

Would Dan ever change his own baby's diapers? Would there even be a baby to wear them?

"I'll be right back."

Inside, Avery heard a phone message, a stop, and then the message again. She closed the laundry room door and headed toward the voice. Dan was sitting still at the kitchen counter. As she asked him questions, he looked at her as if he couldn't quite place her.

"Dan? I said, 'What's going on?' "

"I— There was a message."

"Yeah. They were there when I made the coffee. Why did you have to answer them now? They could have waited."

"I was worried about my parents."

"Is it your parents?" She'd always feared the time when something might happen to Dan's parents, because he was so tender about them, which always struck her as odd because they didn't seem to pay any attention to him, to her, to their life together. She knew that if Marian or Bill got sick or died before Dan could fix this estrangement, she'd lose him in some way, into depression or anger. They didn't need that now. They both needed to focus on the baby, on their own lives.

"No. It's not my parents," Dan said.

Avery breathed in and sat on a stool. "Well, what then? Work? Was it Steve trying to get you to come in tomorrow? God, let him stew. He's had you on a leash for months. Right now, we've got guests, Dan. Luís wants the whiskey. Work can wait until later."

"It wasn't Steve. It was a social worker. From Stanislaus County."

She shook her head. "What? Why would a social worker call you? About what?"

"The past. A long time ago. Things." He pushed back in his stool and then swung his legs around, standing up. He began to pace up and back the length of the French doors leading to the patio and pool, his hands in his pockets, his face pale under his dark hair. "I don't know where to begin."

Her stomach tingled with nerves, and she stood up, pushing a stray hair off her face. Whatever it was, it couldn't happen now, and she hoped she could make it disappear altogether. "Look, we can't get into whatever it is now. We have guests. There are people outside waiting for you."

Dan looked over and into her eyes. "There are other people waiting for me now."

Waving her hands in front of her, she backed away. "No. Not now. Later. Later. Let's do the coffee and clean up and, just, later."

"But she called three times, Aves. I can't not call her back."

Avery slapped her hands on her thighs. "It's a holiday, Dan. Remember? God! It's not Steve or your parents. What could be so important in Stanislaus County that in any way involves you? Why do you have to be so nice to everyone? Christ, everyone you care about is outside."

She was breathing fast, and she put a hand on her throat. Maybe she would stop talking. Maybe she wouldn't say anything else, something she would regret and need to make up for, and he would listen and they could go back outside.

Dan shook his head. "Not everyone. My parents aren't out there."

"You said this wasn't *about* your parents."

"It's not." Dan walked toward her. "I've got to talk with you about it. It's about someone I used to know. A long time ago."

Avery backed away. "So we're supposed to leave everyone outside? Dan, think. We can't have some kind of big talk right now. Please, please wait until everyone leaves, okay? I don't want— I don't want my mother to see us like, well, this. Okay?"

Dan rubbed the sides of his face and sighed. "Okay. But after. Right after."

Avery sat on the couch in the family room, listening to the echoing sounds of Dan pulling the grill into the garage, the last of the neighbors shouting good nights across the cul-de-sac, fireworks exploding on some other street. She swallowed and grabbed her knees. This— whatever this was—should not be happening. Her heart pounded, and her head ached, and not from the crack and boom of fireworks or the lingering sulfur. Somehow, this had to be Jared's fault. Dan was always different after his brother was here. Jared had always been so friendly and warm to her—so different from Dan's parents—but it seemed he was holding a secret over Dan's head. So maybe it wasn't really about the call. She'd noticed something was wrong when Dan had stood up, walking away from the table, leaving Jared in midstory.

She breathed in deeply, thinking about Lamaze breathing, the mitigating of pain. But her body still hummed. Stress. Anxiety. She'd have to call that acupuncturist first thing Monday morning.

The garage door rumbled closed, and then Dan was in the laundry room, shutting the door behind him, walking into the family room. He looked at her, his face still, his lips pulled into an expression of— what? Fear? Anger? She rubbed the heel of her palm against her forehead and wished she had taken some aspirin.

"All right," he said, sitting down next to her, his arms crossed.

Avery shook her head, crossed her legs, wishing briefly for a notepad and pen. She felt as if she were at Pathway Solutions, needing to organize the entire day's work, printing up the schedule of calls and client visits, e-mailing directives to her coworkers, reminding them of meetings. Whatever was bothering him, she had to take care of it. Nothing was going to mess things up now. All this worry was ridiculous. She'd fix everything.

"So what is it?" she said.

"This social worker."

"Right." Avery nodded. "You've already told me that."

Dan looked at her, his dark eyes full of tears. "The social worker called to tell me that an old girlfriend of mine died."

Avery breathed in quickly and then let her mouth fall open. "What old girlfriend? The one from Cal? What was her name? Jordan?"

"No, not Jordan."

Avery sat back, her shoulder blades and neck muscles relaxing. Jordan was too close in time to her, a Sigma Alpha Epsilon Pi girl, all waist-long blond hair and tan legs. When Avery had found a stash of photos Dan had kept from that time, she'd put them in a plastic Baggie and hid them in a shoe box in the garage. But a girlfriend from before that, from high school, was different, far away. Easier. He hadn't talked about this girl once in all the years she'd known him, so this grief would be quick and manageable. Over soon. Fine.

"So who?"

Dan sat back against the couch cushion, his body slumped in a U. "Randi. From high school. And after."

Avery patted his shoulder. "I'm sorry. You never talked about her."

"It was a long time ago."

Just as she'd thought. Moving closer to him, their thighs rubbing, she nodded, relief making her feel light. "Even so, it must be strange for someone you know—someone that young—to die." She left her hand on him and felt the blood and warmth under his skin. She wanted all of him naked against her in bed, pushing her stomach against his butt, her arm across his shoulders. She was so tired. It was eleven thirty. All she could think about was taking her Clomid and finishing the cleanup so she could go to bed.

"No, I never talked about her. I didn't want to."

"Why did the social worker call you? Why is social services involved? Seems kind of weird." Avery looked toward the kitchen. There were a few pots to clean and the coffeepot to rinse. She should also go ahead and reset the sprinkler system, having turned it off today so it wouldn't go off and startle unsuspecting kids. And the lights. She had to turn off the front porch lights.

"Because . . ."

"What, Dan?"

He shifted and moved toward her, grabbing her right arm. She almost pushed away, and then stared at him, feeling her body rev up with nerves again.

"Because Randi had a son."

"Oh." She watched his face, saw how the muscles in his lips and under his eyes were trying to tell her something. "Oh. Oh."

Dan scooted closer. "I don't know what it means yet. I've got to call this Midori Nolan back. I don't know exactly why she called to tell me, but you have to know. I was with Randi for all of high school and until I went to Cal."

Avery pulled her arm out of his hand, feeling his imprint even as she placed it in her lap. "I don't understand."

"She was my girlfriend for a very long time. There was some mention of me in her papers. I'm involved somehow." Dan nodded, as if his movement would convince her. What did he think she was? A child?

"All of high school? Before Cal?"

"Yeah."

"That's only a year before you met me." She stared at him, feeling everything in her face gaping, mouth, eyes, ears. "You've never said a word about her! You've never told me one thing. You were with her for—what?—eight years, and you never mentioned it?"

"I didn't want to talk about it. We had a good relationship at first—you know, normal high school stuff, dances and dates, but later it changed."

"Changed how?" Avery asked, wishing she hadn't as his face shifted, his shoulders fell forward. For a second, he looked like his dad. Just like Bill.

"Bad. My life, well, it was out of control. We got into some stuff."

"What kind of stuff, Dan? For Christ's sake, just tell me." Avery tapped her foot against the coffee table.

"After high school we moved into an apartment, and I started working at Lemore's Hardware, and then I got fired—"

"I thought you went to school. Sacramento Valley College."

"Not right away. Randi's parents had kicked her out, and we decided to move in together. My parents—"

Avery shook her head. "Yeah, they must have loved that. They wouldn't even let us sleep together at their house when we were engaged."

"Right." Dan put his head in his hands, and Avery bit her cheek, feeling the soft, pink skin pulse with pain. "So we're living together, and we were—we were drinking. First it was pot. And then coke. And then we didn't do much else but drugs. So, I got into some things I shouldn't have. I did some things that I wish I hadn't. I took— I stole from my parents."

"You stole from Bill and Marian."

"Yes."

Avery looked at Dan as if he were the "Bay Area Report" in the *San Francisco Chronicle,* her eyes narrowing as she tried to figure out the motive for a crime. "For the drugs? You stole from your parents to buy drugs?"

Dan nodded, resting his head in his hands. She watched his breathing, the rise of his ribs, the tense muscles under his shirt. She almost reached out to touch him, not to comfort him, but to determine if he were still the same man she knew, the man without this particular past, this terrible story.

"Why?" she asked, shaking her head. "What happened?"

Without looking at her, he shrugged, mumbling into his hands. "It was a different life. She was— I wanted to be with her."

It was with these words that Avery felt herself float off the seat cushion, lifting slowly above herself and Dan, looking down at the two people on the couch. She could feel her body, but she wasn't connected to it. And it didn't really feel that strange, hovering over the horrible conversation. It was something she must have done before, practiced, learned by heart. Maybe it began when her dad was recovering from exploratory surgery in the hospital, everyone stiff and shaking in the plastic chairs, her body rising above them all, looking down on the rectangle of the bed, the grief that spiraled upward from her mother and sisters.

From up here, it didn't seem strange that Dan had lived with a girlfriend Avery had never heard about before, that he drank, did drugs, stole, worked in a hardware store, had a baby. Why not? It didn't bother her up here; in fact, all she really could see were the pots in the kitchen, the coffeemaker, her pill in its bottle, the bright outdoor lights. From here, there was tomorrow with its litany of pills, phone calls to her doctor, walk with Valerie and Tomás to Monte Veda Park.

"Aves!"

She rushed back inside herself, felt her tight chest, a band around her middle, pulling, pulling. "What?"

"It got worse. My parents—they called the police. Ultimately, they didn't press charges, but they cut me off."

Images ran through her head from movies and TV—dark apartments, people high on drugs flung back into momentary ecstasy on ratty mattresses. Nothing but the need for more stimulus, more high, now, now, enough so that they'd break into relatives' houses, stealing what would give them what they needed.

"I don't believe it." But she did believe it.

"We lived a terrible life. It was like there was no morning or night, just—well, the same awful flatness every day. Jared usually refused to come over." Dan paused, and now Bill and Marian's absence, remoteness, coldness made sense to her. They couldn't trust him yet, all these years later. Despite his degrees—despite her—he still might take what they had.

"Randi started to steal—"

Avery shook her head quickly and stood up. "You know, Dan, this is too much. We get this call from some strange woman and now you're telling me all this? You lived some slimy, drug-addict life, and you never thought to tell me about it? What if you've got some disease? What did she die of, anyway?"

Dan shook his head, his whole body limp. "I don't know."

"Great. What if you have it? What if you've given it to me?" She put her hands over her eyes.

"You know I was tested for HIV and hepatitis and STDs before all this started. This baby stuff."

"But before that! When we got engaged? When we were first married! You marry me with this secret past and don't mention it?"

Dan stood up and tried to put his arms around her, but she shrugged him away and backed up. He dropped his hands to his sides. "I had myself tested then, too. For everything. I was always fine. I would have told you then if I wasn't. I promise you."

"Promise me? I thought we promised each other a whole bunch of stuff. I thought we told each other everything. I thought we were living the same life." Avery sat down on the rocking chair she'd bought at I Bambini and covered her face with her hands, feeling tears pool under her palms, rocking herself into silence.

"I'm sorry. I'm so sorry."

She looked up and her mouth opened, but she couldn't put her lips around words. She closed her eyes again and replayed their life together, seeing what she'd thought was true—how they'd met, their wedding, their day-to-day life, work, so much work, dinners, movies, housework—and then saw what was real. All along, sneaking behind them both had been another Dan. Not the Dan she'd married, the whiz student, telecommunications wunderkind, happy, smiling, so-warm-as-he-held-her Dan. The Dan behind his desk, computer on, phone in his hand, deals spinning out as he spoke. The Dan who had a golf handicap of 6 and a 4.5 tennis rating. The Dan who laughed with Luís in the garage as they put together tables or chairs or cribs. This other Dan held hands with a woman, Randi, their noses numb with coke, their hearts empty. They sneaked into Bill and Marian's house and stole what they knew they could sell. Instead of living, they slumped wasted on their couch, waiting for their next hit or snort. And he fucked her, gave her what he couldn't give Avery, and then just left. This Dan, she saw, was the real Dan.

So nothing about their marriage was true. What had she expected? She should have known better. Nothing good lasted. Good things never survived crashes, weren't what floated up through dark water. They weren't what stuck and poked and woke you up at night, saying, "Yes, yes." She never gasped awake, sweaty from a nightmare, the sheets twisted around her, thinking, "You have a degree from one of the best colleges in the United States. You have a wonderful, attractive, successful, kind husband. A beautiful home. You are so healthy. What medical and dental insurance!" No.

The baby that she and Dan had tried so hard to have, the one Avery had carried in her head, looked at her and then shut its lovely deep eyes, floating away into darkness. All these months she'd wanted what wasn't true, a life and family with her husband, a man she knew so well, who was kind and soft and whole. Not like her. Not brittle and sharp and needful. This was the karma she must have earned after all. So much for all the mean, pointed barbs she'd held in. It was too late to change anything. Who cared that she was smart, could earn a lot of money, and had a nice house? She'd never find what she was looking for after all. And somehow, she'd always known that.

But if she was going to lose everything, she wanted to know why. She wanted to know it all, write it down in the pages of her mind so she could read and reread it her entire life. She wiped her eyes and stopped rocking. "You need to call this woman. Midori Nolan. You need to call her now, and I'm going to listen on the other phone. We have to find out everything."

Dan nodded. "Okay. Fine," he said. But neither of them moved, as if getting up and leaving the room would make it true.

Outside, renegade fireworks exploded on the horizon, bursts of red, white, and blue light flashing up into the night sky and then falling back to earth.

"Ms. Nolan? This is Dan Tacconi. I'm sorry to be calling you so late. We, uh, just got in."

Avery sat on her bed, while Dan talked in the kitchen. She could have taken the portable phone and sat by him throughout the discussion, but she didn't want to see his face. It would be hard enough hearing his voice and then listening to whatever this woman said.

"No problem at all. I'm glad you called, Mr. Tacconi. I apologize for bothering you on a holiday. But it is crucial that we speak."

"Dan."

"What?"

"You can call me Dan."

"All right. And I'm Midori."

Avery wanted to scream, but she clenched her jaw and took the phone away from her mouth so neither of them would hear her impatient breathing.

"So you heard my messages. About Randi Gold."

"I did. When did she—die?"

"About a month ago. She was at Turlock Medical Center at the end. We were first notified about the boy a little less than three weeks ago."

"How did she die?"

Midori paused, and then said quietly, "We should— Well, it was hepatitis C. It damaged her liver."

Avery heard Dan swallow, coughing a bit. She wondered if he was crying. "Oh. Oh," he mumbled.

"But her son is fine," Midori added quickly.

Dan coughed. "So about the boy . . ."

"Yes. This is the important part. When the authorities finally found the boy—"

"What do you mean, found the boy?"

Midori seemed to riffle through some papers. Avery pressed her tongue against the sore spot in her mouth. "This is the difficult part. It seems Randi didn't or couldn't tell anyone about her son. She died, and he was left alone in the home for over a week. Taking care of himself. Finally, one of the neighbors in the trailer park called the police."

Trailer park, Avery thought. *Just figures.*

"Oh, my God. Was he okay?" Dan asked.

"Physically, yes. But after being alone for a week and then being told that his mother had died, he was not in great shape psychologically. It was in the local papers here. I guess the story didn't make it up to the Bay Area."

So what, Avery wanted to say, *does this have to do with Dan? Get on with it. Tell him. Tell him the truth. Ask for it, Dan! Now! Ask for the answers that will ruin our life.*

"That's terrible," Dan said. "Where is he?"

"In foster care. Temporarily. We hope. And that's why I'm calling you."

Here it comes, Avery thought. She bent down to her knees, pushing her body together as if touching her own flesh could save her.

"Okay. What can I do?"

"When we went to the home, we found Randi's papers. Years ago, it seems she wrote a will, and indicated that, well, you were the boy's father."

Avery had known that was what was coming, and yet, to hear a stranger say what her brain had been spinning since she found Dan on the phone made her dizzy. A father. A father already. Of course his sperm had been good, motile, perfectly formed and shaped. He'd already produced one child. It wasn't him that was damaged. There was living evidence of his reproductive health living in foster care in the Central Valley.

"Oh."

"He's ten years old. Does that work in terms of a time frame?" Midori asked.

"Yeah. It does." Dan sounded cold, shut down.

"So, here's the thing. We need to do a DNA test. To check for paternity. And then we can talk about what you want to do. There's not really any obligation—"

"Obligation."

"What I mean is, the boy could stay in foster care. While we want to establish paternity, it doesn't mean you have to take custody. Paternity would necessitate some form of support from you, however."

"Custody." Dan was turning into a robot. Avery sat up and rubbed her forehead, unconsciously looking for a pen and paper. He should be taking notes, not repeating words. They were already talking about money. Jesus! She walked into the hall and then into the kitchen, cradling the phone as she moved. Dan was slumped over the counter, his face pale.

"We assumed you might want to—"

"Of course." Dan sat up when he saw Avery. "Yes. I see what you mean."

"So the DNA testing is very quick, very easy. It involves only a quick swab of your mouth. Once we have those details confirmed, we can talk about the rest. It seems overstepping to go into too much at this point."

"Okay," Dan said.

"Did you have any knowledge about this child?" Midori asked. "Did you have any discussion with Randi after you left Sacramento?"

"No. None. I left for Cal and never talked to her again. That makes me wonder—how did you get my phone number in the first place?"

"Your parents. She'd indicated their names. They were at the same residence, which made it easy."

"When did you talk with them?" Dan looked up at Avery, his mouth open slightly.

"This morning. I was so glad they were home."

They were home because they hadn't wanted to come here, Avery thought. They hadn't wanted to see what this was about. They cut themselves off, one more time, from Dan because of who he'd been, what he'd done, his past that trailed behind him. They didn't like the real Dan, the one she was just beginning to know.

Dan shook his head. "God."

"So, I'm going to FedEx you this paperwork, and the sooner you get to the doctor, the better for the boy."

The boy. The boy. Avery finally spoke, hearing the jerk of surprise in Midori Nolan's voice. "The boy. What's his name?"

"Mrs. Tacconi?"

"Yes."

"Oh. Hello. I didn't know you were there."

Avery pressed the phone against her cheek and brought a hand to her throat. She was here. She'd heard it all. "I am."

"Well. The boy. Daniel. His name is Daniel."

*   *   *

After they'd both hung up the phones—Midori Nolan assured that Dan would get the DNA test, and call the social worker in Contra Costa County who would be handling the case from this end— they stared at each other. Avery wondered how they were supposed to turn off the lights and go to bed. How would it be possible to slip back into the rhythm of a life that was based on lies? But yet, it was Dan in front of her. Dan. She wanted to move next to him and run her fingers through his thick dark hair, comforting him as she might a child.

"Aves," he said finally, standing up from the counter. He stopped, swallowed, ran his own fingers through his hair, pushing it back from his eyes. As long as she'd known him, Avery had never seen Dan hurt, at least for long. Sometimes after conversations with his parents or Jared, he'd flare quickly or stand still for a moment, his arms crossed, but he'd never let her see what she saw in his face now. She wanted to walk to him and comfort him. She wished she could make things better—but did she really? After all the lies he'd told—or was it truths he hadn't said? Avery shook her head and bit her lower lip.

"Don't. Let's not talk about it right now. I can't hear any more. Not one more word. Let's just go to bed."

"But—"

She raised her hand. "Seriously. I can't."

"All right." As he followed her into the bedroom, both of them flicking off lights as they went, she could feel his eyes on her neck, and she wanted to cover it with her hands. He couldn't look at her bare skin, when she'd never seen him at all.

He knew everything about her. He knew that the very inside parts of her wouldn't do what they were supposed to, and during all her confessions and pleas and talks, he'd never said, "We all have pasts." After any one of her crying fits about something or another, he could have launched into the story of Randi and their eight long years together. And he wouldn't have had to lay it all out at once. A casual remark, leading to details. A remembrance. A recollection. A confession late at night after lovemaking. Slowly, he could have unraveled the twisted story.

Now she could see why it had happened: Bill so strict, so firm, so unyielding, exactly the father she'd never want for her own children. Of course Dan had been unhappy in that house. So why didn't he tell her, letting her know about the drugs and the stealing and the police? If he'd revealed it bit by bit, piece by piece, she could have put his past together with the person he was now and still believed in him. But to hold it all in! Why?

Avery went into the bathroom and closed the door, leaning against it and staring at herself in the mirror. In the bedroom, she heard Dan's shoes thunk to the carpeted floor, drawers opening and closing, the quiet squeak of the bed. Now, she had to sleep with Dan and the past in one bed. She didn't know if there was room for them all.

In bed, her arm pressing down the blanket between them, she stared up at the dark ceiling, points of streetlight or moonlight slicing between the curtains. Dan was awake, his breath inaudible, not the deep, snoring rumble that he made each night until he turned on his side and tucked her arm around him. Her eyes felt red and rough, as if she'd been up for days. But she couldn't close them. She didn't know what she would see if she did.

"Aves?"

"What?" she whispered back.

"What will we do?"

She brushed her hair away from her forehead and turned to him. "You'll make the calls you told her you would. You'll go to the doctor."

"No," he said. "I mean, what will we do if he's mine?"

Her stomach lurched in the same way that had often made her think, for an instant, she was pregnant. "I don't know."

"If he's mine—"

"Dan, we don't know that yet. From what you've told me, maybe she wasn't the most . . . What I'm saying is, maybe there was someone else. Or someone just after you. You can't even think about it until you take the test."

"You're right. But why would she name him Daniel, Aves? And why would she do that and then not call me? It's not like she did it to lure me back. She was giving him . . ."

Avery closed her eyes and listened, even though she wanted to pull the blankets over her head and block out the sound of his sad voice.

Yes. Of course. He was right. Why would Randi do that if she had no intention of trotting a toddler up to a frat house and saying, "Here he is. Your son!"

When Avery was a teenager, one of her classmates had gotten pregnant by one of the most popular, talented seniors, a guy who approached her at a party, handed her drinks, and then had sex with her out on the lawn as the party raged inside. Nine months later, she named her son Bryson, after the guy, Brian, who had ignored her from the moment he pulled out of her and walked off the lawn. Avery's friend told everyone about her baby, told them his name, hoping that Brian would take the name as a calling and recognize the baby as his son. He never did.

Randi had never done that. She'd never called, not in ten years. There had been no awkward visit, Avery opening the door to a stranger and baby. No requests for money. No clue to lead Avery sooner to what she knew now.

"You're right," she said, her voice muffled. "He probably is yours."

Dan was silent, and he turned to the ceiling. "Yeah."

When her father was dying in the hospital, she and Mara and Loren had sat in the waiting area. No one came in to tell them anything. Their mother stayed behind the closed door of their father's room. One minute they were all sitting around his bed, trying to ignore the fact that the surgeon had told them there was nothing he could do. The cancer was everywhere—liver, kidney, bones, intestines. The next minute, the girls were rushed out by a nurse because something—blood pressure, heart rate—was wrong, off, weird, and then the door closed, and they were alone.

In her bed now, Dan on the other side, with her arm pressed firmly between them and the truth in the air above them, Avery felt the same as she had in that hospital room fifteen years ago. Whatever was behind her father's door, whatever the DNA tests would prove, would change her life forever. And there was nothing she could do about it but wait. Again.

In her dream that night, she saw her father's pale face, his dark hair pushed back, his brown eyes closed. But she knew he was alive. There was still hope. A chance. A voice—she didn't know if it was hers or someone else's or just a thought—told her to pull the needles out of his cheeks and chin and forehead in less than five minutes and he would live. That was when she noticed the thin, quivering needles. So many of them. But she had to do it, and the voice told her to start, and she pulled and pulled and pulled. There were so many. Her fingers began to cramp, but she kept at it, even as the light began to fade. Her father's face dissolved into the background, everything a smooth, pale gray.

She woke up, her body rigid, her eyes looking into the dark room that could have been any room, any place, perhaps her bedroom back in 1987. Breathing in and out—*inhale, exhale*—she slowed her thoughts, saw the shadow of her dresser, the fluid swaths of curtain, the ridge of Dan's body on the other side of the bed. Avery grabbed at her chest, trying to stop her heart's wild beating. She couldn't save her father, even in a dream.

Dan turned, his arm falling between them. Avery looked at the ceiling, knowing that she couldn't fix this either. There was no way to keep alive what she had wanted.

The next morning, Dan still asleep, Avery slipped out of bed, into the hall, and then pushed open the door to the room they called the nursery. Or at least, she did, saying, "Oh, I had the bassinet delivered. Could you put it in the nursery, Dan?" For him, the word—not to mention the purchases—was presumptuous or simply bad luck, she could tell, but to Avery, the nursery's existence meant that her pregnancy could happen, just as easily as when she said, "I'm a Cal graduate" months before graduation, or, "I'm Mrs. Avery Tacconi," long before she and Dan were engaged. If you said something and meant it, it could come true.

The air was still and smelled of plastic wrapping, cotton, and wood. In the corner of the room, she'd stacked paint cans. Martha Stewart colors: Viburnum, the palest off-pink white, and Linen for the trim. She and Valerie had decided that with these colors, she could add any color of wallpaper trim, blue or pink. As they stood at the cash register at Kmart with brushes and tape and paint trays, Valerie had rushed to the back wall and picked up wallpaper samples. "You never know. We might need these tomorrow!" That shopping trip had been a day before a visit with Dr. Browne but then, as usual, the results were negative. No baby that month. She hadn't gone back to Kmart since.

Even though Dan always shook his head slightly when she read the advertisements in the *Chronicle,* she went to the sales at I Bambini, Macy's, Nordstrom, Toys "Я" Us, Mervyns, Target, Emporium. In the past two years, she'd found the bassinet, a crib, a complete layette, Diaper Genie, bathtub, stroller, car seat, baby shoes, playpen, changing table, dresser, a baby names book. She'd kept some of the stuff in boxes, tucked neatly away in the closet, but she'd made Dan put the crib together and she'd filled the baby's dresser with clothes and supplies, the top covered with ointments and lotions. And only a week ago, Valerie had handed her a bag full of tiny newborn T-shirts and sleepers, things that Tomás at only three months had already outgrown. "I want you to have them," she'd said. "I want your baby to be the one we hand down to." With each purchase or gift, Avery crossed off an item on the list she kept in the bottom drawer.

She'd also picked out the baby names she liked best. Of course, there were the inevitable but unlikely and slightly ridiculous family combinations: Isabel Marian and Marian Isabel or Walter William and William Walter. She would touch the crib and imagine Sophie, Ana, Mackenzie, Keegan, Connor, Brandon, Julia, Jordan, or Ashley.

Now, she walked over and rubbed her hand on the sheet that she'd put on the mattress, the bumper that softened the edges of the wood, its ruffles between her fingers, the wool blanket with its soft pastel threads. How stupid. How presumptuous, as Dan would have said if he'd dared to say anything about the baby to her. What was she thinking? What was this room anyway? She looked around at all her purchases, some of them two years old, some out-of-date, out-of-style, useless, already replaced with other, more clever baby gear. Here it was: Avery's sad museum of desperation.

She slipped down the wall, her butt on the floor, and hugged her knees. These past two years had been a game, a mirage, a fantasy. Dan had played along with her as had Valerie and Isabel and Loren, but, as her father used to say, she'd "put the cart before the horse." A huge, stupid, ridiculous cart with no horse in sight.

Wiping her eyes, she thought of what she used to do when she came home from high school her freshman year. Mara was in college at Wellesley, Loren was at cheerleading practice, and her mother was in her nest in her downstairs room, her face pressed flat against the pillow, her hand tired and limp on an open book. The bedroom was always hot and smelled like Oil of Olay and Caress soap. Quietly, Avery would open the window, bending down to breathe in clean air, turning back to her mother, who never moved a muscle, not until at least six when the darkness woke her.

Going back upstairs, Avery would flick on the television and listen to the shows as she cleaned up the breakfast dishes and the sad half-empty glasses of water and coffee and plates of uneaten soda crackers and toast Isabel had left around the house. Once a week, Avery would vacuum everything, the machine leaving straight, comforting lines in the red carpet. She would feed their dog, Pippin, change the water in her steel bowl, and drop flakes into the aquarium, feeding the last of her father's exotic fish. The sad fish swam in the murky water as the filter burbled. Then she would take out a pad of paper and make lists: her homework, her dream boyfriends, her perfect life. She'd never gotten the dream boyfriend—her long legs and full breasts were hidden in the folds of Loren's too-big hand-me-downs—but she'd always finished her homework, and then her perfect life had just about come true.

Now the list she had been keeping for the past two years needed to be torn up. Standing up and walking around the nursery, Avery touched everything and then began to pick things up and place them in the closet and dresser—the animal mobile Valerie had found for her while shopping for Tomás, the case of baby wipes from Target, the Diaper Genie, the boxes and bags of teething rings, Desitin, Johnson's Baby Lotion, Burt's Bees Baby Bee soap. She put the paint and brushes by the door so she could take them to the garage. She stripped the mattress of the cute sheep-and-duck sheets and bumper, folding them up and putting them in the closet, as well. Upending the mattress, she leaned it against the wall. Later, she'd have Dan come back in here to dismantle the crib. Maybe

Luís would help him. Or maybe it was too sad a task to invite anyone in for.

Finally, she opened the window, the plastic, cotton, wood smell leaking out into the morning air. She breathed in and turned around, as if expecting to see her mother, sleeping.

Later, after she made the coffee and emptied the dishwasher, she clicked on her Palm and looked up the number. Dr. Browne and his staff would be out of the office because of the holiday weekend, but she could leave a message. It would be better that way. She wouldn't have to talk with Mary, who would ask questions and try to commiserate and cajole. She wouldn't have to explain to the well-meaning nurse that she'd made a mistake, made the wrong kind of list, prepared for the wrong set of circumstances altogether.

Avery dialed and then listened to the long options, irritated by the answering system. She didn't want to talk with the answering service. All she wanted was the nonurgent voice mail. As she waited, she looked to the hall, hoping Dan wouldn't come out now. Finally, she pushed 1 to leave a message, walking into the family room as she did.

"Hi, this is Avery Tacconi. I need to cancel all my appointments for a while. I found out I need to deal with a family situation, and we won't be doing the next round of IUI. I will call to reschedule when things are settled. Thanks. Thanks for all your help." As she pressed the phone off, she saw Mary's face, heard her say, "You don't know what I've seen here."

It was done. She put the phone down and stared out at the pool. A twirl of squawking starlings flumed up and over the fence, their feathers dark and slightly iridescent in the morning light. Next door, either Valerie or Luís was taking a shower, steam rising from one of the vents on the roof.

"What did you do?"

She jumped, breathing hard. "What?"

Dan walked over to her. He laid his hands gently on her shoulders. "Why, Aves?"

She turned, pulling herself away from him, still holding the phone to her chest. "You're asking *me* why?"

"You want this so much. That's all we've been talking about for years. We don't have to change anything we're doing yet."

Avery bit her cheek, winced, and looked at Dan. Yesterday, she couldn't imagine that the Dan of the past and her Dan, this Dan, were the same person. But this morning, now, she could. She'd just missed the wounded, worried look around his eyes because he smiled so much, said the right things, assured her, his colleagues, everyone. His parents had known, so had Jared, and if she'd paid attention, she would have been able to see who they were really looking at. If she'd listened at all, she'd have been able to see Marian and Bill holding back, scared to give him their hearts again, knowing exactly what he was capable of. Avery would have seen the man she'd talked to last night, the one with the kind of past she'd seen only on news programs; he'd been one of those teenagers hauled out of parental homes, struggling against handcuffs and shame.

She had married both Dans, the past and the present, and he wouldn't be who he was now unless the other had happened. Nothing was for good or for real. Her father's death had taught her that. She shouldn't have forgotten.

"Let's be realistic," she said, flipping her hair off her shoulder and stepping away from Dan's hands. "We can't do this right now. We are going to have to deal with this boy. Daniel. If he's yours, you aren't going to want him in foster care."

"What do you mean?"

"I haven't been realistic for about two years. Maybe longer. I've been living in some kind of fantasy world. No one stopped me. It's time I stopped myself."

"Why was it a fantasy, Aves? We want a baby like everyone—"

"Everyone doesn't get news like we did last night, do they? We have to be serious now. We've seen *Sixty Minutes,* the news. You've read the stories of five hundred kids to one caseworker. All that. You know what happens. The abuse. The neglect. Kids disappearing and no one noticing. If you don't take him now, you'll never get to know him. In eight years, he'll be grown up. If he can have a father, he deserves one."

Dan shook his head and licked his lips. "But, you're okay with this?"

Without thinking, she barked out a jagged laugh. "No. Absolutely not. I'm not okay with it, Dan. I'm not okay that you didn't tell me about your life. I thought we were married. I thought we shared everything. I deserved to know about you. To *know* you in the first place."

Dan shook his head and breathed out slow and light. "I didn't think you'd want me if you knew what I'd been like—who I was. What I'd let myself become with Randi."

"Is there anything else you want to tell me? Any other secrets you're hiding?"

Looking up, he seemed to think, replaying all the years before her. Avery's stomach tightened, a hard, dark knot inside.

Finally, he said, "No. That was it. That's what I didn't want to tell you because I knew you'd take it like this. So angry. I knew you'd turn away." His voice was sharp, the tone she'd heard him use with coworkers when a system wasn't delivered as promised or a client was upset. How could he talk to her like that, now, when he was the guilty one?

"Maybe you were right," she blurted. "Maybe I wouldn't have wanted you." She put her hand on her hip, fighting back tears. She closed her eyes and saw their wedding, everything perfect except that her mother's brother Lloyd gave her away instead of her father. But her simple, white silk dress, the cascades of white roses, baby's breath, ivy, the cake from Katrina Cazelle, and her groom were what she'd pictured, listed, imagined: Dan in his black tux, his face tanned and gorgeous over his white shirt, Jared behind him, his parents actually smiling in the front row of the Saint Stephen's church, her mother in her lilac dress, Mara and Loren standing next to Avery in their bridesmaids gowns. That's what she'd wanted. She'd never signed on for the dark twin in the back row sitting with his skanky girlfriend, both high as kites, laughing at how stupid this was.

Avery opened her eyes. "I lost my father. I know what it feels like to really lose two parents. I could never— It would be terrible to leave your son out there, alone, without anyone."

Dan crossed his arms over his chest and looked her in the eye, an explanation on his tongue. There. There he was, the man she knew, who could fix what was broken: a bad grade, a conflict at work, an overpayment on a bill. In this instant, he was the husband she thought she knew. Her love. Her hurt love. "Aves."

The coffeemaker hissed, and Avery turned to pour two cups, trying to keep her hands from shaking. She walked to the fridge and took out the milk, pouring just the right amount for Dan. Handing him the cup, she picked up her own, closed her eyes, and sipped.

"Aves?"

"What?" The coffee was black and strong in her throat, the same feeling that was in her heart.

"I'm surprised, that's all. I don't even know if I can do this myself. There's so much to think about."

Avery breathed out. "Do you think you could leave him out there? Wouldn't you spend the rest of your life wondering about him? What he was doing? How he looked? If he was safe? You left him once Dan. You can't do it again."

Dan put down his coffee cup and rubbed his forehead, leaning against the counter. "Yes."

"So that's it. That's what we'll do."

"And the baby?"

"There is no baby. Not yet. Later. We can do it later. Dr. Browne, Mary, my mom, Loren, everyone says there's time," she said, her voice hitching on the words she hated.

"Aves. I don't know," Dan said. "What about all the stuff you've bought?"

"What good does it do when there's nothing in here?" she said, putting a hand on her belly. "And anyway, I've packed up the nursery."

"You did?"

"Where else is he going to stay? Your office? The couch? I need you and Luís to dismantle the crib. Everything else is in the closet." Avery dumped the rest of her coffee in the sink and rinsed out the cup. She looked out the window, the air already full of heat and summer. If she didn't get out of the kitchen this instant, she wouldn't be able to survive into the next minute. Her skin felt hot, her face full of prickings as if it were covered with needles. "I'm going to go work out. Then I'm going with Valerie to the park."

"Aves," Dan said, looking up. "Don't go."

On her way out of the kitchen she turned. If she was seeing him for the first time at Peet's this moment, she'd walk right out the door and not look back. "I have to."

"Did you know?" Dan held the phone against his cheek, listening to his brother's breathing. "Did you know this was going on?"

"Mom called me and said some social worker had called about Randi, but either she didn't tell Mom about the kid or Mom didn't tell me."

Dan pressed his lips together. If they were twelve and ten again, he'd punch Jared in the stomach. If they were seventeen and fifteen, he'd clock him, as he'd done a couple of times. He closed his eyes. Of course. Dan had deserved this for years: Jared finding a way to punch him back. Jared kept the secret because he wanted to. Because he could.

"So you brought all that up last night about the pool and everything. . . ."

"Look, I'm sorry. I should have told you. Warned you. But there wasn't a good time with the party and everything. It's not like we had a minute of privacy, and you get so mad when I bring up anything. Anyway, I guess Mom's call made me think about you and Randi. Before it got weird. I used to do everything with you guys for a while, remember? I was half in love with her, Dan. In the beginning, she was a beautiful girl."

Dan slumped down in a chair in the living room and scratched his knee, liking the hard feel of his nails against his jeans. "I know. But what am I going to do now? You didn't see Avery this morning. She's pulled down the nursery. She's not going to try for the baby. She called the doctor. And I've got to go and get cells scraped out of my mouth for a DNA test. What am I going to do about that?"

Jared sighed, and Dan could hear all the years of advice he hadn't listened to in his brother's breath. Jared had occasionally visited his and Randi's dark apartment despite their parents' disapproval, sat on the couch and watched sitcom reruns, and tried to get him to quit taking drugs, enroll in college, find a job, apologize to their parents, and admit to stealing the coins and the credit card. Dan had laughed out loud, scooting over as three of Randi's friends walked in the apartment without knocking and slipped between the brothers on the couch, giggling and leaning toward Jared. Dan had rolled another joint and turned the channel. After a while, Jared stopped coming at all.

One hot, end-of-summer morning, Dan had awakened to find that Randi—after a long night of Long Island iced teas and sticky, thick joints—had thrown up in her sleep, her face clammy, her body sweaty and hot. He had leaned over her, afraid, his palm cupping her mouth, checking for life, and when her steamy, putrid breath puffed against his skin, he had stared at her. Her body was warm, but he imagined she could be dead all the same, like Janis Joplin or Jimi Hendrix, someone so wasted that not even stomach contractions and vomit scared her awake. Pushing her damp black hair away from her skin— it was so pale and thin, Dan could see her veins—he watched her pulse, a rapid one-two, one-two beat on her temple. She was fine. Maybe she'd be hungover and grouchy and heavy-lidded for the whole day, but okay. By ten or eleven at night, she'd probably be sitting on his lap and lighting another joint, the day repeating itself over and over again, as it had for months and years.

Dan had moved away from Randi, and leaned against the wall. He had a headache and cotton mouth—his arms were sore from some kind of game he and his dealer, Ingram, had played, a kind of arm wrestling for hits on the bong. Who really won that one? he wondered, when all it gave you in the end was a pounding head and a girlfriend sleeping in her own barf.

He rose to get a towel to start cleaning her up, and then he sat back on the mattress. Dan looked at the dirty sheets, the bare white walls, clothes in piles on the green carpet, the red bong on the dresser. Out in the living room, Ingram was probably naked and asleep, either Lucy or Joelle (or maybe both) next to him. Staring at his pale hands, Dan knew he couldn't live this day over again. He had to start to move, and not just out of the bed.

The next day, without saying more than "I've got to go somewhere," he drove down to Sacramento Valley College and stood in line with kids who'd been sophomores when he'd graduated from high school. At the window, he enrolled in freshman composition, humanities, chemistry, and California history.

When he finished all the requirements for his AA degree two years later, he didn't tell Randi about his acceptance to Cal until the week before he moved out. But really, he'd moved out long before, going to bed early while Randi went out with her friends, studying Greek mythology or calculus or chemical reactions as she sat on the couch, flicked the channels on the TV, and lit another joint. And when he was gone for good, for real, she'd never called. Not once. She must have been pregnant the day he said, "I'm sorry. I've got to go," and drove to Berkeley, his used Ford Taurus filled with boxes. He'd been so busy with himself, he must not have noticed that her periods had stopped or that she was sick in the mornings or that her stomach stuck out in her tight jeans.

Dan hadn't wanted to see or hear anything back then. He had been so scared, he'd refused advice, especially Jared's. He had stopped listening to anybody.

But now that his old life had found him, he needed help. Now, for the first time in twenty years, he needed his brother.

"Do you really want me to say anything?" Jared asked.

"Yeah. I do." Dan swallowed, waiting for words.

"You're going to call the social worker again, and you're going to get the full story. Avery's not home right now, right?"

"Right."

"Find out what happened to Randi. Find out about the boy. Get the details. And then do what the social worker says. Take care of it. Clean up your own mess."

That's what their father had always said, year after year, problem after problem. "Clean up your own mess, dim bulb," Bill had said, cuffing Dan on the shoulder. "Figure a way out of this," he'd say after a bad report card, a principal's phone call, a three-hundred-dollar speeding ticket. But how could he clean up a life? His father had barked and shouted, but he'd never taught them what to do, assuming that his words were rule enough.

"So if he's mine, I bring him home."

Jared sighed. "Of course."

"Right."

"Dan, it's not like you haven't been thinking about how to be a parent for the last two years. My God, you and Avery were desperate for a child. You two have every child book in the universe in your living room. Maybe it's not the way you wanted it to be, but it's the way it is. You can't just walk away from him."

That's what Avery had said, exactly. Dan needed Excedrin. He needed to think. "Okay. I'll call you back, all right?"

"Dan, you've got to listen to me. For once."

"I know. I am. Thanks, Jared. Okay?"

"All right."

He was about to hang up when he caught his breath on a thought. "Wait. Um, should I call Mom and Dad?"

Dan could hear Jared putting the phone back to his ear. "What?"

"Should I call Mom and Dad?"

"I would— I think you should wait. Wait till it's decided. Until you meet him. Daniel. Wait until . . ."

"Until I do something right?"

His brother said nothing, but Dan knew he agreed. Why would his parents want to know the terrible details of Randi's life and death and child—a story they'd hated from the beginning—when they hadn't wanted to hear the good stories of his life since Randi? What was he thinking?

"Never mind. Thanks. I'll call you later."

They hung up, and Dan walked to the kitchen cupboard, opening the Excedrin bottle and popping two pills in his mouth. Since he'd awakened, his forehead had felt crushed by a large hand. "The hand of God," he could imagine Reverend Rawson saying, his frightening Bible tales ringing through the children's Sunday school class. No wonder Dan had refused to go to church when he was thirteen. Who needed the hand of God squeezing your head shut?

He put the bottle back in the cupboard and walked down the hall into the nursery. But when he opened the door, he knew it wasn't a nursery anymore. Avery had put all the clothes and toys away, stripped the mattress, and leaned it against the wall. The crib was just a piece of furniture now. Nothing that they would fill themselves. No baby.

Dan slumped against the wall and shook his head. Goddamn it. What was he expecting? Why had he ever imagined the past would disappear? Instead, it had followed him like a shadow, its black tail whipping all the way into the Central Valley, into Turlock, into a trailer park, into a medical center where Randi had died alone.

"Buck up, Junior," he heard his father say. "Keep cracking."

Dan breathed in and wiped his face. Fine. He'd buck up. He'd call Midori Nolan. He'd call Luís for help taking the crib apart and carrying it into the garage. He'd stop crying. He wouldn't call his parents. He'd finally do as he was told.

"So she contracted hepatitis C how?" Dan asked into the phone.

"I wanted to talk with you about that, but I felt . . ." For the first time, Midori Nolan seemed to falter, her crisp sentence breaking off in his ear.

"What?"

"I was going to tell you that you might want to get tested for that. It's contracted through blood products or shared needles and can be dormant in the bloodstream for some time, I hear. But then your wife was on the phone. She must be having a hard time with this."

Dan nodded and looked out the living room window. Avery's Land Rover was back—parked out front—but she'd walked over to Luís and Valerie's, their front door closing behind her. "Yeah. Both of us."

"Of course. But the facts about hep C are clear. It can be hidden, and then it can cause problems."

"I'm not worried about it," Dan said. "My wife and I, we've been going through infertility treatments. I've been tested for everything a couple of times. Randi must have picked that up after—after me.

After the baby." Dan leaned back against the couch. What had her life been like after he left? Had she given up the drugs when Daniel was born? As she closed the thin apartment door, what did she decide? To keep the baby, that was one thing. To go back to her drugs. That was another. And when had she contracted hepatitis? That was through blood. Needles? Sex? He didn't think he'd ever be able to ask Daniel any of these questions.

He sucked in air. "But the boy? He's healthy, isn't he?"

"Daniel? Oh, yes. He's a little small, but his doctor said physically everything is great."

"Physically. What about, you know?"

"I did mention to you that he'd been left alone for almost a week, right? The story is that Randi went to the hospital—or someone called the ambulance. She was critical at that point, and Daniel ended up taking care of himself. Not going to school. Feeding himself. Worrying. A neighbor finally figured out what was going on, though it took him a while because Randi wasn't always home in general. Let's put it this way: Daniel has some 'issues.' "

"Issues," Dan repeated. Who didn't have issues? He himself had ten years of "back" issues. He had a year's subscription of issues. Avery did, too. Luís. Valerie. Even happy people had issues. Problems. Sad stories. But most people didn't have to stay at home in trailers while their mothers died of blood diseases in hospitals. Most people had family and friends to take care of them. Most people weren't completely alone.

"How has he handled all of it?" Dan asked.

"He's really a great little kid. I think he took over the parental role in some ways, making him overly responsible but still upset. This happens with children of addicted parents. He fights sometimes when he doesn't have words. Acts out. It's hard for him to open up."

A chip off the old block, Dan thought. He hadn't opened up either, and now he had no words, the pause in the phone staticky and long.

"So is your wife pregnant?" Midori asked finally.

"No. Nothing's worked."

"Oh."

"She gave up. For now. This morning. Called her doctor, canceled all the appointments. Do you know what that means?" he said without pausing. "That's like giving up a life. She's saying no to the process that she's followed to the letter since we started two years ago. I can't believe it."

"Dan."

"We've been trying for fucking two years. And this morning she rips up the nursery, calls the doctor, and then leaves."

"Dan," Midori said, "this hasn't likely been easy for her to hear. I'm sorry I had to dump it on you like this. If it hadn't been—"

"It's not your fault at all." Dan paced the living room. "It's all about me and how I screwed everything up long before I even met Avery. How did I think things could be normal? I just left Randi. I left her, and she had to take care of our son. I know he's mine. Randi might have been a drug addict. She might have partied and been a lazy mother or something, but she was true. My God, she was true to me. She never called me, even when things must have been complete shit for her. She let me have my life."

Dan leaned against the smooth wall and then slid to the floor, bouncing on his knees, his head hanging. "She never even called me."

"Dan," Midori said, her calm voice raised. "Listen. This is difficult. No matter who you are in the situation, this is difficult."

"Especially for Randi. She's the one who's dead." He wiped his eyes and tried to breathe.

"Yes, that's true. But really, it's harder for you and Daniel and Avery. You're the ones who have to live now. There is so much that all of you will have to adjust to. But first things first."

Right, Dan thought. One thing at a time, the way he'd lived since the day he woke up to find Randi asleep in her own vomit. Take one day at a time and do it. He'd bucked up, like his father had always wanted. He kept cracking.

"First, do what we talked about last night. Make the appointments, okay? And I'm going to give you another number. I want you to call today, right after we hang up. I bet he's not in the office, but you need to see someone."

"You mean like a psychologist?"

"Yes. That's exactly what I mean. His name is Bret Parish. He's in Berkeley. We've known each other since college. He's worked with a lot of families."

Dan blew out a trapped breath and stood up, pushing his hair back from his forehead. Outside, Ralph Chatagnier was sweeping the remnants of sparklers and firecrackers from his driveway and talking to Frank Chow, who was watering his slightly crushed Jerusalem sage and purple penstemon. Just beyond this window, life was going on as it had for years. How would he ever be able to open the door of his house and merge into it as if nothing were different? Avery had managed to keep moving, work out, talk with friends. Here he was. Stuck. That's why he loved her, why he'd always loved her. She knew how to go on, to take plain air and form it into action and substance.

"I'll take the name," he said, walking over to Avery's organized desk and picking up a pen. "Give it to me. I'll call." He would go anywhere to stop feeling like this.

Luís opened the nursery door and poked his head in. "Hey, man. I've been knocking on the front door."

Dan shrugged, staring at the crib. "Sorry. I'm . . ." He trailed off, not knowing how to finish the sentence.

Luís opened the door the whole way and walked in, putting his toolbox on the carpet. "Well, Avery sure had at it in here."

"Are they still at your house?" Dan swallowed, wiped his face, and stood up. "Or did they go to the park?"

Putting his hands in his pockets and leaning against the wall, Luís shook his head. "Man, they hightailed it out of there. Packed up a lunch that will last them for days. Thank God it's cooled down some, or I'd have to go rescue Tomás."

Rescue. That's what Dan should be doing already, finding his poor boy and bringing him home. Going to Breuners or Sleep Train to buy a big-boy bed, going to Mervyn's for clothes and shoes, calling up the school district to get him tested this summer so he would be ready for school. Rather than calling Jared and Midori and the doctors and this psychologist, Bret Parish, and making all his appointments, he should be gone, halfway to Turlock by now, halfway to the foster home.

"So, like, what happened, man?" Luís sat down on the carpet next to him.

Dan looked into Luís's brown eyes. If he'd been able to look at eyes like that instead of his father's or even Jared's eyes, he knew he'd never have had to lie. Tomás was lucky if this was the gaze he'd get when he cut school or blew up a mailbox or skinny-dipped at Larch Bank Pool. Or became, God forbid, a pot fiend or lived with a live-wire girl or stole family-heirloom coins to buy drugs. He sighed and pulled his knees up, wrapping his arms around them. "The past. It caught up to me. Big time. And it's bad."

"Avery said there was a kid, man."

Dan nodded. "I had a girlfriend. For a long time. All of high school and four years afterward. She died. She died a month ago, and she had a ten-year-old kid. They think he's mine."

"Shit, man. Unbelievable."

"Yeah."

Luís leaned against the wall. "You know, this happened to my father's family. In Mexico City, where my grandfather is from—Tacuba—he had another family. Like, four girls. My grandmother knew about it, but it was this terrible family secret, a giant skeleton in the closet. When my dad finally found out, he wouldn't speak to my grandfather for years."

"What about your grandmother? Did she forgive him?" Dan thought of Avery, her sudden, early-morning rearranging of this room, her clipped, tight voice, her rigid back as she walked out of the house.

"It was ugly, man. They lived in a house that has a courtyard, house on all four sides. My grandfather stayed on one side, my grandmother on the other, only meeting for meals. When my father went down, he'd stay on my grandmother's side. At fiestas, they would ignore each other or say things like, 'Would you ask your *abuelo* to answer the door' or 'Tell your *abuelita* that we have run out of rum.'"

Dan looked around the room. Maybe he would end up in here, alone or with his boy, Valerie acting as intermediary, saying, "Avery wants to know if you paid the gas bill" or "Did you call Terminix about the repair on the pool deck?"

"So, what happened?"

Luís shook his head. "My grandfather got sick and called all his family to the deathbed. My father and his brothers and these four girls—women, at this point. My grandmother made a big wailing deal about forgiving him, hugging the four girls, and then he died, my grandmother holding his hand. And now, I have this huge extended family. Valerie and I visited them all when we went to Mexico City after we graduated. It all ended up okay in the end."

"But," Dan said, "it wasn't easy during."

"No. My grandmother and grandfather lost a lot of years. Could have been good years. My dad, too."

"I've lost ten years of this boy's life. And with Avery and the baby we don't have, I'm losing more time."

"But," Luís said, patting Dan's knee, "man, you didn't even know. My grandfather knew about his 'surprise' other children. You weren't even warned. You are acknowledging this right away. Not like my family."

"So what? It all boils down to the same thing. Look what I've lost."

Luís leaned forward and opened his toolbox. They sat in silence as Luís picked up and looked at his wrench, screwdriver, and hammer, finally putting them down and sighing. "I can't pretend to really know how you feel, man. But you don't have to lose any more, Dan. It doesn't have to be that way. We're not in Mexico. It can be a different story."

"What do I do? What should I do? I don't know how to do this. No one seems to be able to tell me. I've been listening to advice, but I'm sitting here in this room. Waiting."

"What are you waiting for, man?"

Dan looked up at his friend, his mouth open. He was waiting for it to be over. He was waiting for the test results, the foster care visit and reunion or "union" with Daniel, the move home, Avery's reconciliation with his past and his son and their new life, his parents' blessing. A baby, his and Avery's, born after Daniel settled in. He was waiting to not have to live through it. "I just need it to be over."

Luís stood up. "It's not going to be over unless it starts."

Dan stood up, feeling a new ache in his bones. "You're right."

"So let's take this crib apart."

"Fine."

"And then take a shower, man, so I won't get arrested if I haul you out of this house. We'll get some lunch, and we'll do what you need to do today. Maybe I'll barbecue tonight. I've got some leftover *carne asada.*"

Dan bent over Luís's toolbox, trying to choose a screwdriver through the blur in his head. "Yes," he whispered, and they began, taking apart the thick, rich wood of his baby's bed.

Even though she hadn't been invited, Randi Gold sat between Dan and Avery at dinner. As Valerie and Luís passed dishes—*carne asada, salsa verde, arroz con elote*—Avery handing plates to Dan but not looking at him, he felt Randi sidling in, leaning her elbows on the table, saying, "What's this shit? God, Dan, what in the *hell* are you eating? Do you have any hamburgers or something? A plain old hot dog?" As she said the words, she looked at him, her fine, thin freckled skin crinkled at the corners of her eyes. Her hair was pulled up in a puffy ponytail, wild curls spilling to her shoulders, the right one bare, her purple shirt pulled down off it. She kicked him under the table with her sharp, black heel and then wrapped her leg around his as she used to do, pulling him close.

"This is even better the next day," Avery said, holding up a forkful of *carne asada*. "I could eat this constantly if it weren't for the cholesterol."

"Who is she trying to impress?" Randi dug an elbow in his side. "She doesn't even know how to spell it. Like, can't you just see her, all '*a-s-e* . . . whatever.' I bet she really wants some of that wiggly-shit Jell-O salad."

"My mom, man, she would cook this for days," Luís said. "That and soup. Soup with different noodles each day. It's called *fideos*. Maybe she thought if there were wagon wheels one day and macaroni the next, we wouldn't notice. But we did. I can't bear to even smell it now."

"I wish she'd stay with us and make that soup every day," Valerie said. "I can't even open a can of Campbell's, I'm so tired."

Randi pushed closer. "Let's get out of here. Why are you with these people? Who are they, anyway? Some boring couple? And, like, your wife? She's all perfect and shit. I don't know what you see in her. Look at her clothes!" Randi swished her skirt, the smell of synthetic fabric flowing into his nose. "Khaki! A polo shirt. God. There's no way she does what I did to you. Remember, Dan?"

Dan wiped sweat off his forehead and sat back. The room was

pulsing with heat and talk, Avery telling Valerie about some recipe she read in a magazine, Luís cooing at Tomás. No one was talking about Daniel or what had happened less than twenty-four hours ago. Not one of them said the words *DNA* or *paternity* or *custody*. None of them mentioned the crib reduced to parts, folded up and leaning against the garage wall next to the dresser and cans of paint. No one mentioned the drugs, the stealing, the police.

Randi moved behind him now, hugging him around the neck, whispering in his ear. "Let's blow this joint. You know you're bored out of your mind. What's your problem? Come on." He breathed in quick, swallow breaths, drowning in Randi's scent of cherry lip gloss, Charlie perfume, and cigarette smoke.

"Kind of anticlimactic around here after last night," Valerie was saying. "I think we'll have to wait for Halloween for any excitement like that in the neighborhood."

Dan almost jerked out of his chair, certain Valerie was talking about Midori's call. He leaned back, trying to find a resting spot on Randi's arms, but all he felt were wooden chair rails.

"Frank and Ralph have an idea for some kind of Christmas tree lane," Luís said quickly. "You know, with lights." Luís jiggled Tomás. "Ralph will probably put on some kind of suit."

Valerie glanced at Avery and then Dan and pushed her food around on her plate.

"Halloween. Christmas. Who needs it?" Randi tightened her grip. "Boring! A real bore-o-rama!"

Blinking, the room swimming out of focus, Dan tried to stand. He grabbed on to the table, the placemat under his fingers. "I . . . I—" he began, but he saw stars, orbs of white circling the room. Everyone, even Randi, stared at him.

"Dan? Dan?" Avery stood up and grabbed on to his arm. "What's wrong?"

"It's all my fault," he said. "I didn't know."

Avery looked at him and pulled him close. "Do you mean the boy?"

He felt his legs trembling and let her help him sit back down. "Yes. And Randi. I didn't know. I didn't know she was going to die."

"Oh, that's fine. Worry about me now." Randi loosened her arms from his neck, but her long, purple nails dug slightly into his collarbone. "Not a call the whole time you were in your fancy college with the prepsters and fluffy sorority sisters. She was one, huh? I can tell. Don't lie to me."

"You didn't know," Valerie said. "No one let you know."

"It's my fault," Dan said, wishing Randi would let go, her nails so sharp.

"For Christ's sake! Get over yourself," Randi said, sitting on his lap, her hand overlapping Avery's. "It was my life, Dan."

"It was her life," Avery said slowly, as if she'd been thinking about that exact sentence all afternoon. "She made her choices. She chose not to tell you about anything. You made choices, too." She looked at her plate, and he heard what she didn't say: *You chose to not tell me a thing.*

"Yeah, man," Luís said. "Don't beat up on yourself. It's done. Water under the bridge."

And then Dan realized it was actually Avery hugging him lightly, her skin, her touch pushing Randi out of his lap and away from the table. Her smell, her creamy soap, her Redken shampoo, her Green Tea perfume. Avery. His wife.

"I'm outta here," Randi said. "Just, like, take care of shit, will ya? I mean, God. That's all I wanted, after all. I wrote that letter for a reason. Duh!" She flicked her hair behind her shoulder, put her hands on her hips, and gave him one last look. "Jeez, Dan. Get on with it. Like you did ten years ago. Move. Just get on with it. Take care of your son."

As she walked away, he thought to wave, but she was already gone, and the only thing left was Avery in his lap. Not Randi. Not the past, but the future. Closing his eyes, he hugged Avery back, the room still again, the stars gone, his breath deep and slow.

Five

Monday morning while Dan was in the shower, Avery went into the kitchen and grabbed the portable phone. Her old boss, Brody Chovanes, was bound to be in the office early after a holiday weekend, ready to pounce when other people took off the week following the Fourth. As she dialed his number, her hands stiff and cold in the sealed air-conditioned air, she could see him sitting at his desk, pressing through his contacts on his BlackBerry, searching for the one person who would land him an account.

Back when she worked with him, she loved the mornings as much as he did, knowing that when a vice president in charge of technology wanted change, he or she wanted it fast. All week, while Lanny was working on specs and packaging with the staff, Avery would be organizing a PowerPoint presentation that would dazzle even the most stolid accountant. Meanwhile, Brody was visiting the site, charming the client, making promises Avery knew they could keep. In the afternoons, they would all confer about the deal, the excitement building as they continued organizing over dinner at Andrés. At ten, Avery would straggle home, her calves aching from her high heels, the small of her back tense, Dan already asleep.

But by Friday, if the sales meeting went well, the client nodding and clapping and shaking their hands, they'd won. How sweet a Friday evening after that! How wonderful the weekend. But by Monday morning, they were back at it.

Even as she waited for the voice mail system that would eventually allow her to dial Brody's extension, she could feel the old excitement, the one she'd traded in to have the baby. By watching Valerie, she knew that a baby didn't provide the roller coaster of the workweek, the flush of adrenaline during negotiation, the thrill of the sale. Being a mother was a long, slow day, full of sleepiness and dirty diapers and crying.

That life wasn't for her, she knew that now. It wasn't what she would have. It wasn't what she was allowed.

"Brody! It's Avery."

"Avery! My God, woman, why are you calling? Aren't you supposed to be doing the housewife thing? Shouldn't you be scrubbing the sink with Comet? No, wait. You should be at the club working on those thighs. Are you fat yet?"

"You ass!" Avery felt herself smile, from her mouth down into her chest, her muscles letting go just a little. "I should sue you for something. Maybe for being an idiot."

"Too late. Alix already has that lawsuit covered. I'm surprised we're still married."

"It's only a matter of time before some office assistant nails you," she said. "And then, wham, you'll be out. Way, way out. And guess who they'll hire? Guess who really knows how to play the game?"

"Right. Like you want to be here. Soon you'll be knee-deep in kids. So what's up?"

Avery looked over her shoulder, paused, heard the shower echo down the hall. "I want my job back."

For an instant, Brody was still, the hum of his computer in her ear, but before she could say anything else, he said, "Fine. I'll just fire Lanny."

"You know that's not what I meant. Well, sure, I'd like my exact job back, but really, I'll do anything."

"But," Brody said, his voice soft, "what about the baby?"

Don't think about it, she thought, swallowing down her sad story. And even if she did tell Brody, she wouldn't be able to finish it, because neither she nor Dan knew how it would end. She held the phone between her jaw and shoulder and wrapped her arms around her chest. "It's not going to happen right now. And I want to come back. So are you sure you won't fire Lanny?"

"Lunch. Tomorrow. Twelve?"

"I'll be there."

"Wear a short skirt, or I'm not hiring you back."

"If you show up in your underwear, it's a deal."

Avery hung up and looked back over her shoulder again. Dan had finished his shower, and now she could hear him walking around in the room, opening and closing dresser drawers. He'd called in sick at work, and she'd promised to come with him to the doctor and then to see the Contra Costa County social worker, the one Midori Nolan had referred them to.

"I guess we'll learn more about him. Daniel," Dan had said last night in the voice he'd seemed to develop since all the phone calls—light, sad, and stuck in his body. Avery bit her cheek every time he spoke. She wanted to shake him and yank his voice out of him. She wanted to shout, "Stop feeling so fucking sorry for yourself! What about *our* baby? What about what *I* wanted?" But when she saw his dark, full eyes, she couldn't say a thing. When she saw his eyes, she imagined the boy's, his eyes wide in the empty trailer as he listened to the wail of the ambulance taking his mother away. She felt him in the way she'd felt herself sitting in the waiting room of the hospital as her father's blood slowly stilled.

After the dinner at Luís and Valerie's, Avery had left the house only to work out or go to the grocery store, ignoring Val's and Isabel's phone calls. She and Dan had taken the rest of the baby clothes and furniture out of the nursery, cleaned the rest of the house, and eaten silent meals together at the table. At night, she listened to him fall asleep and kept on her side of the bed, fearing his unconscious touch, a circling arm, a searching thigh. If he touched her, she imagined he might suck her dry, like the terrible monster on the *Star Trek* rerun on channel 44 she'd watched as a child.

Years ago, during the long afternoons after school when their mother slept, Loren and Avery would sit on the couch in the den and watch *The Partridge Family*, *Little Rascals*, *The Three Stooges*, and *The Brady Bunch* reruns. In this one *Star Trek* episode, the monster could change into a pleasing shape—a trusted friend, a devoted wife—but when the sad *Enterprise* officers got too close, it placed its greedy sucker-pad fingers on their bodies and slurped up every last bit of juice, leaving nothing but fluttering skin and bone.

She couldn't do more than what she was doing now, every minute the new story flashing through her head: HUSBAND FINDS CHILD, PLANS FOR BABY SCRAPPED. As she emptied the dishwasher, worked out on the StairMaster, shopped at Safeway, she thought of Daniel, of Randi, of an eight-year love affair Dan had never told her about. *How?* she thought as she lay next to him, listening to his sleeping noises. *What else don't I know?* Even though Dan had promised he'd told her everything, she held herself back, away, knowing that one more thing would knock either one of them loose, send someone running from the house. Alone and for good. The more time she spent here, turning the corners of her house that suddenly seemed unfamiliar, the more opportunity she had to think about Dan's past. That was why she had called Brody.

"Are you ready?" Avery jumped and turned to face Dan. He'd put on a suit and tie as if he were going to work instead of going to talk with a stranger about a boy who may or may not be his—all dressed up to have cells carefully scraped from the inside of his cheek. If they'd had to test her mouth, Avery thought, there would be no cells left, just grooves all along it from her teeth, the biting.

"Sure. Yeah." She smiled slightly, feeling how hard she had to work to make her muscles pull up the corners of her lip. Looking briefly in Dan's eyes, she let her gaze fall to his tie, the one she'd bought at Nordstrom only last week, before any of this had happened.

"Okay. Let's go, then." He cocked his head, trying to find her gaze. She breathed in and looked up, let herself be taken in, seen, without looking away.

"Are you okay?"

At his question, she dropped her eyes. "Yeah. Let's go." She picked up her purse and put it on her shoulder.

He opened the door to the garage for her, and she pressed the opener. "Were you on the phone? I thought I heard you talking to someone."

Opening the Lexus's passenger door, she slipped into the leather seat. "Oh, it was someone from the damn United Bank," she said, putting on her seat belt. "Nothing really."

After providing the DNA sample as well as two glass tubes of blood—*to check for disease?* Avery wondered but didn't ask—they went to the Contra Costa County Social Services Department and waited in a bright, noisy waiting room on aqua plastic chairs. Avery crossed her legs, jiggling her foot, and Dan sat with his elbows on his knees, seeming to find the white flecked linoleum interesting. Rather than watch the way he creased his forehead and rubbed his hair back periodically, talking slightly under his breath, she watched a mother and son arguing in a corner.

"You can't tell him about your daddy coming over. What did I tell you? What did I say?" The mother jerked her purse strap up on her shoulder.

The boy, who seemed to be about twelve, had a green-and-gold A's cap pulled down almost to his nose. He kicked at the legs of the chair in front of him. "So?"

"Now think about what's going to happen. Goddamn it!" She squeezed an empty pack of cigarettes, the wrapper crinkling in her hand.

"I don't care." The boy pulled his cap down even farther, and the mother slammed back in the chair and looked up at Avery.

"Going to be the death of me," she said, and then turned to stare at the long line of people inching toward the clerks behind the counter.

The death of you, Avery thought. There it was again, a mother who didn't appreciate her child. For two years—really her whole life— Avery had wanted her own child. Just last week, she would have done anything to have a part of her and Dan brought forth into this world. How she would have cherished that child! How she would have loved it, whatever its sex, whatever its health. Of course, it wasn't fair that there were mothers like this woman or like Randi. Sure, it wasn't fair there were kids like Daniel. But Avery shouldn't have to be the one to fix Daniel's life, amend Randi's, clean up the ugly mess she'd made. Dan's mess, too. She didn't want a damaged kid, a scared, scrawny boy in a baseball cap; she didn't want some low-life mom's leftovers.

"Mr. and Mrs. Tacconi?"

Avery almost cried out, startled, standing up awkwardly as Dan walked over to a man and held out his hand. She looked down at her pumps, breathing in slowly, trying to cool her red face, trying to think of something that wasn't judgmental. Karma. She still needed good karma.

"I'm Dan. This," he said, looking back, "is my wife, Avery."

"How are you? I'm Vince Brasch. Let's go to my office." Vince adjusted his pants around his thick waist and pointed toward the hall with his thumb.

Dan reached for her hand, but Avery pretended not to see it, fiddling with her purse strap and clipping along behind Vince, who led them down a bright, white hallway, past offices with glass doors on either side, each filled with someone behind a desk and one, two, three people on the other side, papers on the surface between them. As if it could all be that easy, life messes arranged into words, sentences, paragraphs, checks sent out, custody agreed upon, work arranged. All they had to do was sign and leave, and poof! Magic. Trouble gone.

Ha, she wanted to blurt out. *Ha!* Do you know what's happened to us? But she didn't. She sat where Vince told her to, tucking her feet under her seat, waiting as he began to flip through a pile of folders and papers, the new story of their life.

Dan sat back and then leaned forward. "I don't need a lawyer, do I?"

Vince looked up over his file. "A lawyer?"

"Yeah. I was thinking while we were waiting. I feel like there are legal things that are going to happen. Financial matters. Almost as if I need someone to advocate for me."

"What do you mean?" Avery asked, cutting in. As she looked at Dan, the muscles in her back pulled tight. "Why on earth do you need someone advocating for you? You didn't do anything wrong!"

"Whoa," Vince said. "Let's start at the beginning. First let me say that if this case proceeds as I think it will, yes, you will eventually need a lawyer."

"Why? What are you saying?" Avery said.

Vince held up a thick hand. "For legal custody. For filing those papers. Formalities. Official documents. Custody. Support. Those kinds of things. But no, you don't need an advocate. Not now."

"Oh," Avery whispered. She sat back in the chair and crossed her legs. Dan still leaned forward, his elbows on his knees, looking up at Vince, as if this heavy, overworked man could actually make sense of this tangled family. Family. Custody. She would have control of a child not her own. The work she would soon have again, her house, and her marriage would spin around a kid she had no investment in, except he was Dan's. Or was probably Dan's. But because he was Dan's meant she *should* be invested, unless there was something so sick and twisted inside her that she should never have a kid at all.

"Did . . . ? Was there a will or something? Midori mentioned there were documents," Dan said.

"Yes. Not a notarized will or trust, drawn by a lawyer, but a written document—a letter—specifying who should be notified at her death, who should care for Daniel. That kind of thing. She wrote that you were the father and there was no one else to care for the boy."

"What about grandparents?" Avery asked. "I mean, other than Dan's. Or aunts or uncles."

"Aves. Come on."

"I just want to know. Even if he lives with us, we will want to know who his family is."

Vince sat back in his chair and pushed away from his desk, crossing his legs, his nylon pants shushing and slipping as he moved. "Randi had no living parents. Or siblings."

"Randi didn't have brothers or sisters," Dan said. "But what happened to her parents?"

"I know the grandmother is deceased. I'm not sure what happened to the grandfather. Ms. Nolan will have that information."

"You're telling me that if Dan isn't the father, there is not one single living relative who would want to take care of this boy?" Avery leaned forward, feeling her purse cut into her stomach. She pressed harder, liking the feel of the stiff leather against her clothes and skin, the hard press of the metal clasp. "And if Dan is the father, we are the absolute only place he could go? There's nowhere else?"

"Other than foster care. There's adoption, of course, but for a ten-year-old boy with some concerns, there's not much likelihood of that."

"Adoption," Dan whispered. "Concerns."

Avery ignored him, leaning in closer. "What are these concerns? These issues? What's wrong with him?"

"Avery!" Dan said sharply, turning to her, his eyes dark. She swallowed and wished she could suck back the questions, but there they hung, mean-spirited, in the air.

"Let's see." Vince ran a hand through his thin blond hair. In a year, he'd be sporting pink scalp, Avery saw, his male-pattern baldness covered by only a thin layer of light hair. All the strange talks he must have with people like us, she thought, brought it on early.

"Schoolwise, he's tested below grade every year," Vince said. "He's going into the fifth grade, and last year, he tested third grade in reading and spelling. Math was a little better. His teacher recommended testing for learning disabilities—dyslexia—but that wasn't done. I don't know if you know the term—IEP. Individual Education Program. The teacher and the special-education teacher and the school administration get together and determine the best course of action for the child. Curriculum, goals, support. Maybe psychological support at the school, tutors—that kind of thing. When he starts school here—" Vince paused and glanced at Avery. "When he starts a new school, that will have to be done. Right away."

"Does that take long?"

Vince rubbed his nose and shrugged. "A couple of weeks. A month. The child is taken out for testing during school time. Then everyone meets and decides on the best plan."

Dan nodded. "We have a good friend, a neighbor, who's a teacher. My friend Luís. He can give us some ideas. My brother's a teacher, too. He'll know about all this." He looked at Avery and then added, "I mean, if Daniel's mine."

Avery wasn't listening, remembering the class at the end of the hall at Pine Hollow Elementary, the room full of kids with braces and padded headgear, the kids who were dropped off in the special, smaller bus. The ones no one wanted to talk to or play with. Benny Roticelli, who sat on the bench and wished he could run with the other kids, but he had a huge dent in the side of his head and dragged one foot behind him. All the kids whispered that he was supposed to die really soon, and sometimes, Avery and her friends would watch him sit, as if expecting him to keel over right there during morning recess.

"And he's had a real trauma," Vince continued. "Ms. Nolan told you about how they found him."

"In the trailer. After Randi died," Dan offered. "Alone."

"Yeah. But imagine this: He's alone for almost a week, finding what he can in the fridge, putting himself to bed, getting himself dressed in the morning. After a couple of days, he got hysterical. Confused. By the time the police found him, he was weeping in the corner of the trailer and wouldn't come out. Basically, he's not adjusting well. At first, he was silent, but now he's fighting with the other children at the foster home."

Dan dropped his head into his hands, and Avery looked out into the hall. In the office across from them, the mother and the son from the waiting room were sitting silently while a woman in a blue suit held up a piece of paper and pointed. Avery read her lips, "And item four says *blah, blah, blah* . . . and then there is this, item five. Very *blah, blah, blah*."

"Is he okay now? I mean, from the trauma?" Dan asked.

"No." Vince scooted his chair closer to his desk. His eyes were circled in white, and Avery could almost see the sunglasses he wore on the weekends. To do what? She looked at the photos on his desk: a boy, a girl, a wife. Swim meets. Picnics. A normal family.

"To be honest, no. He'll need therapy or counseling. It's not just Ms. Gold's death that's upsetting him. Apparently—apparently the home life degenerated in the last few years. The drugs. The people in and out. He hasn't had it easy. This department can provide some of the counseling, but if you have the wherewithal, I'd recommend a private psychologist. If you can afford it, he'd also benefit from activities that put him in proximity of other children. Maybe martial arts. It's social and develops hand-eye coordination. That kind of thing. It's going to take a lot of time."

That's all everything takes, Avery thought, watching the mother across the hall stand up and yank her son with her. Time. Time for her father to die. Time for her mother to recover from grief. Time for

Avery to begin to forget her father's eyes as she left the hospital room. Time for her uterus and vagina and fallopian tubes and ovaries to be tested and scrutinized and observed. Time for her not to get pregnant over and over again. Time for Randi to get hepatitis C and for her son to be totally screwed up.

All Vince and Dan were asking from her now was her time, and she sat back in her chair. Waiting felt like lying in the middle of the street with her arms spread wide, knowing that a truck was coming. Waiting was like a cold hand on her spine, squeezing. Waiting was her egg floating in the red darkness of her body, sperm nowhere near it. Waiting was a cold hospital room, her father somewhere down the hall. Avery had waited and waited, and as they went over details about the visit with Daniel, Avery didn't know if she could wait again.

After a silent ride home, Dan went into their room, changed his clothes, and went out to the backyard. In a few minutes, Avery heard the lawn mower start up, and then she smelled the heavy green of fresh-cut grass. Ever since she quit her job, Dan had wanted to econ-omize, and instead of Ramón and his crew coming every week to mow and trim and prune, her husband did the work on the week-ends.

Avery decided she would go work out at Oakmont, but before she changed into her workout clothes, she wondered if she should call her mother. She didn't want to, fearing Isabel's judgment, either against her or Dan. Or maybe it was simply Isabel's words she feared, the incessant flow of support and sympathy that Avery knew she wouldn't believe, couldn't feel, didn't know how to take in. Or maybe it was that Avery knew Isabel might side with Dan, understanding how things needed to be hidden, just like anguish under blankets.

But during the ride home from social services, Avery had wanted her mother against her skin, the comfort of her soft neck, forearms, palms, the softness of her blouse against her cheek, the way her mother would stroke her shoulder, and say, "It's fine. Oh, sweetie, it's just fine." How long had it been since she'd let her mother say those comforting words? Since before her father died? When she was little and was hurt, Avery would unconsciously call out, "Mommy. I want my ma-me," holding tight her bruised, skinned knee, her fractured arm, her hurt feelings after Bonnie Randall or Megan O'Reilly teased her or Mara threw her Disco Barbie into the street and Mr. Baumgartner ran over it with his AMC Rambler.

Now, when there was *good* news, the first person she called was Isabel. But when the news was *bad,* she walked over to Valerie's or telephoned Loren, protecting Isabel from fights with Dan, arguments with Brody Chovanes, trouble with refinancing the house. The images of Isabel weeping in bed were still too fresh, even eleven years later, to risk saying the words Avery had now: "Drugs. Eight-year relationship. Boy. Daniel. Ours. No more IUI. No baby now."

Standing by the kitchen window dressed in her tight, black workout pants, sports bra, and T-shirt, Avery held the phone to her chest. She watched Dan unplug the lawn mower from the power cord and then walk into the garage, returning with the hedger. He would be out there for the rest of the day, the shrubs whittled to bone, the lawn nude, all the perennials deadheaded to stems. She watched his arms, still as smooth, dark, and strong as they had been the first time she'd rubbed her hands over them, surprised by his muscles. "Do you work out?" she'd asked, and he'd laughed, flexing his biceps.

"I'm a he-man," he'd said, pulling her close.

He still said that, all these years later. A he-man. Was that what Randi had thought? Did she love his arms and shoulders and chest and thighs and penis as Avery did? Did she love his soft, kind eyes and curly black hair? Did she love his voice in the bedroom at night, telling stories about work and friends and the future, their future, the future where he would always be the same, strong and true, coming home from work every night?

And yet, both she and Randi had been betrayed. He'd left Randi standing in the doorway of their shared apartment, pregnant. He'd left her to her drugs and her hidden responsibility. And Dan hadn't told Avery about Randi, a woman he'd known for eight years. A woman he'd had to force himself to run away from. Randi had been that magnetic, that important. He'd loved her that much.

Dan was somebody Avery didn't know at all.

Avery looked at the phone, dialed Isabel's number, and then hung up before it even rang.

"Mom," she whispered, holding the dead phone to her chest and imagining Isabel's voice. "Mommy."

"Loren? Is Mom there?" Avery said into the receiver, putting her gym bag on the floor next to the couch. She'd tried to find a way to keep the visit to the social worker to herself, but she had to tell someone the story, all of it too strange to imagine. And there was time. Dan, not close to being finished, was digging up a dead wisteria in the corner of the yard, a huge pile of leaves and grass trimmings and roots on a canvas cloth in the middle of the lawn.

"No. Of course not," Loren said. "It's Russian today. Or is it Middle Eastern studies? Do you need her? What's up?" In the background, Avery could hear a cartoon's wild sounds and exaggerated voices.

"Things are happening—"

"Are you pregnant? You are, aren't you? When I left Fourth of July, I was sure something was up. Oh, Aves!"

If she hung up now, she could explain it later as a phone problem. The repairman outside cut service accidentally. Or maybe she could pretend to pass out. Loren would believe that, having calmed Avery down before midterms and the Sadie Hawkins Dance, her date one hour late, Avery sure she'd been stood up. Loren had held Avery through their father's service, not letting her stand a minute alone in the church, letting Mara shake hands, and nod at well-wishers. All she had to do now was say the words. That's all she had to do, and Loren would help her again.

"No. I'm not pregnant. But Dan—Dan has a kid, Loren."

"Say that again."

"A call," Avery began, her throat full. She wondered if she might drown in her own tears before she could tell Loren the story. Finding her throat muscles, she tried to swallow, coughing and then breathing out.

"A call," Loren prompted.

"The Fourth of July. That night. A social worker called to tell Dan that his old girlfriend died. She had a kid, a boy. Ten years old."

"No way. No way!"

"Yeah."

"How do they know—Dakota, give the blanket to your brother—how did they find Dan?"

"Through Marian and Bill. They live in the same place. After they found Randi's letter, all they had to do was call."

Dakota screeched, and Avery heard the refrigerator open and shut, the ripping open of a package of something to get Loren through the conversation. "Randi? Doesn't sound like Dan. What do you know about her?"

"She was a drug addict. She died from hepatitis C. A total loser. But, Loren, so was Dan. Just like her. It's like he's someone I don't know. I've been living with a stranger." Now the tears came, her breath ragged, and she took her mouth away from the receiver.

"No, Aves. No. You know him. There's this incredibly weird thing in his past now, but you know him totally. I know him. We all know him."

"But what if there's more?" Avery was almost wailing. She glanced out the window, but Dan was still digging, sweat ringing his underarms. "What if I find out I can't live with him?"

"Have you asked him? Have you said these things to him?"

"Yes, he's said that's all he has to tell. But what if his craziness comes back? What if he ends up the way he started? I couldn't take that. Not again."

"Again? What do you mean?"

Wiping her eyes, Avery thought of her mother, always asleep, the house so quiet, still, silent. "I don't think I could live with him if he became—if he went back to who he is—was."

"Aves. Don't. Don't do this to yourself. I'm as surprised as you are—I can't see Dan living that way. But look at him now!" As her sister said these words, Avery turned to look at Dan once more. He was cutting up the dead wisteria branches, his face serious, as it always was when he was concentrating. Loren was right. He was the same, exactly as she knew him. But Avery understood that people could change, just like that, in an instant. How could he ever promise her he wouldn't start what he had given up? How could he know what his life would be like? The boy wasn't even here yet.

"Aves?"

"What?"

"Have you told Mom?"

"No. I couldn't."

"Mara?"

"She's too far away. And she'd probably end up telling me how the DNA test works and the chances for a match. Or she'd explain hepatitis C in detail. I can't hear that now."

"So come over. We need to talk about all of this."

"Okay." Avery hung up the phone and, without looking back at Dan, she stood, picked up her purse, and walked toward the front door. She'd go over to Loren's and try to feel better. That's all she could do right now.

Brody Chovanes stood up, snapped his red suspenders, and then put on his suit jacket. "I made reservations at Andrés. I'm in the mood for their halibut. You know me."

Avery laughed, even though she really didn't want to, the sound and air barely making it over her bottom lip. *Who cares what you're in the mood for,* she thought, but she walked behind him, his expensive silk suit *flish-flishing,* and followed him to the elevator.

Behind him, she felt her body morph into the one from two years ago, the body that hadn't gone through medical test after medical test. This body hadn't lain spread-eagle on examination tables, fingers and specula and tiny cameras inside it. This body hadn't been injected over and over again, its butt bruised and sore. No, this was a smooth, quick, sexy body, trim under her expensive St. John's suit, tight in Calvin Klein nylons, perfectly finished with Ferragamo pumps. Awash in Boucheron perfume, Avery breathed in her old self, the one she'd given up, and for what? Months of nothing, that was what. Watching Brody's similarly tight, quick body, she felt like a creature released back into the wild, desperate to search out what it remembered but scared that any minute, the net would scoop it up and carry it away.

As they walked, she breathed in the motion of the office, the whir of action, excitement, commitment. Unlike at home, everything seemed to move here just as it was supposed to, machines and people aimed toward a singular purpose, so much success in sight. Avery waved to her former colleagues—Teresa Licardo, Donna Goodman, Tanner Swenson—but kept going, not wanting to talk with anyone but Brody until she knew if she had the job she needed. Why jinx it?

"So," Brody said, pushing the L button and leaning against the elevator paneling. "What's this all about?"

She adjusted her purse and bit her cheek. "Well," Avery said as they moved downward, "things didn't work out exactly as planned."

"No?" He looked at her, his eyes wide, expecting more.

"No," she said carefully. "It's been harder for us than we thought. I'm still so young—" Pausing, she looked up, making sure he saw her tight, firm face, her full cheekbones, her slim, viable work body. "We don't have to make a decision about what to do next for a while. So, I thought—we thought—why not start working again."

The elevator doors opened, and they walked into the airy lobby, their shoes clacking on the shined marble floor. The doors opened to hot July air, but Andrés was next door, and soon they were inside the restaurant, waiting to be seated. The hostess flicked Brody an appreciative look, and Brody leaned toward her, his hands on the reservation desk, and joked with her about his favorite table by the window.

Avery breathed in and wondered if she would be able to deal with Brody now that she'd had time away from him. It seemed impossible that his wife, Alix, hadn't divorced him yet. He always asked the most personal questions—weight, marriage, embarrassing moments, job screwups—flirted with every woman under fifty, his eyes working an entire body in a flashy figure-eight loop. But Avery had to admit that he and his wife looked good together—Brody with his short, dark looks; Alix a tall, thin, brunette; their trio of children between them. He was a jerk, but Alix knew that. Brody was who he was everywhere, at home, at work, in a restaurant waiting to be seated. That was more than Avery could say for Dan.

After they finished their meals and Brody chatted with their server, who brought them lattes, he sat back and gazed at Avery. "You're looking good. That suburban thing agrees with you."

"How could it not, Brody? While I was working, I used to dream of days like the ones I've been having. You know, working out, gardening, shopping at ten in the morning. But if I'm not going to be a mom right now, then I want to be doing something else."

Brody sipped his latte, leaving a swipe of milk foam on his upper lip. Avery didn't say anything, hoping the server would come back and see him looking like a ten-year-old.

"What does Dan think?"

Avery nodded, trying to find the right words, ones that wouldn't be a lie. "He wants me to be happy."

"And you're not happy right now?"

Picking up a spoon, she tapped it against her water glass. "I'm happy. I just think that if I stay at home now that there isn't a reason, I will be less so."

"How does he feel about not having a kid right away?"

Avery hit the glass again, the sound loud enough that a couple next to them looked over as if Avery were going to give a toast. *Here's to long-lost children*, she would say. *Here's to my husband who keeps secrets.*

"He's fine."

Brody wiped his mouth. Avery held her breath, but when he pulled the napkin away, the milk still swam over his lip. "Okay, so here's the deal. Lanny took over most of your job, but he didn't take the out-of-state accounts. We piecemealed them through the San Francisco and Sacramento offices. We kept thinking we'd find someone to take the whole job over, but then there was the downturn and the possibility of the merger. Ultimately, we never got around to it. So what would be available is exactly that. And you know that involves travel. The reason you quit before. In fact, I was running the details by personnel and the home office this morning, and if you start now, you'll need to be on the road next week. St. Louis. We have a whole new network being set up for Dirland Accounting. Integrated system. The whole nine yards. I know how you love that city."

She nodded, already breathing in the stale air of the St. Louis Hilton, the room that smelled like bologna and perspiration and sadness. The hotel where Avery and Brody, after three rounds of cosmopolitans and a successful deal with Alliance Insurance, had smoked cigars that made her sick for days afterward. So what. It was just a hotel, just a dull city. And she'd be gone from home, busy with presentations and client hand-holding; away from home and whatever was going to happen there. Away from Dan and his guilt and the boy who was going to live in her baby's nursery.

"I'll take it."

Brody looked up at her, surprised. "Don't you want to talk with Dan about it first?"

"I don't have to talk to him about it, Brody. For God's sake. I'll take it. I'll start Monday, in St. Louis. Okay?"

"I'll fax you the info and travel plans. And before you go today, hightail it to personnel. I have all the papers ready."

"So you don't want me to talk with Dan after all?" She put her napkin on the table and stood up.

"I've known you for years, Avery," Brody said, turning toward the server and winking as they left the restaurant. "When you want something, you get it."

After talking to Phyllis in personnel, Avery went to Andronico's and bought a pork loin, bacon, red-skinned baby potatoes, green beans, and salad makings. If she turned up the air-conditioning, it would be cool enough to use the oven. As she roamed the aisles, she realized that if they cooked or ate outside, it was likely Valerie or Luís would look over the fence, swing open the gate, and sit down just as Avery was going to tell Dan about the job. Tell him how she wouldn't be home day and night when he brought this broken child into their lives.

She'd been the one to take the shots, endure the hormone highs and lows, watch the screen as the laparoscope snaked through her insides. She was the one alone in Dr. Browne's office when he came in with the papers that said she'd failed, again and again, every month. She'd put in her time for a child. If Dan wanted his child, she wouldn't stop him. But she wasn't about to go to the school district and sign the kid up for classes, go to meetings to discuss what was wrong with his brain, take him to psychiatrist visits, aikido classes, art therapy sessions. Not her.

She pulled her Land Rover into the garage and closed the door immediately, not wanting to attract Valerie's attention. Usually around this time every day, Avery would head over to Val's because Tomás was down for his afternoon nap. They'd drink tea and chat about Avery's tests or watch *Oprah*. They would flip through the J. Jill, Coldwater Creek, and Boston Proper catalogs. Sometimes, they would go on-line and look for baby furniture or read about infertility treatments or procedures—Chinese hamster ovaries, Lupron, follicle-stimulating hormone levels, egg harvesting—usually ending with the "when" talks: "When you have the baby," and "When your baby is Tomás's age," or "When we both have two." She had told Valerie the whole story about Dan and Randi and Daniel, but now she felt as if she'd sailed away from the house next door and was floating alone on the island of childless women.

When Dan came home, the pork was almost done, and she'd set the dining room table instead of the one in the kitchen, something she usually did only when they were celebrating. Avery had pulled out her wedding silver and china, and the table sparkled. Dan put down his briefcase and looked at her, an eyebrow raised, and hung up his suit jacket in the hall closet.

"What's going on?" he asked, walking slowly into the kitchen. Avery smiled and opened the oven, a waft of bacon and meat juice pouring into the room.

"I thought we'd have a nice dinner tonight." She poked the roast with the thermometer, making sure it was at least 150 degrees, still nervous about Isabel's stories of trichinosis. Most every roast Isabel ever made was cooked to the quick, the meat stringy and tough. But safe.

"Oh." Dan opened the fridge and took out a Corona. "So, what did you do today?"

Avery didn't say anything, sliding the rack back and then closing the oven. She put down the hot pads and brushed her hair away from her warm face. "I want to talk about some things at dinner."

Dan nodded. He probably thought she meant things about the visit next week with Daniel. They would go to Turlock on Tuesday, assuming, of course, that the DNA test didn't show that Randi had lied. They would talk with Daniel, his foster parents, Midori Nolan. Then, they would move on to setting up his room, his new bed, the

clothes that would fill the dresser, the dresser they hadn't even pur-
chased. She had no idea what size a ten-year-old boy wore, what
styles were in, what colors were trendy. As she sliced some tomatoes
for the salad, she shook her head and bit her lip. Stop. Stop.

"I'm going to change," Dan said, waiting for a second behind her
as she sliced. The knife cut into the tomatoes smoothly—one-two,
one-two—juice sluicing up along the sharp edge. She felt his questions rise up behind her, but then he was gone, heavy footsteps in the
hallway.

"So, I went and had lunch with Brody today." Dan looked up from
his salad, his eyes wide. Before he could ask a question, Avery went on.
"We talked about the company. Evidently, Lanny never took over all
my responsibilities. More pork?" She held out the platter, her fingers
in a loose grip on the porcelain, slices of meat sliding toward Dan.

"No. No thanks." He put down his fork. "So you went in to have
lunch?"

"Yeah." Avery shook her head, put down the platter, and looked
at her own plate. She flipped green beans with her fork. "And then
we started talking about work."

Dan sat back and dropped his fork. "What do you mean?"

Her breath grew shallow in her throat, and she tried to swallow.
She'd never felt this uncertain before, not about anything she'd done.
When she'd found this house, she'd told her agent, Brenda Wither-
spoon, that they'd take it, even before Dan had seen the inside. She
hadn't consulted him about taking the job with Pathway Solutions
initially, waiting until she came home from having accepted the job to
tell him about the long hours and the constant travel. She'd known
what to do, felt right about it. Everything fit, like a suit she might try
on at Neiman Marcus.

"Well, I'm not going to try for the baby anymore, am I?" She felt
her skin flare red, so she reached for the salad bowl and piled more
on her plate, even though everything about the meal—the oil slick on
the potato skin, the fat, crackly white rim around the pork slices—
made her stomach contract. She avoided Dan's eyes.

"But what about—?"

"What about what, Dan?" she asked, looking up.

"We don't know about Daniel. And if—if he's mine?"

"What does knowing if he's yours have to do with my going back to work?"

Dan wiped his mouth and put his napkin on the table. He set an elbow on the table, thought about it, and then sat back again. "When he comes here, he'll need—"

"So you think I'm going to sit around here and take care of a ten-year-old boy I don't know? Is that what you had in mind?" Avery moved her teeth to her cheek and then stopped, knowing that one more bite would draw blood.

"No. I didn't say that. It's just that you're here now. You are home. I didn't know that you had plans to go back to work."

"Well, I do. I start on Monday. I'm going to St. Louis to oversee a whole integrated system. I'll be gone for a week right off the bat. And then back and forth during system implementation. You know how long that can take."

"But, Aves. The visit. Tuesday. We're going to Turlock. To see— to meet Daniel."

"This," she said slowly, "is yours to take care of. He is your son— *if* he's your son."

Dan shook his head back and forth. She folded her arms, clenching her jaw. *There. There,* she thought. *So there.*

"It's summer still. School doesn't start until the end of August," Dan said.

Avery pushed her chair back and stood up, her plate in her hands. "You'll need to hire someone. Enroll him in a camp. He can go to all that art therapy and martial arts and whatnot. Get a baby-sitter for when school starts. I don't know, Dan. I mean, gee! What do other parents do? And I'm not the parent."

She turned and walked into the kitchen, clacking her plate on the counter, leaning against it. She wasn't the parent, not to this child.

Dan stood in the doorway. "I don't know what other parents do, Avery. I've never been a parent before."

She closed her eyes. Right. He wasn't a parent. "I know," she whispered.

He moved closer, and she straightened her back, not wanting him to touch her.

"Look," he said, "I know this is a lot to ask, but I can't believe you didn't tell me about the job earlier."

"You can't believe I didn't tell you about a job?" Avery put her hand on her hip. "Think about what you just said, Dan."

"I know. I know. I can't keep saying I'm sorry, but I am. I'm sorry I didn't tell you. I'm sorry that all of this is happening. But you're my wife, Aves. I need you now."

"I'm a different kind of wife than I was a week ago." She turned on the water, hearing her sentence in her mind. A different kind of wife. A different kind of marriage. A different life altogether. "I start Monday," she said again, but when she turned, he'd already left the room.

Later, as she lay in bed, she heard the noise. After cleaning up the kitchen, she'd gone to the bedroom, closing the door behind her, hoping Dan would give her the night to think alone. And he had. She heard him moving around in the family room and the kitchen, and for a second she wondered if she should completely ignore him. But what if he went back to his Randi habits? What if he started drinking more than Coronas? In her mind, she saw him put on a sweatshirt, jump in the Lexus, and drive to where? Martinez? Walnut Creek? Oakland? He'd find a house, a street corner, a boxy apartment and disappear inside it, coming out with a bag hidden under his clothes. Much later, he'd come home reeking of weed and scotch and vodka and beer.

She turned and spun in a sleepy drift of thought and fear when she heard the noise. It was muffled at first, but then it grew louder, as if Dan had opened the garage door to awaken her. She sat up, holding her breath, and there it was again, the crack and split of wood. The thud of heavy metal on expensive furniture, the wide open whack of painted wood fracturing. At first, she thought it was part of the awful thoughts she'd been jolted away from. But then she closed her eyes and listened. The garage. What could it be? What was he doing? In her mind, she scanned the room and could see only white painted rails, smooth, expensive hardwood, sturdy, safe wooden legs.

She jerked away the covers and ran down the hall, pushing wide the garage door. Blinking against the bright fluorescent lights, she tried to open her eyes wide despite the pain. Dan was moving, his body convulsing over the crib, his arm going up, then coming down, his legs and chest heaving upon the wood. Crack, crack. She blinked again against air that was filled with the smell of wood and anger and then realized that the crib was in splinters in front of the Lexus and the Land Rover. She put her hand to her mouth and wanted to scream, to yell out and stop him. But it was too late; she stood there, her heart pounding.

Dan looked up, but didn't see her, sweat or tears covering his face, his eyes blank. He stopped, wiped his face, breathed out in hard gasps. Sweat ringed his underarms.

Avery gasped silently, her body frozen in the doorway. Outside, she heard a door slam. Probably Luís coming outside to check out the terrible sound. Dan stood up over the crib, each breath visible under his shirt. He wiped his face again and then closed his eyes, and leaned his head back and moaned, a sound she'd heard only when they were in bed, his climax at its height. But out here, in the cool garage, she thought of an animal—wolf, tiger, bear—of something in pain, a leg between metal teeth.

Holding the sledgehammer with both hands, Dan lifted it up over his head again. Avery backed away, flinching at the sound of busted dreams, and closed the door behind her.

Six

On Tuesday, Dan picked up Jared in Lafayette at nine forty-five and then got back on I-680, accelerating past Walnut Creek, Alamo, Danville, and Dublin without saying anything. Jared sat in the passenger's seat, looking at the freeway in front of him, but Dan could tell his brother was searching for words, trying to be of use on this trip that Jared had called in sick at the school for. But no matter how hard Jared tried, there wasn't much he could say that would reassure Dan or fix anything. Avery was in St. Louis. They weren't speaking, the hours following Dan's crazy crib destruction full of silence and reproach, Avery sleeping on her side of the bed, clutching the covers.

And now Dan and Jared were on their way to Modesto and then Turlock to find out about Dan's son. Dan shook his head. He wasn't sure why he had asked Jared to come instead of Luís. His friend would have understood his silence, respected it, while Jared clearly wanted to talk about the exact nature of the appointment with Midori Nolan, what his role would be in the discussion, how precisely he could help Dan. All Dan wanted, really, was a warm, familiar body next to him. That was it. Maybe it was the memory of Jared always beside him at night in the quiet dark house of their childhood, listening as Dan told stories, that had prompted him to ask Jared. Or maybe he wanted to prove that he could do this one thing right. He adjusted his hands on the steering wheel and sighed, Jared taking the sound as an opening.

"So the appointment is at eleven, right?"

"Yeah." Dan changed lanes and passed a VW van.

"So this social worker will have the results? Will we—you—find out today for sure?"

"I guess so. I signed a waiver or something, and the results were going to be sent directly to Midori. She'll be able to start putting the facts and plans together. I don't know, Jared. I've just been following everyone's advice." Dan sighed again, his body seeming to be made of air. Avery hadn't given him any advice at all, but he could hear it all the same: *Take care of the boy, but leave me out of it. I'm going back to work, okay? I want you to figure it all out.*

"Did you tell anyone at work about this meeting? Steve?"

"No," he said, shaking his head. "I just took the day off. I have it coming. I've put in the hours lately." He wished he'd gone in to the office early and stayed late because of the Network Stragegies project he'd been working on for weeks, the deal finally sealed yesterday, a huge coup for the company. But even as he'd gone on field visits and made calls and given a hundred promises, he knew he was working to avoid Avery.

"You almost never take days off," Jared said. "Steve will know something weird is going on. You're Mr. Never-Miss-a-Day."

"It's not like being a teacher, Jared. I can't get a substitute. I can't show a movie when I come back while I figure out what to do."

Jared turned to look out the window, and Dan clenched the wheel, glancing in his sideview mirror.

"Teaching isn't easy," Jared said.

"I know. I didn't mean that. It's just that there's always some deal going down, and I never know what to prepare for. But believe it or not, I landed a big account yesterday. Steve will be treating me like a king for at least a week. I think I can miss one day after that."

As he took the I-580 exit and curled around, heading toward the Altamont pass and its dry, windmill-covered hills, Dan knew that even today, he'd rather be at work. Work was so clear and concise. Sell telecommunications systems. Get paid. Get promoted. Make money. He loved to sit at his desk and make contact calls, chatting up strangers, using his voice to convince. He was good at it. Maybe he'd developed the skill years ago when he'd lied to his parents about where he was and who he was with, assuring them with every slick sentence. But now, at home with Avery, he couldn't form the words that would make her feel better, as if comfort were a foreign language. He cast a glance at Jared, and then pushed on the gas, wanting to make something happen, even if it was only putting more miles between him and home.

Midori Nolan, neither Japanese nor Irish, as far as Dan could figure out, was a thin, tall woman with curly black hair and brown eyes, who sat at her desk without smiling. He knew that if he were on a sales call, he'd somehow get the story of Midori's name and origins out of her. In fact, within minutes, they'd be having a good joke about it. Midori would relate the long story of how her mother loved Japanese culture a bit too dearly, and then she'd buy up a huge telecommunications system for the Social Services Department of Stanislaus County. Steve would call him in for a congratulatory chat and a huge bonus. Dan would surprise Avery with the keys to the vacation home in Tahoe they'd talked about.

Dan almost smiled at the idea of it until he realized Midori Nolan was waiting for an answer to a question.

"Since you signed the waiver, I was able to get the results from your physician beforehand. They were FedExed over. Do you want to discuss them with me and . . ." She looked at Jared. "Your brother?"

Nodding, he turned to Jared, who smiled, nodding as well, everything so *okay* . Dan felt like one of those bobbing toys with the heads that wobbled back and forth on tiny plastic bodies, goofy smiles on their faces. What he really wanted to do was stand up and pace, get back in the car and feel the highway under the Lexus's tires. In four hours, he could be in L.A. From there, Mexico. Who would care? Not Avery. Not Steve, at least not right away. Not his parents, who had pushed him away long ago. Maybe just Luís and Valerie and Jared. And the boy he didn't even know yet.

"Yes," Dan said, exhaling. "Of course."

Midori nodded and opened up the file. "The DNA results are ninety-nine percent conclusive of paternity. That is about as close as you can get, from what I've been told. We've used these tests before in cases."

When Avery had been going through the medical tests and the shots and the monthly IUIs, Dan sometimes let himself imagine what it would be like in the delivery room. Just as in the movies he and Avery had watched together, he would be standing at her side, holding her hands as she pushed, telling her, "You're doing great, Aves. It's almost there. The head is almost there." He would wipe her forehead, staring into the mirror at her feet, following the progress of the slick, wet head moving into the light.

And then, with one last, long push, the baby's head—his and Avery's baby—would break through, its little gnomish features bunched and dark. The doctor would suction out all the fluid from its nose and mouth, and the baby would break free with a giant first cry. Alive. So alive. He would squeeze Avery's hand, whisper, "Everything is great," and then move to the baby. With the last big push, the child would shoot into the doctor's hands. His child. He was a father. Even when he was simply dreaming about it, his heart seemed too large for his entire body, pumping and pulsing in a way he'd never felt before.

Now, with the proof that he was already a father, Dan felt a flat line of panic thrum through his chest. His breath was caught up under his sternum, and all he could look at was the full, leafy plant with heart-shaped leaves on Midori Nolan's desk. He tried to slip on his salesman face, but his lips only twitched when he tried to smile. He should be smiling, shouldn't he? He had a child, a boy, who was past the worst stages, the ones Avery and he had read about in the *What to Expect When You're Expecting* book Valerie had given them. No diapers. No late-night cries. No bottles.

"Wow," Jared said. "Wow."

"Yeah," Dan answered, pulling up the only sound he could find in his throat.

"This will be a big change for you and your wife," Midori said.

"Right," said Dan. "A big change."

"Do you want to call your wife? Avery, right? You can use my phone." Midori started to stand up as if to leave so he could have a moment of privacy.

"No, that's fine. I'll tell her—I'll tell her later."

"What happens now?" Jared asked. "Is there a hearing? Paperwork?"

"When do I see him?" Dan said before she could answer any of his brother's questions.

Midori rearranged herself on her chair. "I called his foster family this morning to see what his schedule is like. He gets out of summer school early today. But that's not until two fifteen. I suppose if you wanted to go have lunch, we could meet back here at about two to drive to Turlock."

"And then what?" Jared asked. Dan flicked a look at his brother. This wasn't really his business, and Dan wished he'd stop asking so many questions. But maybe Jared was doing so because Dan didn't seem able to ask what was important.

"You're right about the paperwork and the hearing. But the paternity test makes it really almost pro forma. We will collect information about Dan. His wife. Their marriage and family situation." She stopped and smiled at Dan. "And then we will present the information to the court, which will approve the change in the child's status, from foster care to parental care. We've already done an initial family background check and searched for other living relatives. We have the DNA test that says it all. It should be quite easy."

Dan remembered Avery's question to Vince Brasch. "It's not really clear what happened to Randi's parents. Did they both die?"

Midori shook her head. "It's kind of strange. The grandmother died in 1993. We know that. Death certificate on file and such. But the grandfather seems to have disappeared. We made many inquiries, but we are assuming—and the court will assume—that he is out of the picture. Randi didn't leave any forwarding address for him, no information at all."

"Could he come back and cause trouble?" Jared asked, leaning forward. "I mean, could he want custody of Daniel?"

"Oh, no," Midori said. "The father takes precedence."

"What do we do if he shows up?" Dan asked. "He and I never got along very well. He was— He's not a good guy."

"Let's not worry about that unless it happens," Midori said, clicking her ballpoint pen. "Vince will help you with that if the situation should arise. We should focus on Daniel."

"So," Dan began, feeling like he was losing something with each word that came from his mouth. "So this could all be over in less than a month?"

"Oh, sooner. That is, if you want him."

Midori and Jared turned to him; he could feel their eyes on him like a tree full of owls, as his grandmother used to say. Owls with night vision that noticed everything.

"Well, yes. I mean, he's my son. I want to meet him, though."

Midori nodded. "You should meet him. We will have a couple of visits before it's all settled. You should think about it carefully."

"Does he know?" Dan asked. "You've told him everything?"

Midori put on her glasses. Under the glass, her eyes were wide and dark and blurry. "We haven't told him a thing. It wouldn't be right until we were sure of the paternity and knew if you wanted custody. At this point, he doesn't know about you or any of your family."

"How has he dealt with his mother's death?" Jared asked, the history teacher in him wanting to know the true story. Dan hadn't told his brother what Vince Brasch had said about the terror, the learning difficulties, the fighting.

"He sees a therapist once a week. But he's a sad little boy. Angry, too. I think he feels very lost."

Dan licked his lips, pressed them together, swallowed. As he listened to Midori and Jared talk, he felt the road under his tires, the slick black asphalt that could take him away. Daniel didn't know him yet. He could still leave.

But then he saw himself at ten, swinging from clenched hands on a sturdy limb of the cherry tree in their backyard, Jared already on the ground laughing. Up and down, back and forth, the air against his face, the leaves against his shoulders, the smooth bark of the tree under his hands. Light dappled his face, and he swung into and out of shadows until he let go, his legs arcing, his arms at his sides, his feet aimed toward the ground. The feeling before he landed! The warm air holding his body! He knew everything around him, the tree, his brother's wide smile, the house where his parents sat at the kitchen table, the town where he'd been raised. It was all his, every part of it. He knew it all. Even if he had later thrown it away, he'd had it once, and he knew what it felt like when he tried to re-create it with Avery. That time was still inside him.

His boy had nothing, no family, no yard, no house. He'd never felt that air buoying him, holding him up through time. He hadn't had that feeling when Randi began to die, right in front of him. As Dan sat in the chair, pressing the backs of his legs against the plastic, and listened as Jared asked more questions about Daniel, he knew what he was going to do. What he had to do.

Dan and Jared sat in the Lexus in front of a plain ranch house on Yosemite Court in Turlock, a once small farming community that had blossomed into streets of stuccoed strip malls full of Kmarts, Cold Stone Creameries, Borders Books. The last time he had been here to get gas while heading down Highway 99, all there had been were fields of corn and almonds. "Ah-mends," said the kid who'd pumped his gas. "That's how they say it here."

Neither Dan nor Jared said much, listening to the music on the radio, something slightly country and soft, the twang of sad guitar chords circling the car. There was a brass 12 on the mailbox in front of the house, though the court held only four houses, all the same, one beige, one yellow, one beige, one yellow, all with painted trim and the exact same patches of lawn and perennials in front. In front of number 12 were two bicycles—one with training wheels, the other slightly bigger. Dan hoped the smaller one with training wheels didn't belong to Daniel; the boy had to know how to ride a bicycle by now. But just as he was thinking this, two boys slammed out of the house and grabbed the bicycles. One was about twelve, blond, his skin already brown from the Central California sun. The other, Dan knew, was Daniel. He was dark haired, with a baseball hat pushed down almost to his nose, and fair skinned, light as the tule fog that spread like glue down the valley in the winter months.

Looking at the bigger boy, Daniel shook his head and said, "No way. I'm not going downtown," and then pedaled carefully down the small slope of the lawn and onto the sidewalk, his skinny legs straining to move the pedals.

The blond boy teased, calling out in a singsong voice, "I'm not *go-ing.*"

Daniel wobbled past the car, his bike precarious under him despite the training wheels, shimmying and teetering with each pull on the pedals. Then Dan saw that Daniel was holding on to the bars with one hand only, the other hand clenched. Turning his bike, he rode toward the other boy, who laughed and jumped out of the way as Daniel flung out a fist.

"Dumb-ass," the other boy yelled, laughing.

"It's a miracle he didn't fall off the bike," Jared said.

"That's him," Dan whispered.

"I know," Jared said. "He looks like Randi. My God, he's just like her."

And yes, he was. Dan closed his eyes, seeing Randi at a nightclub, her tight jeans, her still slightly big eighties hair in a black, curly froth, freckles across her pale nose, cheeks and lips red, sparkly, glowing. She was so thin, he used to think of her hipbones as handles, grabbing her, pulling her to him, on him. She was the first woman he'd had sex with, and they'd done it so often, her skin became his, each mole, curve of flesh, angle of bone completely known to him. When he first slept with Avery, he'd realized with surprise that he was still feeling for Randi's body, even though Avery's smooth, fuller one was wonderful; even though she was the woman he wanted to marry. Now, Avery's was the woman's body he carried with him, but Randi was still there, a shadow wife, the first body his own had understood.

Jared was right. He would have picked the little boy on the bike out of a crowd of twenty, fifty children, knowing he'd find constellations of freckles across his nose, pointy elbows, thin, pale lips that hid a wide, white smile. Even though Randi's two front teeth were slightly crooked, one leaning slightly on top the other, she put on bright red lipstick and laughed at everything.

"He looks exactly like her," Dan said, just as Midori's Honda Civic pulled up behind them.

They both got out of the Lexus and stood on the sidewalk, following Daniel's progress around the court.

"That's a new bike," Midori said, closing her car door. "The Barnetts bought it for him."

"Is the other boy their son?" Jared asked.

"No. Another foster child. They have three. At least, right now."

The blond boy looked carefully both ways and then rode across the street, passing by the group standing next to Midori's car. Daniel made it to the same spot and got off, walking his bike across, the plastic training wheels spinning loudly on the asphalt. He looked up and clearly recognized Midori, stopping in the middle of the street.

"Keep going," Midori said. "Don't stop there."

Daniel's black eyes were wide and anxious, and Dan wanted to say, "Nothing's wrong." But he'd be lying.

Nodding, but not saying a word, Daniel pushed the bike toward them. He didn't look up, his eyes hidden under his baseball cap. Dan didn't realize he was backing away until Jared pushed him gently, forcing him to stand still.

"Daniel, this is Mr. Tacconi, and—well—Mr. Tacconi. Dan and Jared. This is Daniel."

Daniel lifted his head and peered at them from under his cap, his eyes brown slits. "Hi," he mumbled, blinking against the light and then sneezing.

"Bless you," Dan and Jared said at the same time.

Daniel wiped his nose on his arm and kicked his bike tire with his shoe.

"That's some bike you have there," Jared said.

"Can I go now?" Daniel looked over at the front door, where the other boy stood. "I want to play the wrestling game."

"Sure. But later, I want you to talk to Mr. Tacconi."

"Which one?" Daniel looked up again, his nose wrinkling in an almost-sneeze.

"Me," Dan said, lifting his hand and then dropping it by his side.

"Whatever," Daniel said, jumping on the bike and pushing hard for a few spins until he reached the lawn. He dumped the bike and ran inside the house behind the blond boy.

"He's so small," Dan said.

"He's perfectly normal in height and weight," Midori said.

"No, I didn't mean that. It's just, I thought he would be bigger."

They walked slowly to the door, Midori leading them both. Dan looked at the bike with its training wheels. What he'd meant was that he thought there wouldn't really be much work to do. In his mind, a ten-year-old boy was almost finished, baked, good to go. Not like a baby who needed everything: feeding, bathing, watching. But Daniel wasn't ready for anything, even Dan's untrained eye could see that. He would have to be a father. He would have to pay attention.

"He's had a difficult time," Mrs. Barnett—Liza—said. She held a can of diet Coke in her hand, holding it tightly enough so that Dan could hear the tinny echo of her squeeze. Mr. Barnett wasn't home, but Dan could see evidence of him everywhere—in some project on the table, metal parts and bolts and some kind of glue; a shelf in the family room full of books on bridges and tunnels; on the wall, a color portrait of the Golden Gate Bridge.

Liza saw him looking around and nodded at the table. "We take in only older kids. Martin's projects wouldn't go with little kids. He's an engineer. He was actually working on this project with the boys. They love it. Well, Daniel mostly watches, but I can tell he's interested."

"Oh. That's nice," Dan said. He glanced at Midori, who was turning pages in her folder. Jared sat with his hands pressed between his knees, looking around the room. If he was looking for evidence of ineptness or negligence or danger, Dan thought, he shouldn't. Sometimes, you couldn't see it.

Liza sipped her Coke.

"So he's had a hard time?" Dan asked.

"His mother was sick for years and he kind of took care of himself. Actually, when she went to the hospital for the last time, he was alone for several days before anyone figured out he was there."

Dan pressed his lips together, keeping in the moan that had worked its way up from his lungs. "Yeah. We heard about that."

"Daniel's psychological exam shows he has some fears of abandonment," Midori said gently, as if Dan's sadness were visible, leaking out of his skin.

Well, duh. Hit me on the head with a brick, Randi would have said. Of course a test had found that. A human eye alone could find that.

"In some ways, he's been making progress this past month. He doesn't have night terrors as often, and the summer school program has been reinforcing reading and math skills," Midori continued.

"There is the fighting issue with the other boys. But in your home, there won't be other children to take attention away from him."

"How will you explain this new set of circumstances?" Jared took his hands away from his knees and leaned back. "You're going to have to be very careful."

Liza put down her Coke can, the aluminum dented with finger marks. "He knows that we're looking for relatives. Midori and my husband and I have told him that much. But I don't think it should happen too fast."

"Neither do I," Dan said too quickly, the words sliding out of his mouth like ice. "I mean, I don't want to scare him." He felt Jared's eyes on his cheek. As if Jared knew what this was like. As if Jared had ever even been in a relationship long enough to know how it felt to say good-bye. Dan felt the words on his tongue, longed to flick out the truth about Jared's short, varied relationships, one woman at Thanksgiving, another at Christmas. He could go off on those long summer vacations and not have to worry about trying to live day to day with someone else. How could he know what it had been like to look at Randi and know that the view of her in the doorway would be his very last? Everything for Jared had been easy, smooth, on the surface, slick enough to slide away.

"I'm inclined to feel the same way," Midori said, closing the folder. "I believe that we should set up a series of visits over the next few weeks, increasing in length. Not too long—I would want Daniel to get introduced to his new environment during the summer, so that he will be able to make friends. But he has had enough abrupt change. We can make this one smooth."

"Sounds good." Dan brought his hands together and then stood up.

"We should make the dates now," Liza said, picking up the empty can. "Anyone want a Coke?"

Outside, Dan and Jared stood on the lawn, watching Daniel's foster brothers and a bigger boy who had ridden up on a mountain bike run in circles in the court. They were laughing and grabbing one another by the shirt, pulling and spinning until they fell on the asphalt. Daniel stood on the sidewalk, watching, pulling on a lock of hair. A mother from one of the houses called to them to get on the lawn, and they continued the game, this time rolling on the grass. Midori Nolan waved as she drove off, and Liza closed the front door, saying, "Drive careful."

Dan rubbed his forehead, leaning into Jared as he closed his eyes and lost his balance for a second, the world as small as this court, the noise of the children, his brother's shoulder against his own.

"It's going to take a long time to get to know him," Jared said. "To win his trust."

"Yeah, I know, Jared." He righted himself and pushed the hair away from his face.

"No. I mean he's been through a lot. He looks so . . . scared. Tentative."

Dan wished he'd come alone, though he knew he would have barely made it down Highway 99 if he had. He'd probably have pulled over in Ripon and gone home to sit in his empty house, ignoring Midori's repeated phone calls. But shit, did Jared have to know how to do everything, especially when he didn't have any kids of his own?

But he was right. Dan could see his son was not quite sure how to react, standing on the edge of the action, not able to push himself into the fun, not knowing how to join in unless he was trying to land a blow. "Yeah."

"Do you want to say good-bye?"

Sore and tired, Dan cupped the back of his neck with a palm. No, he didn't want to say good-bye, but he knew he should. It would make the visit next Wednesday easier, Daniel remembering him more clearly. "Okay." He started to walk over to the children, feeling Jared move with him. "No. I'll go alone."

Jared kept walking for a moment before stopping, looking at Dan. "Oh."

"I should go. It should be me." Dan reached out for Jared's arm, holding him back.

"Fine. I'll wait in the car." Jared shrugged Dan off, turned, and went back to the car. Dan heard the door slam.

When he made it to the sidewalk next to the lawn where the children were playing, he stopped to watch. Daniel was now in the pile of the wrestling match, yelling, "I'll get you, Mark," his thin, high voice too serious and not at all playful.

Dan waited until their bodies fell away from each other before he called out, "Daniel? I just wanted to say good-bye. Could you come here?"

Daniel pulled his legs out from under the blond boy's and stared at Dan, his eyes squinting against the afternoon sun. "Okay."

Swallowing, Dan waited as his son stood up and whisked grass off his jeans and put his cap back on his head. *Keep it off,* he thought, wanting to see the dark glint of Randi's hair again. What had she looked like in those final months? Had she lost that angry spark that kept her beautiful but also kept her an addict? Dan wanted to imagine her in the hospital bed, still beautiful, still angry, the current of energy that was her personality alive and on fire.

Daniel stood in front of him, and Dan stuck out his hand. "It was nice to meet you, Daniel."

"Who are you?" Daniel asked, keeping his hands by his sides.

"Mr. Tacconi. Dan Tacconi."

"I know that," he said, shaking his head. "But why did you come here?" Under his hat, Daniel's eyes looked like two polished chestnuts.

"I had some things to talk about with Liza, your foster mom."

"I know who she is. You know I live there," Daniel said, and in his voice, there was Randi, live wire, smart-ass, know-it-all.

"I do know that. Anyway, I just wanted to say good-bye." Dan moved his outstretched hand, and Daniel hesitated and then took it, squeezing back. His skin was so soft, with the fine texture of a child, his life not having left a mark there, at least. Dan closed his eyes, resisting the urge to pull this small boy to him, take him in his arms, put him in the car now, now, to save him and himself from the weeks of awkward talks and movie dates and Pizza Hut dinners. But he mustn't scare Daniel, and he stared at the magpie flying overhead, watched it dive and then land on a fence, bobbing its head and then standing still.

"Okay," Daniel said, pulling back his hand. "I'm going to play now."

"All right. Bye, Daniel."

"Bye." Daniel turned back to the kids who were watching them, and by the time Dan was halfway to the car, the court was a swirl of laughter and teasing, Dan already forgotten.

Going home, the traffic was light, all the commuters streaming home in the other direction, pushing up over the hills and into the valley from jobs in San Jose, Fremont, San Francisco. Jared sat quietly in the passenger's seat as Dan tried to form the perfect sentences. "Thanks for coming," he imagined saying. "You were a big help. I really needed you." But he said nothing.

Finally as they passed through Manteca, Jared turned from the window and stared at Dan, who could feel his brother's gaze, as he always had, even from across a darkened bedroom.

"What?" Dan asked.

"I don't know. I guess I don't know if you understand how hard this is going to be. How hard anything— Never mind." Jared let a hand fall hard on his knee, the sound echoing in the car.

"Just say it. Nothing's stopped you before." Dan turned on his signal light and passed a middle-aged man doing fifty-five in a red Porsche Spider.

"What's that mean?"

"You always say what you want. Like at the Fourth. Blurting out everything, even when I've told you not to." Dan moved back into the slow lane, watching the red car fall far behind them.

"Wouldn't this have been a hell of a lot easier if Avery had known the truth? If she'd known about Randi and what went on with her? And you? And the folks?"

"Have you really forgotten what it was like?" Dan said. "And I don't mean me. I mean them, her. Now you've got it all twisted into this story about how I ruined everyone's lives."

"You can blame them all you want, Dan, but you did what you did. You made choices. For you and Randi and Daniel, even if you didn't know it then. Now you're going to have to make the right choices."

Dan moved his tongue through his mouth, feeling the sharp edges of his molars. He shook his head and glanced at Jared. "It must be damn nice to be right all the time."

"That's not what this is about. I don't want to be right. I hate being the one in the middle, the one who hears both sides, every damn holiday and get-together. It makes me sick. All I want is for things to—work out. For a change. I want to have my family back."

And then it was Dan's hands on the steering wheel, the heat and asphalt under the car, the whir of the air conditioner, the dashboard with all its gauges and meters and blinking numbers: 75, 76, 80—25,179—4:59—¼—40. Whoosh went the road, Shell station, FARM FOR SALE, Target, Arby's. Whoosh went the past twenty years. His cheeks felt heavy; his eyes ached. The hair on his knuckles tingled. When Daniel had pushed his bike across the cul-de-sac, he'd seen Randi in him, the white skin, the thick, dark hair. But in Daniel's disappointed gaze, Dan had also seen Jared. At different times, both his brother and his son had the same look in their eyes. Dan had seen it night after night at the dinner table, in the living room as he left with Randi, when the cops came, at every meal and holiday since then. He'd abandoned his brother, just as he'd abandoned his son, leaving them both to clean up the terrible mess.

Dan shook his head. "I—I'm sorry."

"That's what you always say, Dan. But nothing's changed."

"I know."

Dan could see Jared nodding, the nod he must give his students. Sometimes Dan couldn't believe that was what Jared did all day, recounting lines of time and culture and civilization, listening to kids' questions and problems and excuses. He knew kids. More than Dan did.

"Okay." Jared settled back in his seat. "Well, I'm still here."

Dan nodded, pushed on the accelerator, and pulled down the sun visor. "Thanks," he said, the word so full on his tongue, bigger in feeling than sound. "I mean it."

Jared sighed and pushed on the radio, tuning into KCBS and the weather and traffic report. Heavy backups on the Sunol Grade, the San Mateo Bridge, West 680. Delays at the Bay Bridge and Caldecott Tunnel. Partial clouds, chance of rain, early clearing.

After dropping Jared off and driving home, Dan sat in the backyard, the sky full of afternoon heat and purple finches that landed on Avery's bird feeder, pecked at the empty plastic, and then flew away.

No diners tonight at Avery's bird restaurant, he thought, remembering how excited she'd been when Dan had put it up. He'd gone to Orchard Nursery and asked for the special anti-squirrel, anti-jay feeder, a baffle and a metal cage around it. He'd also bought a heavy, expensive sack of peanuts and pumpkin and sunflower seeds that looked good enough to set on the table during a poker game at Luís's. When he brought everything home, Avery's face lit up as it hadn't for a long while during those months of shots and tests, and she refilled the feeder every other day. She went out and bought a bird book, whispering, "A grosbeak! A nuthatch. Let's see. A pygmy nuthatch. Oh, look. That one's yellow. A lesser goldfinch," as she stood by the window, the book open in her hands. Until the Fourth of July, she'd actually kept a list of all the different birds that came to eat, excited by the permutations of male, female, breeding, summer, and juvenile markings.

As he sat in the chair, the portable telephone in his lap, he knew he should fill up the bird feeder. At the very least, it would make him feel that something was normal in this day of abnormalities. But he couldn't. His body felt drained by the long car rides and the pinched, angry look on Daniel's face and the sad set of his dark eyes. When Dan leaned back and stared into the dark blue sky, he heard Midori Nolan's voice, "Ninety-nine percent conclusive of paternity." He heard her say, "If you want him," and remembered the expression on Jared's face, the look that said, "Don't fuck this one up, bro. This time, don't drop the ball."

Part of Dan wanted to drop-kick the past, including the boy and all his baggage, out into space. He wanted to fly to St. Louis and lie to Avery, tell her that it was all a big mistake. Randi, in her drugged-out, desperately ill state, had written a drastic note to try to save her son. Yes, the boy was in foster care, but he could tell her that the foster mother was all right. Liza had said he was doing better. Daniel needed help, and he would get it there, in Turlock, in that school district, with Liza and her eccentric engineer husband. Dan and Avery wouldn't have to do a thing but send monthly support checks and maybe big Christmas presents every year. Case closed, crisis averted.

But that wasn't what had happened, and Dan knew that Avery

needed to know the truth. He looked at the phone in his lap and dialed her hotel number that he'd written out before he came outside.

"Hello," Avery said, the clip of work in her voice.

"It's me." He heard the hum of a hotel room—lights, television, air-conditioning—and something else, like muffled conversation.

"What happened? Did you go?" She seemed more interested than she had on Monday. She'd given him a quick, absent kiss that just missed his forehead and whispered, "I'll call you," before walking outside to get into the BayPorter van. Maybe she did care.

"I went. I took Jared with me. We met him, Aves," he said, imagining the dark eyes in front of him as he spoke. "And he's mine."

"Oh. Oh." She paused, and he heard a door or a drawer open and close. "God."

"I know."

"No, I don't think you do. And I don't know how you feel really, either. We aren't in this together."

"I know."

"Stop saying that! No, you don't. You don't know what this is like for me. You barely know what it's like for you. You just met him, for Christ's sake. You have no idea what the future will be like for us, for him. Oh, God."

Dan sighed and rubbed his forehead. "I'm sorry, Aves."

"So am I. God . . . So what is going to happen? How does this whole thing fit into our lives?"

"He's not a thing—he's a little boy," Dan said, heat flaring in his cheeks the way it had the night he bashed up the crib. He blinked, trying to push the memory of the splintered wood out of his head.

"That's not what I meant. I meant how does the process unfold? Jeez, Dan. What do you have to do?"

"I've set up some meetings with Daniel. Midori and I have to tell him the story. He doesn't know anything yet. He'll be very shocked."

Avery breathed in deeply. "Like the rest of us."

"Yeah."

There was sound in the room again, and he heard Avery's earrings clank against the receiver. "Is someone there with you?"

"No. I just turned off the TV. Look, I'll be home Friday. We have got to figure all of this out. We have a lot to discuss."

Dan nodded, knowing that as of this second, he wished Friday would never come. "I kn— Right. Right. Um, well, how's it going out there?"

"I don't want to talk about that. I'll see you then, okay?" Avery's voice was back to her brisk, get-it-done cadence.

"All right," Dan said, hanging up.

Resting the phone on his thigh, he watched a scrub jay land on top of the feeder, cocking its head down, trying to figure out how to make it to the seed tray.

"Hey," Dan said, but his voice was too low to scare anything, all his pointed words used up in the phone call. Neither of them had said one soft word to each other, the space between them now as cold as the empty plateau in their bed, mattress and blankets smoothed to silence since the Fourth of July.

⟨☀⟩

After work on Wednesday, Dan stopped home to take some measurements, the same way he had measured a year earlier, when Avery and Valerie went out to buy the crib and changing table. Now, he had to find out how wide and long the bed could be. A single bed. He hadn't bought a single bed ever, having left behind the one his parents bought for him years ago. When he went home to Sacramento, he'd walk up the stairs and push open the door of the room he and Jared had shared, staring at his old little bed. He'd never fit in that room or in his parents' house, chafing under all the strict lines his father drew in the sand. "Be home by midnight, goddamn it, or you're grounded! And I mean it this time," his father would say behind the slammed front door.

"Please drive carefully," his mother would whine as she opened the garage door to watch him drive away. "Don't get into any trouble tonight, Danny. He's at the end of his rope."

Even though those years had been terrible for his parents, his mother had left his room unchanged since he was in high school, a testament to trouble. When he'd gone home for the holidays while he was at Cal, he'd found an old stash taped to the bottom of his dresser drawers and another in the shoe box in the left-hand corner of the closet. Thank God, he'd thought then, he hadn't remembered his hidden loot one strung-out night with Randi. Jonesing for a smoke, they would have broken into his own house, and his parents would have had to call the police again. And Dan knew that if he'd remembered, he wouldn't have cared about his parents or the police, needing a smoke that bad.

As Dan pulled out the measuring tape, jotting down the room dimensions, he wondered when he should call Marian and Bill. When was the proper time to announce the existence of their first grandchild? Then he would have to tell them that Daniel was Randi's boy. Randi had been their least favorite person in the world. His father would stop in midaction, his face clouding and stilling as it did every time Dan had brought home bad news, laying it down in front of their feet like a dead rat. This would be worse because it would last as long as Daniel did, which would be for the rest of all their lives.

The measuring tape slid back, metallic and clangy, and Dan stood up and looked around Daniel's room. Bed. Dresser. Clothes. Shoes. Toys. School supplies. And what about all those things kids did now? Video games? Scooters with motors on the back? At least Daniel already had a bike. That was taken care of, but the boy needed everything else. Dan closed his eyes and thought of his boy, short, thin, his pants so big his belt dangled even on the last hole. His stringy hair under the baseball cap, his curious, deep eyes. His mouth, like Dan's, wanting to lash out at everyone, especially some nosy stranger who asked questions. His skinny arms wicking out to strike people who didn't understand him. Maybe, Dan thought, as he opened and closed the closet door, Avery was right to take a job that would allow her to escape. Maybe his parents had been right to turn away from all the pain he'd put before them.

Just as he was about to leave for Target, the phone rang. He hoped it might be Avery, so he answered it instead of letting the machine pick up.

"Dan? It's Isabel."

Dan let a sigh build up in his mouth, but he didn't exhale the sound. "Hi. How are you doing?"

"Oh, me. Well, fine. But—well, Loren finally called me, told me the story. She's worried because Avery hasn't returned her calls. It's just— I want to know how you two are doing."

Dan shook his head. Loren and her damned big mouth, he thought, needing something nasty to talk about. Then he sighed, knowing that she was right to be worried, with Avery suddenly absent, silent, out of the house by seven a.m. "Oh, yeah. It's been strange." He leaned against the kitchen counter, thinking of ways to get off the phone. The doorbell? Luís and Valerie needed him right away? He had to go back to work immediately? Isabel kept talking.

"Of course it's strange. What a surprise. A sad surprise in many ways. But where is Avery? Why hasn't she called me? Why didn't she tell me?"

"She went back to work. She's in St. Louis," Dan said, letting more secrets fly free. Why not?

"What? Now? When there's so much to do and think about? When this big thing is happening?"

"Yeah. She won't be back until Friday."

"Oh, my." For the first time, Dan thought he detected disapproval in his mother-in-law's voice. "Oh, my."

"Well." He stopped, not knowing what else to say.

"This is such big news. Really." Isabel paused, her questions pressing silently against the receiver.

"I can have her call you, then," he said, finding the door handle of this conversation.

"But, Dan, what's the next step? Have you met him? He's yours, right?" Isabel asked, flinging the door wide open again.

"Yesterday. Jared came with me. He's mine."

"Oh, my. That's— Well, congratulations, I guess you'd say." Dan saw Valerie on their deck, Tomás strapped to her chest in a Baby-Björn. She turned to the house, noticed him, and waved. He waved back, as if it were any other day in any other year, another Wednesday evening in a typical week.

"Yeah. Thanks, but listen—"

"What are you planning? Have you decided when he's coming? What about his room? Will you use the nursery?"

"Actually, I was just about to go shopping. He'll be here in a month or so. They want him here before school starts. Anyway, I need supplies. I need everything."

"Can I come with you? Pick me up, Dan. Please, let me help."

Dan thought of how much Isabel talked, her inane questions, her refusal to let anything slip by without comment. Then there was the feared Jell-O salad that everyone scooped up on their plates and ate in big bites on the Fourth of July. Avery had been stunned and then annoyed every time anyone said, "Oh, Isabel. This is so good. My mother used to make it, and it was always my favorite. I just love the walnuts. And what is this secret ingredient? Cottage cheese?" No one had noticed Avery's grimace and closed eyes, all nodding at Isabel appreciatively, asking for the recipe, handing over e-mail addresses and phone numbers, saying, "I need it for a picnic," or "Now, don't forget!"

Dan rubbed the back of his neck. "Okay. Great. I'll pick you up in twenty minutes. I have a long list."

"Wonderful. I'll be waiting."

Isabel pushed the big red cart down the aisle that cut through the clothing section. Dan checked off pants and shirts, and then looked up. "Okay. Underwear."

Isabel followed the hanging signs and pushed the cart forward, both of them soon standing in front of a rack of boys' underwear.

"What are all these cartoons?" Isabel asked. "My, underwear has changed. My friend Elise has four grandsons, and she says that everything these days is commercial. My girls had flowers, a little lace, and maybe colors. But look at these." She pointed to a pack of underwear with Spider-Man's large webbed face on the front. Next to that was a pack with Daredevil; next to that, X-Men. Dan smiled, remembering how he and Jared would read comic books in their room, one after the other, over and over again.

"It's a whole marketing thing." Dan picked up a pack and read the back label. Weight. What was his weight? He closed his eyes and imagined picking Daniel up under his arms, lifting him up and down. Seventy, seventy-five pounds? He was so skinny, his knees must look like knobs, his elbows pointy and dangerous. Dan opened his eyes and then found the correct size for the weight and threw five packs in the cart.

"Well, he'll be in underwear for a long time." Isabel moved the cart toward the socks. "I can't imagine what socks will look like if underwear has cartoons on it."

The socks weren't half as exciting—rows of white athletic socks, short, white skate socks, and a few brown and blue dress socks, but Dan couldn't even imagine what size shoe a ten-year-old would wear. Isabel looked at him, her eyes wide.

"I had girls," she said, shrugging. "We should have called Elise. Well, let me ask the young woman over there."

She walked over to the counter and leaned up against it, laughing with the clerk, who began to ask questions about her grandson. Isabel didn't miss a beat, providing the information, and then she was back, taking the right size from the rack and putting pack after pack in the cart.

"I've heard," she said, "that boys are a little rougher on clothing than girls."

"You aren't kidding," Dan said. At ten, if he and Jared weren't helping Bill trim trees, stack bricks, or mow someone's lawn, they were up trees, in huge holes they'd dug in the backyard, or with the neighbor kids running through the streets. For one summer, none of his pants had knees, his mother ironing on patches, saying, "I refuse to buy you any more pants until just before school starts. Really, Danny, what do you do outside?" But she was smiling when she said it. Dan remembered that, even all these years later.

"Well, let's move on." Isabel looked at Dan's list. "I can see we've barely started. And when we're done here, I'm going to take you to dinner. My treat."

Dan followed her past the socks and belts and girls' tights, accepting her kindness, surprised how the colored underwear and small, white socks reminded him he needed his mother, a mother, any mother, right now.

"Oh," Isabel said, pushing away her plate, only one bite of hamburger and two French fries left. "I am fully sequansified and have had a genteel sufficiency."

Dan smiled. If Avery were here, she'd roll her eyes at her mother's strange family expression, *sequansified* not even a word at all. But as he looked at Isabel's satisfied face, he could see that she meant it, was glad to be out, to be of use.

"Me, too," he said. "And I don't have any leftovers." A tall boy with swirls of acne on either cheek took their plates, brushing the fry and hamburger bun crumbs off the table with a damp rag. Dan sucked on his straw, pulling in the last of his Coke.

"Dan, I have to ask. I know it's not my business at all. But is . . . Has Avery left for good? I want to know. Her asking for her job back seems, well, strange. Especially after all the hard work both of you put toward having the baby."

"No. She didn't," he said. "I mean, she hasn't moved out. It's just the job."

Isabel shook her head. "I really can't believe she gave up on the baby, even with your news. When she wants something, she sticks with it."

"That's why I'm nervous. She didn't stick here with me, Isabel," Dan said, the words pulling on his lips, his eyes filling. Not here. He wouldn't break down here in front of Isabel and the teenaged waitstaff. Dan rubbed a finger under his nose and sat back. "I think she feels like I've abandoned her. Like I abandoned her before she even knew she was abandoned. I know I should have told her about Randi, but I didn't know how."

Isabel shook her head and spun her milk-shake glass on the table, nodding. "It's my fault."

"What?"

"It's my fault. It's because of me."

The boy waiter circled their table, looking at the empty space, the drained cups. Dan took one last sip of his Coke and stood up. "Come on. Let's take a walk to the park and back."

Isabel nodded, and they pushed out into the night air, the temperature exactly right—seventy-eight or eighty—the shadow of the Berkeley Hills dark and rolling against the purple sky. They walked in silence for a while, past the new library and into the park. Other people strolled the path that looped around the wide lawn, their voices thrown across the grass like softballs, easy to catch.

Isabel looked at him. "It's because of her dad," she said quietly. "I didn't— Times were different then. I guess today I would have been in therapy. You know, a support group." She paused. "It was during those four years when Avery seemed to just push forward on her own. She went from being a girl to a woman and made decisions that shaped her life. I wasn't there to help her with any of it. I was like a shadow, present but not really. She figured everything out, and then she was gone to college. Before I knew it, she'd met you, graduated, was married."

Dan listened, his eyes on the path, holding Isabel's arm as a boy on a bike whooshed past them.

"One day after she'd left for Cal, I found a note in her room. I was just on my feet again, seeing things for the first time since Walt died. I'd gotten a job, you know, at the library. So I went into her room. I'd started doing that, sitting on her bed, trying to figure out how she'd gone ahead and grown up without me, when I opened a dresser drawer and found her note. It was a list, really. It had all the steps she was going to take for the future. The title of the list was 'Perfect Life.' She'd written it when I was in my—my slump. She hadn't had me, so she'd gone ahead and found what she needed in herself. But I know that's not enough. She needed me, and I wasn't there. Her father wasn't there."

"But I've always been there for her," Dan said. "Through all the pregnancy stuff. I went to every appointment I could. Read everything. Watched the videos."

Isabel shook her head, turning to Dan. "You didn't tell her about Randi. Or about you. Who you really were. You didn't let her in. And now when the bad news keeps coming, she feels like you aren't there, even though you are. Even though you didn't mean for this to happen. She can't take that, Dan. That's why she's gone back to work. She doesn't know how else to deal with it."

Dan thought of Avery as a teenager, sitting on the floor of her childhood room, writing the list of accomplishments that would make her life perfect. He'd always thought she was perfect. Her list had come true, except for him.

"I should have told her about Randi. About my life before I went to school. But how could I? How could I tell it in a way that wouldn't make her—?"

"Run away?"

"Yeah."

"But she ran away because you *didn't* tell her."

Dan watched his feet on the asphalt path. "I should have told her."

"Probably," she said. "But things happen. Things you can't predict or explain. I know that now, but I didn't know it when I was your age. Look at Walt. One day he was fine. I kept thinking to myself just before his diagnosis, 'My how wonderful it's all turned out.' Mara was going to go to Wellesley and wanted to be a doctor. Loren was popular, a cheerleader, happy. And Avery was going into high school, had a lot of friends, was smart as could be. Walt and I played bridge with friends, went on vacations, still loved each other after all the struggles that a long, full marriage can bring. The next thing, he had stomach cancer. Within months, he was gone. How can you predict that? Sometimes I used to think that because I had the nerve to think that things were perfect, they turned sour. Like God was telling me to stop taking things for granted because they can be ripped away with one word: *cancer.*"

Isabel wiped her eyes, and they stopped walking for a minute, letting another pair stroll past them. "I never talk about this because it upsets Avery so much. After I recovered, I started to mention her father's name, and she'd walk out of the room. From that point on, I never brought him up. I don't think we've talked about him for years." Isabel exhaled.

"What?"

"How can I tell you that you should have told Avery about Randi? Look what happened when I tried to talk with her about Walt."

"It's different. I mean, she talks about that time with me. A lot," Dan said, thinking of how the conversation usually started with "When my mom checked out." He wouldn't tell that to Isabel, at least not tonight. "But I really don't know anything about Walt."

"She was his favorite. I know I shouldn't say it, but it's the truth. She was the baby. Our last chance to do it right. We were struggling a bit financially when we had the first two, but those four years between Loren and Avery made all the difference. He would come home from work and pick her up, sit at the kitchen table with her on his lap and feed her Chex mix. When she started school, he wanted to know everything she did. He must have gone over hundreds of pages of homework with her. She looks just like him, you know. Same face, same eyes."

Dan shook his head. He thought of the photo of Isabel's three girls on the living room couch, in order of age and height, Mara, Loren, Avery. "I always imagined Mara would have been his favorite. Didn't she get the best grades? A doctor from the get-go?"

"Yes, she did get good grades. Oh, my, did she. She studied at night when she was in the third grade. I couldn't get her to play. But no, it was Avery. Loren was always with me. Mara didn't really need either of us. Maybe Walt was older by then, softer, finally knew what to do. I certainly did. Or at least I thought I did. But after he died . . ." Isabel stopped and pulled Dan to the edge of the thick lawn, letting another couple pass them. Cool air rose from the lawn and pressed against their faces. "After he died I realized I didn't know how to do a thing. I didn't know how to get up in the morning, how to make a cup of tea. Everything was so hard, so I let it all go. The girls just survived, somehow. I don't remember one thing about Loren applying for college or Avery's dances or family holidays. It's all a blur. Even now, when I fall asleep, it's the first thing I think about. Those awful years. The ones that made Avery who she is."

They walked out of the park and back onto the sidewalk that would lead to Dan's Lexus. The streetlights had come on, buzzing as they pulsed bright. "It's not your fault, Isabel. Look at me. When I was in high school and then especially afterwards, I did things . . . you know. Look, sometimes I want to blame my parents. I do, actually. I get on a roll, thinking everything that happened to me was because my dad was too hard on us or my mother had no backbone. It's not like I don't think about it, but how I ended up—with Randi and all— is not their fault. Jared was saying— Well, I know I made decisions on my own. So, it's not your fault that Avery acts the way she does. I think we come out wired a certain way, that's all. Or things or people—" For an instant, Dan saw Randi walking ahead of them, the back of her knees so smooth, her feet tiny in her high-heeled sandals. "They help us do the things that are inside, right or wrong."

"It could be we're wired to be a certain way," Isabel said, "but what happens to us—that can change us. That can make us who we are. Avery's dad dying, my slump, your dad's feelings. All those things came together."

"Then we can change. I changed. Or maybe I just hid. Maybe that's all Avery did, hid. She hid from her father's death, from you, and now from me."

"Oh, my, Dan," Isabel said. "Yes, she changed. Walt's death and my depression were what pushed her forward. It's so hard to see your child change because of something you did."

"What you did, but also who she is inside," he said, knowing that his own son, his Daniel, the boy with a baseball cap sliding down his skinny head, a fighter, a poor learner, was who he was because Dan had walked down the apartment steps and into his packed-to-the-brim Ford Taurus. He knew what Isabel was saying, and he hoped the changes in Avery and Daniel weren't permanent.

"So what should I do?" Dan asked. "How do I make her see that no one could have put this on a list?"

Isabel walked on, her face down, her arm through Dan's. "Who am I to tell you?"

"Just what do you think?" He felt some of Avery's impatience, a flick on the corner of his lips, and then breathed and held her arm tighter.

"Okay," she said slowly. "Well, I think—I think you need to go on. That's all the advice I can give you. It's what I finally did. Make this work with your boy. Fix up his room and visit him. Get to know him. Bring him home. Somehow, Avery will see that it's not like when her dad died. It's life, Dan. Life."

He couldn't speak, so he nodded. Life. It was life. It was what wouldn't happen in Avery's womb. It was more, not less. It was fuller, not smaller. All he had to do was open his arms and pull it in. If only Avery could, too. If only he could bring both Daniel and Avery back to him. This was what he had to talk about with Bret Parish when he had his appointment Friday. All this fear, all this need.

"And Dan," Isabel said.

"Yeah?"

"You might not want me, but I want to be there. For you. For

Daniel. When you go to buy the bed, I want to come. I want to help paint the room. I want to be a part of this new life. Okay?"

He nodded, his tongue thick with thanks he couldn't speak. He squeezed her arm, and he and his mother-in-law walked down the street toward his car, moths and mayflies looping around the lights like satellites, the moon hanging yellow and heavy above the hills.

Seven

When the BayPorter van pulled up in front of the house, Avery saw her mother's Camry parked out front. Inside, all the lights were on, the house like a birthday cake on the dark street.

"You have some party in there, miss," the van driver said, opening his door and sliding out.

Avery waited for him to open her door as the BayPorter drivers always did, and then she stood at the back doors as he took out her single black suitcase.

"Thanks," she said, pressing a fifteen-dollar tip into his hand.

"It is nothing. Thank you for using BayPorter, miss."

As he drove away, Avery rolled her suitcase up the driveway toward the garage, her belly like a clay bowl, heavy, hard, and holding her organs uncomfortably. She had to pee, and she felt dirty, her clothes all needing a rinse or a dry cleaning.

After Dan had called to tell her that Daniel was his, she hadn't talked much to her husband, the couple of conversations tense and short and awkward. It had been wonderful to hang up after a minute or two, lie back in the soft bed, and watch shows and movies on HBO and Showtime. During the day, she'd overseen the preliminary steps of the implementation of the computer networking system, talking with executives and employees, and in those conversations, she'd felt like the woman she wished she were all the time: strong, knowledgeable, focused. Avery appreciated the thanks she'd received, the glances men had thrown her way, the admiration in the women's eyes. And then there had been Mischa Podorov, who oversaw the computer systems for Dirland Accounting nationwide. Mischa was from Georgia, the Georgia in the former USSR. "Not the peaches and the cream Georgia, you know," he'd said. "I am from the original. The best."

When she opened the garage door and pulled her suitcase up into the laundry room, she stood still and listened. Echoing down the hall from the nursery—the spare room, Daniel's room—she heard her mother's high-pitched laugh, Dan's slow, calm voice, and then something falling. Luís said, "Pick it up, man, or we'll never get this contraption together."

Valerie laughed, and Avery thought about turning around and leaving. They were all in on it together, wanting whatever was going to happen next. Wanting Daniel. But then the door closed loudly behind her, and she heard the collective pause from the back of the house and then footsteps. Too late for so many things.

Avery sighed and pulled her suitcase into the kitchen, looking up at Dan standing in front of her, his hands on his hips, a screwdriver in his front shirt pocket.

"Hi," she said, taking off her suit jacket.

"How was the flight? Here, let me take that." He grabbed her jacket and then the handle of the suitcase, rolling it back and forth gently on the Spanish tile, as if the sound could be confused for the normal conversation they used to have when Avery came home from business trips.

"Fine. No problems. So, what's going on in there?"

Isabel peeked in the kitchen. "Oh, sweetie! Hello! I'm so glad you made it home safely."

Avery found the spot on her cheek she'd bit so often that it felt worn, callused, ready for her teeth, eager to help her avoid saying the words she otherwise would, like, "Of course I'm home safely," or, "How do you think it went?" If they would only let her go to bed, but that would be impossible now. Her mother would pump her for information on her starting work, the trip, whom she'd met, what they wore, what she ate and where. And even though he was being careful with her, Dan was clearly excited, whatever was going on the room lighting his eyes, his cheeks reddish under his summer tan.

"No problems," she repeated. "So what's going on in there?"

Isabel looked at Dan, her face wobbling between truth and a soothing lie. She blinked, said nothing. Dan coughed and said, "We're putting together a bedroom set. Desk, bunk bed, dresser. Luís and Valerie are here. Dolores is watching Tomás. It's a bigger job than we first thought."

"Oh, my, yes," Isabel agreed. "So many parts. And the directions are written in Sanskrit as far as I can tell. Come see. Then you can tell me all about your trip." She smiled, but her lips quivered as she tried to hide that she knew about Daniel. Dan must have told her everything already, not leaving anything for Avery to do.

"I think I'll go and unpack," Avery said quickly. "Change. Okay?" She walked to Dan and took her jacket and the suitcase. He put his hand over hers, but she pulled away, rolling the suitcase down the hall. "I'll be there in a sec."

She shut the bedroom door and closed her eyes, leaning her head against the wood. Her heart pulsed in her head and throat, and she wished she could open her eyes and find herself back in the soft hotel bed, a delicious meal on a table, the television tuned to a first-run movie, Mischa calling her from his hotel, laughing about Ed from Dirland and his sad toupee. "It is a backwards carpet, you know, *ptichka?*" he'd say. "How will I look in it, A-vary?" Her name was birdlike on his tongue.

But when she opened her eyes, she was still in Monte Veda. Her husband was down the hall, fixing up a room for the ten-year-old boy who was moving in with them. His son.

Avery threw her jacket on the bed and unzipped her suitcase. She tossed her dirty laundry in the hamper and was hanging up blouses when Valerie knocked on the door.

"Aves? It's me." Valerie knocked again and then pushed open the door. "Hey, girl."

Avery turned and smiled. "Hi."

Valerie sat on the bed and fiddled with Avery's jacket buttons. "So, how are you? I barely saw you before you left. I didn't even know you'd gotten your job back. Dan had to tell me that part."

Avery swallowed and pushed her hair away from her forehead, turning to look at Valerie. "I know. I'm sorry. It just seemed like something—"

"Something we couldn't what? Talk about? Aves, come on! We've talked about everything. Remember, I used to work, too."

Unpacking her makeup and jewelry bags, Avery nodded. "I know."

"And then Loren called. She told me about—Social Services."

"So which one of you told my mom about Daniel?" Avery threw the bags on the bed and put her hands on her hips. "Don't you think I should have done that?"

Valerie breathed in, her collarbone visible under her T-shirt. "I don't know how she found out. Maybe it was Loren. Or Dan. But we are all worried about you. I'm glad she knows."

Avery took a couple of hangers from the suitcase. "Great. But maybe I could have made that decision. She's my mother. And now look at this circus."

"I'm sorry," Valerie said softly. Avery couldn't look at her, closing her eyes instead and feeling the fabric under her hands: silk, rayon, cotton. "But now that it's out, we can all talk about it."

"You're supposed to be on my side!" Avery slapped closed her suitcase.

"Come on. What would you have done if the situation were reversed?"

Avery wanted to turn and say, *I wish it were reversed. Take it! Take all of it. I'll take your baby, and then I'll call your mom and sister and build a bedroom set for Luís's bastard son and hang out with your family.* But as she thought the words, she knew she would be worried about her friend and would do inappropriate things, like calling Valerie's family and passing on the sad stories.

"I just need you to be there for me."

"I am. But Dan's my friend, too. He's hurting."

Zipping up the suitcase, Avery untucked her blouse and unbuttoned her skirt. "Great. Fine."

"Avery? I want to be able to talk about all of this."

"I know."

"You didn't want to go back to work before." Valerie crossed her legs and put her hands in her lap. "This wasn't a career move."

"No," she said, walking toward the bed and resting against the tall, oak bedpost. "No, it wasn't."

"So, what happened? When we talked right after this all started, you were going to go along with it. It seemed like you were ready to . . . see what was going to happen. And then you just left." Valerie looked up, and Avery could tell she was on the brink of tears, her eyes glassy and full. Avery had never imagined she was leaving behind more than just Dan and all his horrible news.

"Oh, Val." Avery sat down next to Valerie and grabbed her hands. "I'm sorry. I should have told you. I don't know. I can't take what's going on. Everything's out of whack. Terrible. Now you all are building him a room. It's like—"

"It's real?"

"Yeah," Avery whispered. She'd hoped it would somehow not be real. Like a dream she could shake herself awake from. Like a list she could rip up and throw away. "It's happening. Dan said that we're going to visit Daniel on Sunday. The first "get to know the dad" visit. I have to go, but I don't want to. I don't even want to be home. It was so peaceful in St. Louis, and I hate St. Louis. I didn't have to think about any of this. It was like it wasn't even part of my life."

"What do you want, Aves?"

Before she could stop herself, she blurted out, "My baby."

"Oh, hon. I know."

"No, you don't," said Avery, looking at Valerie. "There's no way you can. You have your baby. You got him right away. I was strapped down on tables like Frankenstein's monster, and even then my body wouldn't work. You don't know what that's like at all."

"Oh." Valerie pulled her hands away from Avery's. "But, Avery, you gave up. You called Dr. Browne and stopped everything. That's not going to help you get pregnant. That's not going to give you your baby."

Avery stood up and took off her skirt. "Yeah, well now it doesn't matter anyway. I'm not going to get what I want, am I? I've got a strange, damaged kid coming my way. I've got a husband I don't know. I'm going to focus on work. I'll take that instead." She slipped off her skirt and hung it up. "It's all I have left."

"Oh, please!" Valerie stood up and shook her head. "Look around you! Come on. Can't you see what Dan is trying to do? He's trying so hard to make it work. He loves you."

"Right," said Avery, flicking her skirt straight. "If that were true, he'd have told me about Randi and his past from the very beginning. He would have trusted me."

"Have you said that? Have you told him how you feel? Have you told him anything?" Valerie looked at her, more softly than Avery could have looked at her, especially if Valerie had told her she'd resented her pregnancy and baby.

"Sort of. Not really. Anyway, it's done, isn't it? There you all are, fixing his room. What can I do?" Avery turned to the closet and hung up her skirt, grabbing on to the hanging clothes to steady herself. She could see her life was spinning away from her. She was like a faraway comet that came close to the earth only every few years. The next time she orbited, Daniel would be a teenager, his friends in her house, Dan barbecuing them steaks; Tomás would be a five-year-old with a three-year-old sister, both playing on the lawn, while Valerie rubbed her pregnant-again stomach. It was like the view she had of her family life before her father died. Now every year, it grew farther and farther away, her dad's face a blur under his dark hair, her own teenaged body barely a memory.

"It doesn't have to be like that," Valerie said. "You can come back. You can help make decisions about the room and everything." Valerie moved closer to her, and Avery could smell her friend, the slight, sweet scent of breast milk, baby lotion, soap. She wanted to lean against Val, pull her close, believe her as she had about the infertility treatments, the crib, the paint, the clothes in the catalogs. Val had been her truest friend since Joanie Frankel in high school.

How Avery had loved to run next door and sink into the Delgados' red couch, sipping (pre-Tomás) Kendall-Jackson Chardonnay and eating cheese and crackers. She loved her friend, but the pattern of their friendship had changed, starting really from the day Valerie found out she was pregnant. It was their shared desire and circumstances that had brought them together, and nothing Valerie had envisioned for Avery had come true, and now Avery was on her own because Luís did not have a secret son or a drugged-out, dead ex-girlfriend. There was nothing for them to talk about anymore.

Sighing and standing straight, Avery turned to Valerie. "It's confusing, that's all. I'm sorry. I'll get better. Listen, I'm going to go to the bathroom and clean up. I'm pretty tired. I'll be right out, okay?"

Valerie moved forward a step and then stopped, something in Avery's eyes telling her what her words had not. "Oh, all right."

Avery turned back to the closet and listened as Valerie walked out, closing the door behind her, leaving Avery alone, the noises of laughter and planning and building as far away as a distant planet.

In the kitchen, Avery put on the kettle, leaning against the counter as the gas burned blue under the steel. Isabel came into the kitchen, her face slightly red and moist.

"I haven't put something like that together since . . ." She trailed off and opened the refrigerator, taking out a bottle of Crystal Geyser water.

Avery turned toward her, her arms folded across her chest. "Since when, Mom? Dad put stuff together. And then I don't remember you doing much of anything. Most stuff was just delivered, and then, you know, not delivered at all." She felt heat under her skin and moved away from the stove.

Her mother looked at her and nodded. "You're right. So I'll say it differently. I'm glad to feel like this now. I'm glad to be of use. That's all I've wanted recently. That's all I want now."

"Oh. Oh. Oh, that's great." Avery's lips trembled, and she took the teakettle off the flame, watching the blue tips of fire lick the air. "Wonderful. Just flipping wonderful."

"Avery, can't you see this might be what you've wanted all along?"

"Are you crazy, Mom? Do you really think—" She stopped, hearing Dan's voice travel down the hall. She began again, whispering. "So you think that finding this out about Dan is what I've always wanted?"

Isabel shook her head and sipped from the water bottle. "No. That's not what I mean. It's the child. Daniel. He's yours. He's what you've wanted in a strange way. He's not a baby, of course."

"And not mine, Mom."

"But he's Dan's. And Dan is your husband. Things don't always work out as planned, you know."

"Yeah, Mom. I know that. Look at us. Our life. Look—look at Dad!"

Putting down her drink, Isabel turned toward her and moved closer. Avery shut her eyes and imagined her first-class seat in the jet, her body hurtling through the air somewhere over Tulsa, Boise, Reno. Anywhere but here, with her mother suddenly wanting to talk, in this house where everyone was working away from and against her.

"Listen, sweetie, I should have talked more to you, let you know how I was feeling when your father got sick. And later." Isabel paused, the hum of the fridge like an annoying bug. "We just never talked about it."

Avery looked up quickly and waved her mother's words away. "And now isn't the time, Mom. God, I'm so glad I came home. Everyone is all over me." Again, she thought of Mischa, the night he knocked on her hotel door, holding a bottle of Dom Pérignon and two ounces of beluga caviar. She'd opened her door, staring, thinking, *What? You keep jars of caviar around? Spares for going to women's hotel rooms? Your cultural calling card?* She half expected him to whip out bottles of Stoli and a couple of Russian nesting dolls, an ambassador of seduction. Then he'd smiled, brushed his thick blond hair up over his forehead, his blue eyes on her, on her, on her.

She could call Brody and concoct an excuse to get back to St. Louis, a plane trip only days away. Mischa would still be there, working on the office system, his next stop Dallas. She could end up there soon enough, organizing a system for Sherman Wilson Insurance or Home Spot. Avery blinked, breathing out, breathing in. Her kitchen, her mother. How she should be acting? What she should do. She shook her head. "What is this, the month of revelation? I've gone all these years without knowing about Dan. Without you talking about Dad. Why now? Whenever I've said something before, you've ignored me."

"I was talking with Dan—"

"Dan? About what?"

"About that time." Isabel stared at her softly, the skin around her eyes full of lines. Avery blinked and swallowed, clutching her stomach that still felt hard and full and weighty.

"Mom. Please. I'm so tired. I'm sorry. I can't talk about this."

"That's exactly what I told Dan. Every time I try to talk to you about your father, you leave the room."

Avery ran a hand back and forth on the kitchen tile, running a finger down a line of grout, her tongue circling in her mouth for the least angry words. "*I* leave the room? Me? I don't think so. You never keep the discussion going. I want to. So does Loren. Probably Mara does, as well. But from the very beginning, you were too zonked out, and then it was like forbidden territory. No one could enter without the map no one could find."

They stared at each other. Avery felt like she was seeing her mother from another perspective, the same way she felt all those years ago while leaning against the bedroom door, Loren next to her, the mound of their mother's still body under the bedclothes. She clenched the bridge of her nose with a thumb and index finger, squeezing the skin as if pressure could push away this conversation. And then, as if in answer, Luís walked into the kitchen. "Okay! Come see it. It's all done."

Avery stared at her mother, who was almost old now. For so long, she'd seen her mother as she'd been throughout her childhood: short, clipped brown hair; smooth, pale face; dark, full eyes. But the mother she saw now wasn't that same woman. Her hair was almost totally gray in front, a patch of dark in the back, her eyes tired, a story of a dead husband and children who grew up and moved away.

Pushing a strand of hair behind her ear, Avery sighed. "Okay, Luís. We're coming." Avery grabbed Isabel's hand, and they walked together into the hall, the bright kitchen swallowing up their words. How many more times would she be able to hold her mother's hand? Even if they were walking toward something she didn't want to see, couldn't look at, hoped she could forget as soon as she turned away.

After her father had died, she had thought of all the times she'd turned away from him, said, "No way! Like, I'm not going to the store with you," "I don't want to play cards," or "I don't want to see where you work!" At night for years, she replayed those moments, and said yes to them all. Yes to his hand, his offer, his smile. Yes to everything she'd passed up.

Dan and Valerie sat on the brand-new bunk bed, which was made up in blue-and-yellow sheets and a comforter. Dan saw them and stood up, holding out his arms. "What do you think?"

"Oh, my," Isabel said. "You got that last drawer together! I am impressed."

Avery looked around the room, all traces of her imaginary baby gone. The walls were a vibrant yellow, the molding white. She could smell the wood furniture they'd all put together, the dresser and desk and bed gleaming oak in the light of the new red lamp. This wasn't a room she knew.

"Nice," she said, pulling her cheek between her molars, pressing, pressing. "I have water on. Anyone want tea?"

Not waiting for a reply, she turned and walked back into the fluorescent light of the kitchen, glad she didn't hear one single footstep behind her.

They didn't talk until Modesto. Avery sat with her legs crossed, knees pressed against the dash, and leaned against the passenger's-side door. Closing her eyes, she placed her cheek against the window. For the rest of the evening on Friday and all day yesterday, she and Dan had said very little to each other except for the basics. "Yes, the visit's on Sunday. . . . They're expecting you. . . . I can take only an hour or so. . . . That's fine. . . . Turn up the air conditioner. . . . I'm going to bed."

Dan spent most of the weekend shopping for Daniel's clothes and toys, buying a PlayStation and the brand-new Spider-Man video game. "Luís tells me all the kids at his school love this," he'd said, avoiding her gaze as he hooked it into the television in the family room. Avery had peeked into the spare room once and saw that the desk was full of paper and pencils and thick pink erasers, the kind she'd always bought before school started and never used; the nightstand was lined with books Isabel had bought; and the bed was dotted with a couple of sleek, boy-looking stuffed animals. *He's doing what I did for our baby,* she thought, tears in her throat. She couldn't hate him for that, but she closed the door and promised herself she wouldn't look in the room again.

At one point on Saturday afternoon, she'd checked her cell phone for messages, and there was Mischa's voice. "I am imagining your phone in your pocket, my voice next to your skin. I am thinking of standing in your doorway, and your eyes asking me a hundred questions. Call me."

Ugh, she thought as she erased his words, *how cheesy. Who on earth talks like that?* But then she imagined his hands on her thighs, as close to her as her cell phone, rubbing back and forth. Her body argued with her voice, sucked back all her words. Something warm grew in her throat and spread into her chest and stomach. *Um,* her body said. *Yes.*

But she hadn't called him back—the only person she'd called was Brody, checking on the reaction to the St. Louis meetings. She didn't call Loren or Valerie; she didn't listen to her mother's messages. She cleaned her house, did laundry, stared out the kitchen window, watching red-winged blackbirds drink water from the drain around the pool and chickadees land on and then fly away from the empty bird feeder.

"We're almost there," Dan said, nodding toward the Modesto sign, population 194,390. "It won't be more than fifteen minutes."

"Okay." She looked at her flower-print shirt, the red poppies vibrant in this strangely overcast day, the sky low, dark with clouds, full of heat and humidity.

"Midori talked to him this week, and so did his therapist. He knows. He knows who I am and who you are. He was angry at first. He said that we'd all lied to him, but then after a while, he seemed to adjust."

Better than I am, Avery thought, her chest tight. "Good."

"He really wants to meet me. I mean, he met me already, but meet—"

"I get it," she said. "He wants to see you in terms of who you are now."

Dan nodded. "Yeah."

"I'd want to see you, too." Avery thought of her father, his glasses sliding down on his nose, the space between his teeth, his constant laugh. If he walked into a room, she'd want to run her hands down his face, smell his neck, press her cheek against his chest. She'd open her mouth and swallow a waft of tobacco smoke, take in what may have killed him. She'd remember what she'd forgotten.

Daniel, who'd had nobody for so long, would need flesh that could teach him how to live, even if the flesh belonged to Dan, the father who had been promised to Avery's unborn children.

Dan looked at her, searching for sarcasm or anger, but Avery held still. "So," he said. "What we'll do is have kind of a meeting at Liza and Martin's. And then they and Midori will let us talk with Daniel alone. Maybe we'll be able to go out for ice cream, depending on how he acts."

Avery shivered. "Whatever."

Dan turned to her again, and for a moment she thought he was going to pull over on Highway 99 and throttle her. He had on the same face her father had worn the few times she'd misbehaved, gone one step too far, asked for the twentieth time if Grace Szudelski could spend the night. His eyes would narrow, his lips would press together into two strips of solid white. With Mara and Loren, his face transformed much more quickly, after one "I don't know what happened to the fender," or "I did too get home at eleven." Then there were quick, loud words followed by silence. Avery had always hated the silent time, even when it was one of her sisters who was in trouble. She would step slowly into the room where her father sat smoking a pipe, gently touching his knee, shoulder, hair, hoping that everything could go back to normal again.

And now Dan looked at her with the same slitted eyes, his hands tight on the wheel. "You might as well say 'fuck you,' Avery," he said. "I know you don't want to be here. But for Christ's sake, could you help me out a little? I've waited for days for you to show me one tiny bit of interest. Shit. Anything. I'm going to meet my son. If it were your son, I know I'd be more interested than you are."

To Avery, Dan was farther away than even her dead father, the air hard and solid between them. "If I'd had a son, you'd already know about it. I would have told you even if I'd had an abortion. Or a miscarriage. How you can think that I could do any more than I am already doing is just flat-out amazing."

She sat back hard against her seat. Dan stepped on the accelerator and wiped his forehead with his hand. "I'm nervous, Avery. Yeah,

I should have told you. Everything. I know that. Yes, you needed to know I lived a terrible, awful life before I met you. I've been thinking about it since the phone call. I know I've screwed up everything. But I thought you loved me. Who you married is who I really am, Avery. I had stuff in the past, but that became part of what I am today. Don't you see? I thought you really meant what we said to each other. Better or worse. This is the worse part we were talking about. We've had the better."

Turning to him, she felt her mouth hang open, the past two years a jumble of unarticulated anger in the pit of her stomach. Month after month of examinations and exploratory surgery and hormones, failure after failure after failure. That had been bad enough. "So I'm just supposed to take it all in. Your drug use. The drug addict you lived with. Her poor, sad son who now has a room in my house, in my baby's nursery?" She tried to breathe down her tears, but there they were, unwelcome and hot in her eyes. "I'm supposed to be some kind of mix between Deepak Chopra and Martha Stewart, able to deal with all humankind's crap with kindness and be a goddamned whiz at redecorating and furnishing a boy's room. You want me to accept it all. But what about me, Dan? What happens to me?"

"It's just not about you, Avery. Christ!" Dan clutched the steering wheel. "It's about a boy. A boy who's been abandoned. His mother died! You said you understood that."

"I do!" she cried, remembering the first dream she'd had about her father after he died. He was standing at the mantel talking to her, his pipe in one hand, the stem moving up and down as he made a point. When she woke up, she smelled tobacco for just a second, and then she remembered what was real, what she was left with. "But how can I possibly be expected to be anybody to him?"

"You're supposed to be somebody to me," Dan said more quietly. "You're supposed to be my wife."

Avery closed her eyes and leaned back against the headrest. She felt the hum of highway under the car and in her feet, and she remembered the airplane, her giddy nerves as she flew home, Mischa's voice still in her ear. She thought of her and Dan's bed, the forbidden zone in the middle, the way they'd been talking in shorthand for two weeks. Was this a marriage? Was this what she'd agreed to at St.

Stephen's Church, with their friends and family all around them, listening to every word of their wedding vows?

Smoothing her pants, Avery imagined today like a project at work, a company that had to be sold Pathway Solutions equipment and software. She could do that. She knew she could smile and charm the clients, make them think she wanted nothing more than to come to Tulsa and stay for two weeks at the Doubletree Inn while she introduced the networking system. Avery could convince all the clients—Lawrence and Claire and Simone and Perry—that her life depended on that very thing. She didn't have to mean it. If they didn't buy in, she would walk out the door with only one tiny regret, the loss of commission.

So today could be like a sales meeting. She could sell herself to Midori and Daniel and Liza and Martin. They would think she was the most amazing wife of all time. Dan would get off her case and stop making her think about her father and Mischa. If they left her alone, she would have time to breathe. She would have time to decide what she was going to do.

They all sat in a dark living room, a conglomeration of strange metal gadgets arranged on the coffee table and bookcases. Behind the couch where Avery, Dan, and Midori Nolan sat was a row of Bavarian beer steins. Liza and Martin Barnett sat in two dark red chairs across from the couch. Liza had a diet Coke in her hand, and Martin pushed his glasses back against the bridge of his nose. When he spoke to Midori or Dan, Avery stared at him, wondering if he were one of those sick men who took children in to abuse or dominate them. But he seemed simply like a scattered, intelligent man.

"After some confusion, I think Daniel took the news pretty well," Liza said, squeezing her Coke can, the small tin sound pinging in the room. "Once he got over us keeping a secret, he was amazed! In fact, he has been acting much better since then. I think he's really excited."

Avery cast another glance around the crowded room, knowing she'd be glad to leave this house, too. Martin crossed his arms and nodded, his glasses sliding down his long nose.

Dan smiled. "That's good to hear. So when do you think he can come home with us?"

Midori looked up from her notes. "We have the official papers to deal with first. But not long. A matter of weeks. Maybe only two. Hopefully, he'll have the time he needs to adjust to his new home before school starts. That will be a major transition for him."

One breath in, one breath out, yoga breathing, calm breathing, centered breathing. Avery tried to keep her eyes open, but all she wanted to do was close them and drift away. Transition. Everyone's life was a transition. Hers was, and she'd been waiting for the one defining moment to mark her passage. But into what? What was she supposed to turn into? Pushing a child into the world would have been clear, true, pure. Her child was inside her, and then it was outside her. Easy to see the black-and-white of it all. It was either in or out, life or death, the darkness or the light. Not like the mess her life had become.

"Avery? Is that okay?" Dan was looking at her, waiting.

She wanted to say, "No, it's not okay." She wanted to give Midori Nolan, Martin and Liza, and Dan a terrible face, something pruned and squished and angry, or maybe she'd blow a raspberry with her lips, spit and sound everywhere. Then she would stand up and walk out to the car, sit in the driver's seat, and take off. She wanted to cry.

Instead, she nodded and said, "Yes." And then, remembering how she had to sell this moment as if she were a product, she lifted her lips, feeling the muscles press into her cheeks. "Of course."

Liza and Martin looked at each other doubtfully, so Avery added, "It's been a shock, all of this. Truly. But a boy needs his father." Liza leaned forward. "And a mother," Avery tacked on, knowing she was supposedly the mother. Liza leaned back in her chair, and Avery turned to Dan. He was looking at her with such gratitude, she immediately wanted to take her words back, stuff the lie into her mouth, and chew it gone.

"Well, let's bring Daniel in," said Midori. "Why don't you all have a good discussion? He will ask about you and Randi, Dan. He wants to know how you met. I suggest you tell him the basics. The details can come later. It's up to you, though."

"Okay." Dan sat on the edge of the couch, his hands slipped between his knees, as if he were waiting for a teacher to pass out a final exam. Avery held on to her cushion, trying to find the breath she had counted out before, but every inhale and exhale was in halves or quarters. Her stomach was scratchy with acid, her heart pounding.

Liza stood up and walked into the hall. Avery heard her knock on a door and then a muffled conversation. If this were a scary movie, Avery would close her eyes and put her fingers in her ears so she wouldn't have to listen to the music that was now rising in intensity, cellos and singular piano notes as the monster or murderer or ghost slid silently down the hall, ready to kill or shock or damage. At the movies, she would throw herself into Dan's side, hold her face against his shoulder, search for his open hand. Now, she looked at him on the opposite end of the couch, his eyes on the hallway, and she knew he wasn't watching the same movie. He was watching the end of a drama, the characters reunited and redeemed. He wasn't in the same theater at all.

Daniel came down the hallway and stood in the doorway, looking at Dan. He was a small child, skinny, his elbows white and pointy. His jeans were new, but way too big, caught at his middle in a belt that hung down below a T-shirt that said QUICKSILVER on the front. He wore all-white shoes that Avery recalled having seen on television, a famous basketball star jumping up to the basket, the shoes brilliant on the screen.

Starting with his dark, still-wet hair, she searched Daniel, looking for Dan. At first, it seemed that the test had been wrong. He was so pale, none of Dan's olive skin in him at all. If she bent down, tilting up his jaw, she would see all the veins that kept him alive, his skin revealing that for him, there had been no swim lessons or playdates at the park, no vitamin D.

And then there were the freckles, points of color flowing across his cheeks and nose, running down the tops of his arms. If she made him take off his baggy jeans, she bet there would be more on his thighs and shins. That wasn't from Dan's family, and neither was the body, all bones and sinew. Dan and Jared came from bigger parents, full of muscle and flesh, strong and ready to work. Bill still maintained his yard every weekend, mowing and hedging and cutting. Marian walked every morning with her neighbors, women in visors and sensible shoes, charging down the lanes.

But this boy? He would be sucked under a lawn mower. He would fall to earth from the weight of a chain saw. He would begin to whine after a half-mile walk. He was the kind of kid who was laughed off every playground in the United States, and Avery closed her eyes, pushing back nausea and delight. They were wrong. Completely.

But then Midori said something to him as she walked out of the room, and he responded. Avery opened her eyes, watching his mouth, the slight tip of chin as he spoke, his lips, full and Italian and Dan's. This was how Dan's genes mixed with another woman's. This was how his had failed to mix with hers. Here was the child he couldn't have until death and Social Services brought him one.

After Midori left, Daniel stared at Dan, and then looked toward Avery. She almost flinched and pulled her gaze away from his eyes but managed instead to look back, finding the awkward smile she'd used earlier. "Hi," she said, breathing away her nausea. "I'm Avery, Dan's wife."

"Do you want to see my room?" he asked.

Avery looked at Dan, and he stood up. "Sure we do."

"I want to take my things to your house. I don't want to leave anything here."

Great, Avery thought as she stood up, imagining more strange metal gadgets and mini beer steins. Or worse, Randi's collection of what? Heavy metal CDs? *People* magazines? Leather halter tops?

"I have my own room here," Daniel said, leading them down the hall. "I was supposed to share, but I have my own room." He turned to Avery and Dan, his legs apart, his face turned up. "Do I have my own room at your house? Am I near you? Where will I be?"

"We've got a room all ready for you," Dan said, leaning over, trying to look into Daniel's eyes. "It's just down the hall from our room. Kind of like how all the bedrooms are here."

"But much bigger," Avery said. She brought her hand to her mouth and turned around, glad that Liza and Martin weren't behind them.

"Bigger than like this?" Daniel asked. "This house is way big."

"Oh, much," Avery said. The dark walls seemed to close in around her. Liza and Martin needed a skylight in here. She felt like Alice following the white rabbit down hallways, both searching for the way out. "Can we go in?"

Daniel nodded and pushed open the door. The room had obviously been cleaned for the visit—the bedspread tucked tight, the board games, plastic action figures, and comic books arranged in neat piles on the dresser. Daniel stood in the middle of the carpet, his tiny arms at his sides. "This is my room."

Dan walked over to the dresser and began asking Daniel about his toys. Avery closed her eyes and breathed from her center, or the center she imagined, never having quite found it despite the yoga teacher's coaching. But after a few breaths, her heart began to beat like it did ten minutes into kickboxing class, one-two, one, one-two, one, one, one.

She walked over to the desk and sat in the wooden chair, looking up at the mirror that hung on the wall. A black-and-white photograph of the blond actress in the show *Friends* was taped to the right corner.

"You like her?" she asked, turning to Daniel.

He shrugged. "Yeah . . . I want to meet her. I want to go to the show. But I don't want to marry her or anything."

"Oh, well, that's good. She's already married to one of my favorite actors."

Dan shook his head. Why? Did he think Daniel had had enough disappointment, too much for him to know the pretty actress was married to an even prettier actor? He'd better get used to it, Avery thought. Everyone had to. She looked up at Daniel, who was pulling on a lock of hair above his left ear. When he dropped his hand, the tuft stuck out straight. "Do you have a girlfriend?"

"No," Daniel said, pressing his lips together. "I don't think about that stuff. That's what girls think about."

Avery turned back and noticed an open math book on the desk, the problems completed in pencil right on the pages. Vince Brasch and Midori had both said Daniel had learning "issues," but here were all the problems done correctly, at least as far as she could see. "You seem to like math, too."

"Math makes sense," Daniel said, his dark eyes on her, and she nodded. Work was the only thing that made sense to her now. Keeping busy. Problems A, B, and C solved by six p.m., and then they could celebrate at Andrés for one or two or three hours.

"So do you want to go get an ice cream?" Dan asked.

"No." Daniel sat on his bed, crossing his arms, his mouth pulled down. "Liza says I'm not supposed to have sugar."

"A hamburger, then? We could walk right down to McDonald's." Dan leaned over, his eyes wide. Avery felt the nausea creep back up her throat.

"No."

Standing up, Avery walked past the bookshelf and stood in front of the closet. "What do you want to do, then?" she asked.

"I want—I want to go home with you now."

Avery looked at Dan, her eyes wide, and shook her head slightly. Dan stood up straight, his hands nervous fish dangling at the ends of his arms. "Well, Daniel, um, I think we have to wait for some paperwork to go through. There are some legal matters. Official stuff, you know?"

Daniel pulled harder on the lock of hair. "But Midori said the test meant you were my father. If you're my father, then you can take me home. I lived with my mother. She was my mother in the real way. I didn't have to wait for that."

Dan seemed to think about what Daniel was saying, and Avery wanted to run to him, lean on his shoulder, say things like, "I was wrong. I'm sorry. I'll quit my job. Just come home. Leave him here for now. Please?" She thought about the long drive back to the house, the words she could use to fix this, to stop this boy from changing everything. Then she closed her eyes. Daniel hadn't done a thing wrong. He didn't deserve anything that had happened to him. If Avery was going to drive away from anyone, it should be from Dan.

"Do you like it here?" Dan asked. "You do like your room."

"I'm going to leave anyway, right?" Daniel's lock of hair stood out from his head like a horn. "I'm going to come live with you, right?" He looked at Avery, his Randi eyes full of tears. He wiped at his face quickly, as if they wouldn't notice, crossing his skinny arms across his chest.

"Of course you are," Dan said, leaning down again and putting a hand on Daniel's shoulder. "You're my . . . son."

"Then I want to go now."

Avery pushed back against the closet door. It was happening. Life was cracking clean open and changing in front of her. Before, she had tried not to notice it. Each morning came, and she'd get up, her list of activities clear, while all around her people turned on others whom they'd adored the day before, scientists made discoveries, men and women fell in love. In this room, though, like in the hospital waiting room with Mara and Loren, she could feel it. No matter what she did, the earth turned toward the sun, and—poof!—it was daylight. Poof! Here was her stepson, and she could feel him in the backseat of the Lexus as if they were all driving up Highway 99 right now.

It wasn't this moment, but the living afterward that would hurt. It was all the time from this second on that would twist her life into another shape. A flare lit in her chest, small but angry. She hated Dan for doing this to her, even if it wasn't his fault. Even if he had no choice.

"I'll go talk to Midori," she said. Before she turned to the door, she saw Dan reach for Daniel, pull him close, take his small bones into his man body and hug him. As Avery walked down the hall, she wept for Daniel. For Dan. Maybe even for Randi. For herself and her father, for the hug she wanted from a ghost.

TWO

Eight

At his second appointment with Bret Parish, Dan sat silent for long moments. Bret asked questions, and Dan mumbled short sentences: "Yes. I think so" or "No. Not yet." Strangely, he'd been eager for this appointment, desperate to have all this feeling inside him uncorked, but now, with Bret looking up at him with wide, interested eyes, Dan had nothing to say.

"So, Avery's not happy? You said, 'I think so.'" Bret tapped his pencil on his yellow legal pad.

"It's hard to tell."

"And Daniel has been home how many days?"

"Eight. The first day was theoretically a visit. They couldn't just give him to me. To us. But Midori pushed everything through the following Monday, and he's home." Dan was almost panting, this sentence requiring too much air.

"And Avery's back at work."

"Yes."

"And you took that paternity leave? Like we discussed."

"Yes," Dan said. On Daniel's first day home, Dan had called Isabel after Avery had left the house and asked her to come over to baby-sit. Then he'd driven to work and sat down with Steve and told him the whole story, beginning to end. Steve had sat still in his seat, his mouth open, his fingers beating out a quiet rhythm on his desk.

"Christ," he'd muttered a couple of times as Dan spun out the story, all of it.

And then, even though it was unheard of and strange and a ridiculous career move, Dan had requested his six weeks of paid paternity leave, a benefit he never would have considered using, not even when Avery was trying so hard to conceive. He promised Steve he'd take client calls from home, advise the sales staff when problems arose, which they would, every day. Even so, he wasn't surprised when Avery had stared at him that evening, her face reddening as he told her what he'd done.

"What?" she said. "No one really takes that."

"I have to. Who's going to take care of Daniel if I don't? I'll have enough time to get him ready for school and then keep an eye out the first few days of school if there's trouble. It's the perfect solution."

Avery shook her head, her lip trembling. "I suppose you think I should stay home. That's what you wanted. I told you I wouldn't!"

Dan looked over his shoulder, not wanting Daniel to hear. Lowering his voice in hopes that Avery would get the hint, he said, "I know. I'm not saying you should now. But I am."

"But what will they think of you at work?" Avery said just as loudly as before. "I know they give paternity leave, but no one on track takes it. What if Steve leaves? Do you think they'll give you his job now? Some guy who takes six weeks off from his career? Someone who leaves and makes his colleagues pick up the slack? Everyone will hate you."

"I don't care," he said. "Not now."

"And," she said, almost snorting, "you told him about everything? What were you thinking? How could you let Steve know what happened? How stupid."

"I had to, Avery. I can't pretend anymore. It's too late to pretend it didn't happen."

Avery pulled her hair back in an imaginary ponytail, and then let it fall back to her shoulders. She tapped the kitchen counter with her fingers. "I'm not Mother Teresa, Dan."

"I don't want you to be."

"Yes, you do. You want me to be someone else! Someone who's

nice. I'm not nice, Dan. You don't see me adopting twenty special-needs kids, do you? I don't know what you want from me."

"What are you talking about?" he asked.

"I'm not the kind of person who can do this! You're not the kind of person who should be on paternity leave. You weren't going to take it when we were going to have a real kid. Our kid."

Avery crossed her arms, pressing against her chest, tears in her eyes. They stared at each other until they heard the footsteps, the soft, small kind trying not to be heard. The kind going backwards, away from what was painful.

"Shit," Avery said. She glared at him, her eyes the blue of the fake frozen block at the bottom of the Igloo cooler. "I'm going to bed." She brushed by him and went to their room. Dan breathed in, his lungs so heavy, they felt wet, and then went to go find Daniel. But when he got there, Daniel was under the blankets, the Spider-Man night light on, his breathing slow and steady. *He knows how to pretend,* thought Dan. *He's just like me.*

Now Dan crossed his right leg, his ankle hard on his left knee. He looked at Bret and sighed. It seemed to him that therapy would take forever. Two visits weren't enough to get at all the stories, the ones involving Randi, his parents, Avery, and now Daniel. Midori was right to send him here, but maybe this wouldn't work. Maybe he wouldn't come back. He didn't have time. If it weren't for Isabel and Valerie watching Daniel for him, he wouldn't be here now.

"So do you like being home all day?" Bret asked. Dan blinked, surprised by this easy question.

"Yeah," he said. "I've been able to talk with Daniel a lot. He's told me stories."

"About what?"

"About his life. About Randi. What her life was like after—after me."

"What did he tell you?"

Dan scratched his knee. "There was a baby-sitter for a while. A friend, really. A woman who lived in the trailer park. Susan. She moved away a couple years ago, but she seems to have taken up a lot of the slack. When Randi wasn't feeling good, Susan and Daniel would go down to the park or to the library. There were other times, though, when Randi was sick and Susan wasn't around. Daniel had to take care of her. Make her meals. Get ready for school by himself."

"What else?"

"They were on welfare. Daniel talked about going down to an office for money. Sometimes they ran out of food at the end of the month."

"How does it feel to hear those stories?" Bret tapped his pencil a bit harder, one-two, one-two. The fountain outside spilled water onto rocks. Dan closed his eyes for a second, opening them to find Randi on the couch against the far wall, her legs crossed, one swinging a purple leather high-heeled sandal.

"Tell him," she said. "Come on, big guy."

Dan cleared his throat. "Daniel told me that at the end of the month when they ran out of money, Randi would go at night to a peach orchard, pick a basket, and then sell them on her corner. Made a sign and everything."

"Tell him what I bought with the money, Danny," she said, rubbing her hands over her black nylons, adjusting her sandal strap.

"Daniel said she would buy him a bag of candy and a hamburger at Burger King."

"Is that all she bought?"

Dan looked at the couch, but Randi wouldn't look up. She clacked her gum and pulled a dark curl with her forefinger.

"He said she also would buy drugs. Even when she was really sick. Midori told me that Randi died of pancreatitis and something with her liver. I didn't even know what that was. Daniel said she was yellow at the end."

"For crying out loud, Danny." Randi stood up and adjusted her leather skirt. "Did you have to tell him that? Jee-sus. I'm outta here."

"How does Daniel feel, talking about his mother?"

Dan watched as Randi tippled to the door in her high heels, her shoulders white and smooth in her strapped shirt. "You better change your tune, Danny, or I'm not coming back." The door opened and slammed. Dan jumped.

"Dan?" Bret stared, looking over his shoulder.

"He tells me at bedtime. When he's tired. Sometimes he cries. During the day he's pretty quiet. He watches everyone. Even me. I keep thinking he imagines it's all going to disappear. I don't know what will happen when he goes to school."

Bret glanced at the clock on the shelf behind Dan's head. "How do you feel when he tells you about Randi?"

Breathing in deeply, Dan could still smell Randi's Charlie perfume, the amber, fruity smell of the Longs Drugs aisle where she would slip boxes of cologne, perfume, and after-bath splash into her coat pockets. An ache of old tears pulled at his throat. "Not good. I just left her, Bret. She was on her own. I didn't even call. How can I tell my son that? How can I tell him that his mother died because of me?"

"Would you have done anything differently? Really? Didn't you have to get out of there? Wasn't that life toxic for you?"

"But I could have helped her."

"Sometimes, Dan, the only person you can help is yourself." As he stared at Bret, Dan heard Avery saying, "I'm not Mother Teresa." Maybe Bret was right. No one really was always good. Nobody did everything possible. But for his boy? Randi? No matter what Bret said, Dan knew he could have done something. One small thing.

"We're almost out of time. But I want to know if you've talked to your parents."

Dan scooted forward in his seat, resting his elbows on his knees. "Not yet. Jared's come over. But we decided to wait until Daniel is more settled to bring anyone else in."

"Who's we? You and Avery?"

"No. Jared and I. We decided. Avery didn't have anything to— She didn't have an opinion."

"Really?"

He shrugged. "Daniel's already met Avery's family and our good friends next door. I think he's kind of overwhelmed." Even though this was the truth, Dan felt the words as slick on his tongue as a lie. He was scared to call Marian and Bill. If Jared told him to wait, he would wait. As long as he could.

That night, before Avery came home from work and long after dinner, Dan sat in a chair next to Daniel's bed, holding *Julie of the Wolves*—the book Luís had recommended—in his hands, reading aloud. Daniel looked up at him, his face blank, taking in the story of young Miyax who ran away from home and ended up lost in the Alaskan wilderness. They'd finally gotten to the part where Miyax was accepted into a pack of wolves, and Dan couldn't help but think that Daniel was in exactly the same situation. Only in this house, there was an alpha female who bared her teeth at anything that came too close, even at the alpha male.

As he read, adding character to Miyax's thoughts with high and low intonations, Dan tried to remember if his parents had read to him past the picture-book stage. Sure, he could still envision *Where the Wild Things Are* and *Green Eggs and Ham*. But later? Nothing. He and Jared read comic books with flashlights in their dark bedroom, trying to stay as quiet as possible so that Bill wouldn't push open the door and yell something about lights out. And it wasn't until college that he'd picked up a book, a novel, and then it was only because he had to read *Catch-22* or *One Hundred Years of Solitude* for a required English class. Maybe it wasn't too late for Daniel to like words, to use them to forget what had been real.

"Dan?" Daniel was all eyes, peeking from under the blanket. "Dad?"

Dan put his thumb on the page and looked up, his mouth open, his eyes smarting. *Dad. Dad.* He cleared his throat and said softly, "Yeah?"

"Am I here for good? I mean, will I have to move again? Will I have to go back to the Barnetts?"

Leaning back against the chair, Dan closed the book on his thumb. Miyax's somber face stared at him from the cover. "No. This is where you live now, Daniel. Midori and Vince Brasch are making sure all the papers are in order. Everything's just about set."

"But she doesn't like me."

"Who? Midori? Of course she does."

Daniel shook his head on the pillow, the reading light picking up the red in his hair. Randi's red. The red that snaked through her black curls. "No, not, like, her. I mean your wife. She's hecka mad."

Dan's mouth puffed full of denials and cover-ups, but then he nodded. "She is. She's really mad."

"Why? I didn't do anything to her." Daniel sat up and leaned against the headboard. "I don't even know her."

"It's not about you, Daniel. It's me. I didn't tell her some things I should have."

"Like what?"

Dan put the book down on the nightstand and rubbed his face with both hands. What would have happened if his parents had told him the truth when he'd asked questions? His parents had fought behind their bedroom door, his mother running out of the room and down the hall, her eyes red. For the rest of the day after a fight, Bill sat in his favorite living room chair watching a ball game or car races or a golf tournament. If his mother had said, "I wanted to take you two boys to visit my parents for two weeks and your father said no," would Dan have been damaged beyond repair? Why did parents want to hold life away from their children? All it did was make it more frightening when things did happen, childhood slamming against adolescence, truths falling like dead bodies to the ground.

"I never told her the story about your mom. That we were a couple. How we met. All of that."

"How did you meet my mom?" Daniel asked, crossing his arms across his thin chest.

Dan smiled. "I met her during freshman orientation. The very first day of high school. She was sitting in the middle of the quad with some friends. And I said to my friend Tim, 'Look at her.' "

"Was she pretty?"

Dan looked over at the picture of the blond actress Daniel had immediately put on his mirror. "It was 1984, so styles were different. She had this big"—Dan put his hands on top of his imaginary hairstyle and patted it—"hair. Big hair. But it was dark and curly, and she was thin. Not skinny. Thin."

"Kids call me skinny. The other boys at the Barnetts' called me Bone Boy."

"Listen," Dan said, rubbing his stomach, "later on, you'll be glad you pulled from that side of the family. Trust me."

"What do you mean? Who else is there?"

"My parents. Your . . . grandparents."

"Did they like my mom?"

Again, the easy lie bloomed in his mouth. How much easier it would be to say, "Oh, they adored her. My mother and she went shopping together. Your mom learned all my mom's recipes. My mother's one best wish was that Randi and I have kids. Wait until they meet you! It's Grandma's dream come true." But it would take what? Another day? A week? before Daniel would see the lie for what it was. There would be no spontaneous, joyous reunion with Bill and Marian. Nothing like the picture postcard Dan's lie would create.

"They didn't like us together. They didn't like us as a couple. We did some things that made them mad. I guess you could say they are still mad at me because of them."

"What did you do that made them mad?" Daniel asked.

Looking around the room he, Val, Isabel, and Luís had put together, Dan sighed. "Do you know how your mom died?"

"Midori told me it was her blood. A disease in her blood that was bad for her insides."

"Do you know how someone gets that disease?" Dan asked, hoping Daniel would nod, and the conversation could move quickly toward its end. But he didn't, shrugging his shoulders up to his ears.

"Well, you can get it—it's called hepatitis C—from blood."

"Oh, sort of like AIDS?" Daniel said. "We learned about that in school. A lady came in to talk with us about it."

"Oh? Well, yeah. Just like AIDS."

"So from another person. She got it from another person?"

"Maybe. Or from taking drugs with a needle."

Daniel thought, his eyes looking toward the nightstand and the book. He blinked and then looked up at Dan. "Okay."

"You know about that?"

Daniel adjusted his legs under the covers and picked at an imaginary scab on his arm.

"You know what I'm talking about, then?" Dan persisted.

"So why haven't your parents come to meet me?"

Dan sighed, exhausted. He'd forgotten how children talked, asking what was true and close to the bone, words like the sharpest knife filleting away the bullshit. When had he himself changed from a kid like Daniel to the young man who stole from his parents? When had the truth disappeared into a fog of lies that swirled so tight around him and Randi that Dan saw only shadows?

"I haven't told them yet. I thought—we thought . . . Your uncle

Jared and I thought," Dan said, thinking of Bret Parish and how he made Dan clarify everything, "that you'd met enough people this week. You will meet them. I promise."

"If they didn't like my mom, I don't like them."

Dan nodded. Just as well. Fine. But unrealistic. Somehow, he'd have to make that meeting work.

"Did you ever meet your other grandfather? I know your mom's mom died."

"He'd come over sometimes. But then Mom said that he'd 'high-tailed it away from hell.' "

Dan hid a laugh. "Oh."

"That's what she said, anyway." Daniel looked down. "*Hell* isn't a bad word here, is it?"

Picking up the book again, he smiled. "No, it's not."

"Mom wouldn't let me swear at all."

"Really?"

Shaking his head seriously, Daniel said, "One word, and I had to go to my room. Once I was in there the whole day because I said *shit.*"

Pain fell down Dan's ribs like stairs. The whole day? What was she doing while he was in there? "Were you upset?"

"No. She gave me a puzzle to do and a bag of M and M's. Then in the evening she took me out for chicken. She was really happy. I liked it when she was happy."

What could he say about that? Dan thought, gripping the book too tightly in his hands. He tried to imagine Randi that day, doing what? Drugging? Recovering? Having sex to earn the money that would take them out to dinner and pay part of the rent? Closing his eyes for a moment, he listened to Daniel's soft breathing. Shit. What else could they do now but move on? "Do you want me to read more?"

Daniel shrugged but looked up expectantly, and Dan continued reading. Outside, the light shifted from light gray to black, houses lighting up, darkness settling on the neighborhood. As he turned the page, he swallowed, realizing that for the first time, this house held a family, parents and a child, like all the other houses.

That night around eleven, Dan startled awake, staring at the ceiling, his ears taking in the round, dark sounds of the house. There!

Kitchen counter. Keys. Avery. She was just getting home, putting her things down, filling a glass with water once, twice. She was thirsty. Did that mean she'd been drinking? She'd called at seven to say she had a dinner meeting with Brody, Lanny, and someone from that accounting firm in St. Louis, but before when she was working, she didn't drink at those meetings. "Alcohol doesn't help in business," she'd said. "It only gives everyone a headache."

Later, when they had first started trying for a baby, she'd stopped drinking altogether. During the weeks following each IUI, she wouldn't drink coffee, tea, hot chocolate—she refused to pump her own gas, sit in the hot tub, eat canned tuna (mercury levels) or Camembert or Brie cheese (*Listeria*) or fresh broccoli (toxoplasmosis). If any can in the pantry was dented, she tossed it into the trash (botulism). Once she sent a large bowl of sizzling rice soup back at the China Garden because she was sure the mushrooms were canned not fresh, and she hadn't been able to inspect the can personally.

She drank only bottled water, ate vegetables (except broccoli) that were high in folic acid (protects against neural tube defects), and took the yoga class at the club. She went to bed before ten, aiming for nine good hours of sleep. Instead of using Roundup on the weeds that crept up in the cracks in the patio, she pulled them with her fingers. She wouldn't even help Dan with the pool, fearing the chemicals. Dan laughed at her, calling her Bubble Girl and threatening to put plastic around the house, but she hadn't laughed back.

"Everything I do makes a difference. You should be on the same regimen," she'd said. Fearing a weeklong caffeine withdrawal headache, months without the sulfites in pepperoni and pastrami, and weekends without a Corona or two with Luís, Dan had shut up and let her go along, winnowing out anything that might hurt her chances for conception or the health of the possible pinpoint-sized child growing inside her, or both.

But in the weeks since she'd begun working, that old, careful Avery had been replaced by business Avery, who wore high heels despite the possible damage to her Achilles tendons, stayed up late, worked ten- or twelve-hour days, and drank cosmopolitans or martinis after work with colleagues. All her desire for a baby, for a family, had evaporated, and in a way, Dan felt she had become another kind of Bubble Girl. Her inner life was shrink-wrapped and hidden from him, her oxygen coming from a distant planet.

Avery opened the bedroom door quietly and slipped in. For a minute, Dan let her think he was still asleep, and he watched her dark figure move toward the closet and then the dresser. He heard two quiet ticks of her earrings on wood, the slow unzip of her skirt, the *shush-shush* of her nylons sliding down her legs. How long had it been since he'd really touched her? They'd had sex once since Midori's first phone call, and it was the type Avery used to love. In the middle of the night, Dan had found himself inside her, both of them moving, making noises, kissing each other as if nothing had changed. This used to happen all the time, a dream arousing him, making him reach out for Avery, who had probably been too tired for sex when they first went to bed. He'd probably felt the same way—early in their marriage, both of them had worked long hours, and after dinner, all they wanted were clean, smooth sheets and a dark room. But at one or two or three in the morning, both of them were ready, even if they didn't remember their lovemaking until sometime during work the next day.

"You sex machine," Avery would say, calling him from her desk. "You wild man."

Dan would flush, feel himself harden, remember her body under his. "Me? What about you?" And for a second, she was all long tan body, her arms around his neck, her breasts in his hands.

Dan didn't know if Avery remembered this last time. The next morning, she was shut down, quiet, apprehensive, knowing their life was changing and she could do nothing to stop it. They hadn't had sex since. At least not that he could remember.

"Avery," he said now, sitting up and leaning against the headboard. "Where have you been?"

"I told you. I had a meeting." She unbuttoned her blouse and let it fall to the floor.

"I know. But it's eleven."

He heard the tiny metal click of her bra coming off, and then she opened a drawer, pulling out a nightgown. "Look, it was business, okay? I had to go out with Brody. This is an important account. I told you that. I might have to go back to St. Louis in a few weeks. We're having some trouble with the system applications."

Dan rubbed his eyes, liking the pressure, the push of his fingers. Then he sighed and opened his eyes wide, trying to see as much as he could. Avery's eyes were reflecting what little light was in the room. She blinked, and the shiny reflection disappeared for an instant.

"But Daniel starts school pretty soon," he said. "We're going to have all those meetings with his teacher and the principal about that IEP Vince was telling us about. I hoped you'd be there. It's really important."

Avery shook her head, her hair whishing against her nightgown. "Dan, you're home. You're on paternity leave. I don't think we both need to be there. Think of all the school meetings that only mothers go to, especially in Monte Veda. I don't think they'll even miss me."

"I'll miss you. I do miss you," Dan said, his voice catching. He closed his eyes and bent his head.

Avery didn't say a word, but she sat down in the chair opposite the bed. A couple of times, he imagined she was trying to say something. He caught his breath, realizing he didn't want to know what it was. But she remained silent, and they sat in silence in the dark, the only noise the whoosh and splash of the pool cleaner outside.

When he and Avery were first going out, Isabel had taken him to her old room and shown him all of Avery's swimming awards, medals and trophies and certificates. There were years of team pictures on the walls, Avery always in the center, other kids leaning into her. Walt had built a display case for her in her room, and Isabel hadn't had the heart to take anything down. "She swam like a fish," Isabel had said. "She was the most beautiful thing in the water. But she quit after her dad died." Now, she didn't even go into their pool, working out in the gym instead.

Daniel didn't know how to swim, and Dan had hoped that Avery might teach him. He'd pictured the entire scene, the way Avery would hold his son in the water, showing him how to float on his back and then his stomach, teaching him how to blow bubbles and then turn his head to breathe. But since the phone call, no one had been in the pool, the cleaner sweeping all day and night for no reason at all.

Avery was silent, her arms still at her sides. She breathed like someone trying not to be found.

"He thinks you're mad. At him."

"Who?"

Dan hit the quilt with his hand. "Who? Daniel, for God's sake."

Avery was quiet again, and then she sighed. "He's not really my deal, Dan. You're home. I'm working. I'm not mad at him. . . . I'm just not here."

"You aren't here. Not even when you are actually here. Like now. You never talk to him unless it's like 'The glasses are in the cupboard over the sink.' You haven't even tried."

Avery stood up. "Do we have to do this right now? I have to get up in the morning."

"When should we do this, Avery? When should we start living again? Are you ever going to get over it? I know I screwed up and your whole life is changed, but you are being so selfish. Such a baby!" Dan realized he was yelling and stopped. He didn't want Daniel to hear another fight.

"Right," she said. "I'm being selfish. Who just went ahead and did what he wanted? Did I really ever have a say in anything? And I mean the little stuff. Did you ask me about his room? No, I come home and our best friends and my mother are here. Do you ask me about appointments with teachers? No, you just tell me."

Dan pushed away the covers and sat on the edge of the bed. "What do you think I'm going to do? Wait for you to snap out of it? Meanwhile, a kid has his entire life ripped open, and I'm supposed to wait for you? That's great, Avery. Real adult of you."

Avery stared at him, silent, her mouth pressed tight. Dan's chest fluttered, his stomach making small gurgling noises. He wanted to run over and grab her, pull her to him, hold her tight, make her change back. If he held her tight enough, he might find the bones of his wife somewhere in this strange woman standing in front of him.

"I don't know if I can do this," Avery said finally.

"What?" Dan felt the panic in his voice.

"You. Us. Him."

"What do you mean?" he asked, not needing to know any more. He wanted the whole conversation to stop, the night to rewind. He would go back to where he woke up and heard her tired coming-home sounds. He wouldn't say a thing. He'd let the days pass dry and silent as they had been.

"I don't know—I don't know if I can stay."

"Are you— What are you saying?"

"I don't know if I can trust you. . . . I don't know if I love you any-more. I don't know if I love you enough now to live like this. To live without everything I've always wanted."

Dan closed his eyes against her words, trying to understand the cracked, strangled sounds she'd made. If it was so hard to say, she must not mean it. If it made her cry, she could change her mind. He imagined that when he opened his eyes, she would be moving toward him, her arms wide. His heart pounded in his throat, head, stomach. When he did finally open his eyes, Avery had already gone into the bathroom and closed the door behind her, a slit of light fanning out into the silent bedroom.

Dan hung up the phone and looked into the family room, where Daniel sat on the carpet watching a cartoon about a sponge who wore pants. Before Dan had called Steve, he'd stood over Daniel, listening to the exaggerated voices. When Jared and he were little, they watched *Popeye, Looney Tunes, Scooby Doo, Captain America*, and *The Flintstones*. All those shows now seemed more entertaining than this sponge, but then he realized that talking rabbits and dogs and lit-erate cave people and a sailor morphed by spinach were probably just as strange.

Daniel laughed at something the sponge said, and Dan leaned his elbows on the counter. Steve had been curt, obviously busy, telling him, "Look, it's a madhouse here. I'm putting out about ten fires at once. Call me later."

At the click of the phone going dead, Dan wanted to call back and tell Steve he'd be there tomorrow. Ready to go. Prepared to fix everything. Able to somehow forget all the events since Midori's phone call.

But how should Dan feel since July Fourth? From that moment, his life had felt as crazy as the cartoon sponge's, all bright colors and loud voices.

The doorbell rang, and Daniel turned back to him, his face white and tight. He stood up and pulled at a lock of hair. "Who is it?" he asked.

Dan walked around the counter and into the family room. "Don't worry. It's Luís. We're going to walk down to the park with him and Tomás. Go ahead and watch your show while I get the door."

But as Dan walked down the hall, he realized that Daniel was following right behind him, matching his strides, staying as close to Dan as a high-noon shadow.

"Hey, man," Luís said. Tomás was strapped to his father in the BabyBjörn, a big smile on his face.

"Come on in. I'm going to get this guy a hat and some sunscreen." One afternoon while they were all hanging out in the front yards, Valerie had given Dan a lecture about childhood sunburn. "And Daniel is so fair. One good burn, and who knows what could happen when he's an adult. You know, melanoma." Dan had sighed and looked at his son. It was too late to chart a perfect life for him. Too much had already happened. Sunscreen was the least of their worries.

Luís nodded. "Don't even begin to think that this guy doesn't have sunscreen rubbed on every exposed millimeter."

They walked down the hall, and Luís put his hand on Daniel's head. "So, *mi'jo*, how do you like it here so far?"

Daniel nodded without saying anything. Dan looked up at Luís and shrugged. "Come on, Daniel. Let's get you ready."

In the bathroom, Dan kneeled before his son, rubbing Banana Boat 45 SPF lotion into Daniel's white, freckled skin. Daniel stared at him and then swallowed hard. "What—what do you mean, get ready?"

Dan squirted another creamy dollop into his hand and worked it into his son's forehead. "For the park."

"Oh."

Clicking the lid closed, he looked at Daniel. "What did you think I meant?"

"I don't know."

"Yes, you do. What did you think I meant? I told you we were going to the park with Luís, didn't I?"

Dan stood up and put the lotion away in the cabinet. He looked into the mirror and saw his son, small, downcast, his face white. A little ghost.

"Daniel?"

"What?"

"Did you think I was going to take you somewhere else?"

Daniel shrugged.

"Daniel?"

"I don't know, okay?"

"Did your mother ever take you places that scared you?"

Daniel looked up at him, eyes wide.

"Were you scared?"

Blinking, Daniel opened his mouth and then closed it, saying nothing.

"Okay. Okay." He reached out to touch his son's hair, and then remembering the sunscreen, smiled and turned to the sink. Washing his hands slowly, looking at his fingers, Dan breathed out. Bret and Daniel's therapist, Jane Bissell, had told him that Daniel would worry about being moved again, about being abandoned, stranded, lost. So Dan tried to explain their every move in advance. But it didn't seem to help. In the grocery store, Daniel wouldn't let him out of his sight, holding on to the cart like a toddler. If he'd been smaller or had less pride, his son might have asked to sit in the little seat, where he'd be able to watch Dan's eyes, touch his hands, keep him in clear view. And even though Dan knew why Daniel was acting like this, he began to get irritated. *Settle in,* he thought. *Believe it. Believe me.* He tried not to let his feelings show.

Turning back from the mirror, he relaxed. Daniel wouldn't look at him, his soft brown hair shining in the bright bathroom light. Dan knelt down again, almost gasping when Daniel looked up at him with Randi's face.

"He's just a friggin' kid," Randi would say. "For crying out loud. Don't be like your asshole dad."

"Don't worry, Daniel." Dan put a hand on either small shoulder. She was right. Bill would have said, "Buck up, soldier" or "Get it together, dim bulb," impatient with emotions he couldn't control. Had Bill ever knelt in front of Dan like this, his hands saying what his voice could not? *Everything will be fine.*

"It's going to be a good day, I promise." Dan squeezed Daniel a bit, feeling his son's heartbeat through his shoulders, his tears in the tenseness of his skin. "We can play with the Frisbees I bought. It'll be fun."

Daniel stared at him and then finally nodded slightly, his eyes full.

At Monte Veda Park, Daniel sat on a swing, not wanting to be pushed. Dan thought he was probably afraid of heights and also afraid of having to admit that. Nearby, a group of other ten- and eleven-year-olds threw a Nerf football around, rolling on top of each other whenever the ball fell to the grass, laughing and playfully hitting each other in the shoulders, arms, stomach. A group of mothers with infants and toddlers sat on the half-moon rock wall, chatting as their children dug in the sand. One woman looked over at Dan a few times, and Luís poked him with his elbow. The men sat in front of the baby swings, Tomás just able to sit in one while propped a little with a blanket. His wide brown eyes tracked clouds and birds and trees.

"Hey, man. You've got a friend. Check that blonde out. She's giving you the high sign. She wants you."

Dan looked, and the blonde turned away and cooed at her baby, who was sitting on the sand and beating it with a large plastic shovel. "Yeah, well, maybe I'll be back on the market soon," he said, trying to joke. The words were ashy on his tongue, and he wanted to weep. Daniel looked at him, and Dan hoped the boy hadn't heard what he'd just said.

"What are you saying, man? What's going on? I thought she was okay with the whole plan. I mean, shit, it's clear she's not thrilled, but she seemed fine." Luís gave Tomás a little push, and Tomás smiled, a swirl of iridescent drool at the corner of his mouth.

"She said she might leave," Dan whispered. Daniel blinked twice and stared at him, reading his lips. "Try the new climbing structure," Dan yelled out. "Look at that bridge on the lower level. It's made for big kids."

Daniel turned to look and got off the swing, walking slowly to the plastic-and-wood structure. He put a small hand on it, as if to test its safety by touch.

"What did she say?" Luís said loudly. Daniel turned around, and then Luís said more quietly, "When did she tell you?"

"A couple of days ago. She came home late from some meeting

with her boss and some Dirland Accounting big shot, and we got into it. She's working late, completely submerged in work, not paying attention to what's going on. I could tell she was still angry about the whole thing. And then she said she didn't know if she could live like this. With Daniel. With me."

Luís shook his head. "Shit, man. I didn't know she could be like that."

"I can't imagine what I would have done if she came home with my news," Dan said. "I don't know how I would have reacted."

"Oh, I know it's not easy," Luís said quickly. "It's just that the Avery I knew . . . *know* could have taken it on. I'm surprised, that's all, man."

Sighing, Dan watched Daniel take tentative steps onto the structure. He was walking as if he were on the moon, the first person to set foot on such a landscape. What had Randi done with him? From Daniel's stories, it seemed that sometimes she was there, playing games with him, driving him to school, decorating cookies, and then at other times, she was keeping him in his room for a day or selling peaches on the side of the road or feeding him only junk food. What had she been thinking? Or had she thought at all? Why didn't Daniel know how to throw a football or interact with kids his age? Had she sat in her apartment his entire life and hoped that he would turn out normal? Had she shipped him off to school, hoping, as Luís always claimed of all parents, that the teachers would pick up the slack? But how could he complain? Where had he been, the man, the father, who should have taught his son to throw and swing and run? It was just as much his fault as Randi's.

"What are you going to do?" Luís asked. "You know Val and I will help out in any way, man. Val is really into Daniel. She thinks he's a cool little dude."

For the first time, Dan imagined the house without Avery, his whole life about his son and his work. He felt his wife's absence like a tear in fabric, but though he had loved his life since meeting Avery, he knew he couldn't go back. He had to stay right here. Not because he didn't love Avery still, even though she was acting selfish and spoiled. But because of the little boy walking slowly on a wooden bridge, holding on tight, as if at any minute someone would tip him off and leave him hanging.

After Tomás had fallen asleep in the swing and Luís had gently taken him out, put him in the stroller, and left, Dan and Daniel went to the middle of the field with the Frisbees. The sun was arcing toward the Berkeley hills and all the bigger kids had left the park, leaving nothing but tufts of upturned sod.

Daniel stood across from Dan, ten feet away, his arms stiff and straight at his sides, his face turned toward the play structure. The young mothers—including the smiling blonde—were packing up their babies and diaper bags and picnic lunches, rolling their strollers up the path to the parking lot.

"I want to play on the structure," Daniel said.

"Let's just throw this a couple of times and then we can go back for a while."

"The bridge is cool. I want to play on it."

"Come on. Let's just try it," Dan said.

Daniel was silent, but he crossed his arms.

"Here, let me show you how to do this." Dan walked over to Daniel's side. "It's easy."

Daniel shrugged and shook his head but looked up.

"Okay, you hold it like this. Take this Frisbee, and we'll throw together." He handed Daniel the neon green Frisbee. "First, hold it like this. Your thumb grips it like this, and you put your index finger on the edge and the rest underneath."

Dan held the Frisbee up as an example and watched as his son tried to put his fingers in the correct position, the plastic sliding around in his hand. Probably slick from all the sunscreen, Dan thought.

He dropped his Frisbee and arranged Daniel's thin white fingers on the disk. "There. That's right. Okay, stand sideways. Now, hold your arm and elbow parallel, level to the ground. Like this." Dan held up his arm, and Daniel did, too. "Okay. All at once, you're going to lean your weight on your back foot, take one step, and transfer the weight to the front. Extend your arm and release. It's really important to follow through. You point with your index finger where you want to throw it. Watch. I'll throw it at that birch tree."

Daniel watched as Dan let the Frisbee fly free, the disk sailing to the trunk of the tree. I haven't lost it, Dan thought. Most fall and spring weekends at Cal, he and his frat brothers would play Frisbee golf up at Tilden Park, aiming at trees, fences, and sign posts, running around without their shirts on, yelling, annoying picnickers and hikers. "See? Nothing to it. You ready?"

Daniel nodded.

"Okay. So, stand right." Dan adjusted his shoulders and tipped up his arm. "One, two, three."

Daniel stepped back and then leaned forward with all his weight, but he forgot to let go of the Frisbee, instead sending it spiraling to the grass by his feet. He slapped his hands on his thighs and kicked at the grass.

"That's okay. It's okay. I really should have said it looks easier than it is. I've been throwing a Frisbee for a long time. Let's try it again."

"I don't want to. It's stupid. No one plays with those things anymore. I'm going to play on the structure."

"It's not stupid. It's good to learn how to throw. And I want to play with you, okay? Come on, let's try it again."

"Whatever." Daniel picked up the disk and looked up at Dan. "But I can't do it."

"Give it a shot. Okay, stand right, that's it. Good. Now, one, two, three."

Again, Daniel set up, leaning back then forward, releasing, but this time he forgot to point with his index finger. The Frisbee flew up above them and then fell back behind them.

As the Frisbee thumped to the earth, Daniel turned to him, his face red, tears already on his face. "I hate this. I'm not going to throw it anymore. It's stupid and you're stupid and I hate this and everything. I want to go home. I want my mom. I hate everything," Daniel said, falling to the grass, swatting away Dan as he leaned down toward his son. "Go away. You don't want me. I can't do anything."

"Daniel," Dan said, looking around, wondering if Social Services had spies waiting for moments like this, when it was clear Dan didn't know how to be a parent. They'd have seen that he'd forced his boy to do something he didn't want to do. They'd see that Dan was just like Bill. "Stop. It's okay. Be quiet. I'm sorry. I shouldn't have made you do that. We don't have to do it anymore."

"But it's too late," Daniel sobbed.

"Too late for what?"

"No-thing. Leave me alone." Daniel wiped his face on his shirt and sat up. "I want to go home."

"Oh, Daniel, you can't go home. You know that."

"What do you mean? You won't let me live with you anymore?" He began to cry in earnest now, his sobs deep in his chest, snot pouring out of his nose.

"No. No, oh no. I meant—I thought you were talking about your mom."

"You are a friggin' idiot," Randi said, her arms crossed as she stood over them. "Jesus Christ on a stick. What are you doing to him?"

"You can't go home to where you and your mom lived, but of course you can go home. We can go home. Together. You're always going to be there. That's where you live. That's where you'll live until you grow up and go to college or get married or whatever." Dan reached out with a hand, and Daniel didn't hit him away. He stroked Daniel's back, feeling each rib under his hand. "I'm sorry. I'm so sorry."

They sat together as the sun hit a row of Monterey pines and then fell behind them, the park full of tree shadows and sudden insects rising from the grass like mist. Daniel sniffed and wiped his nose on the handkerchief Dan handed him. Dan still held on to his Frisbee and then looked up toward the trees. "Watch me lose this Frisbee," he said, standing up.

Daniel stood up, his eyes wide. "What do you mean?"

"Just watch." Following his own instructions, Dan released the Frisbee, and it sailed up, up to the pines, glimmering bright pink against the sunlight breaking through the branches, and then falling into the boughs and disappearing from sight.

Nine

At lunch, Avery sat next to Mischa Podorov in the booth at Andrés, Brody and Lanny across from them. Though they were seriously talking about the possibility of implementing networking systems at Dirland Accounting nationwide, expanding to all two hundred offices, all Avery could feel was Mischa's knee pressing against hers. He leaned into her as if he weren't doing a thing, his flesh constant, warm, textured against hers, the fabric of his pants gently rubbing against her St. John's silk. Avery imagined his knee, his leg, the rounded muscles above the joint, his lean shin, strong calf. She'd seen him running one morning as she took a cab to the St. Louis office, and now those lean, muscled legs were right next to her, along with his runner's torso, his smooth, well-defined arms. From the firmness of his knee, she could bring forth the rest of him against her, the same tight lines, the places of softness, of hardness.

"So what do you think?" Brody asked, leaning back in the booth and wiping his mouth.

"Oh," Avery said, startled. She tried to swallow the desire in her throat, pressing it back inside her, where it needed to stay. "It's completely doable, but we need to get the specs off to the Dirland home office ASAP. Probably before."

Brody and Lanny nodded. She'd said the right thing. Mischa pressed against her. She blinked and took a sip of water.

"Then it is all settled for now," Mischa said. "I will present this information to my superiors, yes? And I will be in contact with you soon. Perhaps Monday. Who knows? These things move fast once the ball is in the rolling."

Brody brought a napkin up to his mouth, and Lanny coughed.

"Fabulous," Avery said.

Brody looked around for the server and the check. Lanny pushed out of the booth and stood up, holding out a hand to Mischa. "It'll be great taking this the whole way with you."

"I feel the same." Mischa smiled.

Brody took the check from the server and stood up. "You two have dessert. Go over the integration plan. I'll go up to the office and start making the calls."

Brody had never seemed like the type to save her, but as he walked away, Avery wished he'd come back and interrupt dessert. He could keep the knees the only body parts that touched. He could stare at her with knowing husband eyes, reminding her of Dan. She sipped her water and breathed in deeply.

"This will be great," she said, turning slightly to look at Mischa.

"I think so. We worked so well together in St. Louis, *ptichka*."

"What does that mean? You've said it before."

"It is bird, but not regular bird. A beautiful bird. Small beautiful bird."

She thought of her name on his tongue, the birds in A-vary, the way she could fly in his mouth. "I like it. It sounds nice. Better than *bird*."

"Of course. What did I tell you about English? Like German. Nothing feminine. No word good enough for you."

Avery smiled. Her mother called her sweetie. Dan called her Aves; so did Loren and even Valerie. Her mouth closed, Avery rolled the *p-tich-ka* against her lips and palate. A word no one else but Mischa could say.

"Well," she said, looking at her napkin in her lap, "I think Lanny and his support staff will be in on a few offices. I know I can't go to all of them." But two hundred other cities appealed to her. Two hundred cities without Daniel, who stared at her from the moment she walked in the house until the moment she left. Just this morning, she'd tried to hand him a glass of juice. There she was, her arm out-stretched toward him, and he'd stared at her, blinking, unmoving. What did he want?

In Tulsa and Atlanta and Phoenix she wouldn't have to duck his dark gaze, turn the corners fast to get out of his view.

"If you don't go, I don't," Mischa said. "I will have that written into the contract. I assure you." He moved closer. He smelled like clean skin and soap and something spicy. One dark blond curl hung over his temple, and she held her hands together in her lap to avoid tucking it behind his ear.

Avery laughed. "Right. I'm sure your bosses will understand that."

"If they saw you, they would."

When she was thirteen and dreaming of the perfect man, Mischa would have fit exactly into her fantasies. He was the kind of man she read about in the romance novels she checked out from the library and hid under her bed so Loren wouldn't find them and start teasing her. In every story, the hero was the same: charming, sexy, attentive, slightly foreign. Not familiar. Not Dan, who seemed to grow heavier and hairier each day, walking around unshaved with an apron on. Not her father. Someone else entirely. But even when she'd grown into her body and attracted male attention, no romance male showed up to sweep her away. No one with the right amounts of charisma and vulnerability, with a perfect body and a keening need for hers. Not even dark, handsome Dan at the counter at Peet's came remotely close. She shook her head. What was she doing? Such perfection didn't happen in real life. But wasn't that what was happening now?

"We'll see about that." She picked up the dessert menu, but her stomach crackled with nerves. "I don't think I'm going to get any-thing."

"I do not think I will either, *ribka*." He smiled and lifted his water glass to her. "Not yet."

Later as she sat in her office, Avery had a hard time breathing. The air refused to go deep in her lungs, and it caught on her ribs. Closing her eyes, she tried inhaling through her nose, slowly, slowly, like her yoga teacher had recommended during particular stretches. Finally, she felt her blood slow, her lungs open to take in air, her thoughts of Mischa fading to gray, nothing in her mind but office sounds—phones, footsteps, muffled conversations. She heard the whir of air from the vent, the electronic beeps of the Xerox and fax machines, and then all the machine sounds faded into the place she read about in the pregnancy books, the calm in mind and body, the calm you could give your child in the womb. Avery breathed in, listened to the sounds in her body, nothing but her blood and heart and organs. No Dan, Daniel, or Mischa, with his hundred enchanting words. No Dirland Accounting. Nothing but gray. Gray. White.

"Jesus!" she yelled as the phone rang, her eyes wide. Her body cranked up with nerves, her fingers tingling, the quiet place a disappearing pinprick in her mind. Her arm shot out for the phone.

"What! Hello!" She put her hand on her chest, willing her heart to beat normally.

"Avery," said Isabel. "Why do you sound so—so surprised?"

Avery rolled her eyes. "I was having—in an important talk, Mom. What's going on?"

"I tried to call Dan, but he's somewhere on the road. I left a message on his cell phone, but you know how his service is. I don't know why he doesn't change to FC and T. I told him about that—"

"Mom!"

"Oh, my. Well, I'm watching Sammy and Dakota for Loren today. Your sister had to go on a field trip with Jaden's class. Anyway, Daniel's school called."

Sitting back in her chair, Avery looked out through the glass at her assistant's desk. If only she hadn't told Joel he could leave early to pick up his sister at the airport. If he'd been here, she could have told him to tell Isabel she was busy. She wouldn't have to listen to whatever was wrong with Daniel. That's what every conversation about Daniel started with. When Dan came home from the IEP meeting at the school Avery hadn't attended, there were pages and pages of recommendations and diagnoses. The psychologist had lists of ideas for Dan and Avery to follow up on: talk about Randi, visit the cemetery, show him pictures of Dan and Randi together, hug him, hold him, read to him, laugh with him. The doctor wanted him to eat more red meat and drink at least two full glasses of milk each day. Even Flora

Alvarez, the baby-sitter Dan had hired to watch him after school, left a good pageful of notes about what Daniel did or didn't do: *Daniel not finish his history homework. Daniel not clean his room after school. Daniel want to eat candy instead of fruit.*

"What now," she said, sighing. "What did he do?"

"He had a scuffle in class, and then later he tried to run away. Or not run away. Hide. He tried to hide so he didn't have to go back to school after lunch."

Avery almost snorted and then held her breath, amazed that she could make such a sound. "Jesus. But why did they call you?"

Isabel was silent for a moment, and Avery understood. She was third on the emergency call list. Maybe not even third. Probably Loren and then Val and Luís were next, but Luís was back at school and Val was visiting her mother in New Orleans.

"You've got to go down to the school right away. He's in the principal's office."

"What about Flora? Did you try to get ahold of her? She could pick him up at the school early."

"The principal wants to talk with a parent. The baby-sitter can't do that sort of thing."

"Shit." Avery couldn't just leave the office now. Brody and Lanny would want to go over the Dirland Account specs and the travel arrangements, Mischa would want a verbal walk-through of the plans, and she had to e-mail her other clients about product updates. But if her mom couldn't go and no one could find Dan, she had to go. She had no choice.

"Avery."

"Fine. I'll leave right now."

"And Avery?"

"What, Mom?" she asked, pushing away from her desk and picking up her suit jacket.

"Be nice. Please be nice."

She wanted to swear and slam down the phone, but that would only prove her mother's point. She wasn't nice. It was true. She wasn't. But she couldn't admit it to Isabel, so she closed her eyes, searching for that quiet place she'd found earlier. "Okay," she said finally. "I'll be nice."

*   *   *

Although she'd driven past the school once or twice every day since she and Dan had moved to Monte Veda, Avery had never been inside. From the street, it looked like most schools in the area, portions of the original buildings surrounded by newer, stuccoed construction, paid for by bond measures and parent activism. She'd heard the women in Dr. Browne's office oohing and aahing about the teachers, the staff, the secretary who knew all the kids by name. Avery had given contributions to the youth choir and the drama club and the "plant the school" campaign when parents and their children rang her doorbell, pamphlets and bumper stickers in hand.

Back when she was trying for the baby, Avery had thought that in five years, she'd be walking down Dias Dorados Avenue with her child, holding in tears on the first day of school. Her child would have a backpack, a new outfit, and stiff, just-out-of-the-box shoes. She would be holding the hand of her youngest child, as well, telling her how next year, it would be her turn. "You'll be the big girl then. So wave to your brother! Say good-bye! Blow a kiss."

Avery pulled the Land Rover into a parking space next to a row of Rovers, Suburbans, and Volvos and jerked up on the parking brake. Instead, this was how she would enter the school she'd fantasized about. Brought by Daniel. Daniel in trouble.

She got out of the car and walked to the sidewalk, holding her hand over her eyes to cut the glare and looking for the office. The September sun was beating afternoon heat into the pavement. Avery tugged at her blouse, feeling sweat trickle down her sternum.

"Avery, right?"

She turned and blinked against the brightness. "Yes?"

"It's Marcia. Val's friend? We're in the baby group together. We met at her house."

Nodding, Avery ran her tongue over her molars, trying to avoid biting the soft bleeding skin inside her cheek. The baby group. Every Wednesday, Val went to a meeting, sat on someone's living room floor, talked about every change in Tomás's eating and nursing schedules, sleeping patterns, and bowel movements. At first, Avery had tried to listen to Val's recap, but after a while, she'd gone home feeling light-headed and sick. Finally, she'd avoided Val's Wednesday afternoon calls, turning down the sound on the answering machine so she could erase it without ever hearing a thing.

"Yes. Hi. How are you," Avery said, and then before Marcia could answer, "I'm looking for the principal's office. Do you know where it is?"

"Right down the hall. To your right. See?" Marcia pointed to a door with a big OFFICE sign above it.

"Gee," Avery said. "Who would have known? Well, thanks."

She smiled and turned to go, ignoring Marcia's perplexed look and obvious question: What are *you* doing here?

Closing the door behind her, Avery walked up to a waist-high counter. Behind it, a woman sat at a desk, talking on the phone, and behind her was an office door with the name MS. ANITA BRISBO stenciled in gold ink. Below the shiny name was the word PRINCIPAL in black. The glass door was frosted but even so, Avery could see Daniel's smooth, brown head, the chair he sat in, his feet dangling over the floor. A quiet conversation seeped out from under the door. At least he wasn't hysterical, Avery thought. She could manage until Flora or Dan got home.

The woman put down the phone and smiled. "You must be Mrs. Tacconi. I'm so glad you could come in. Principal Brisbo is waiting for you."

Avery nodded. The secretary who knew everything. Did she know Avery wanted to turn and leave without seeing Principal Brisbo? Did she know Avery couldn't care less about Daniel and his woes? Did she know that Avery wasn't really a nice person?

"Come this way," the secretary said, lifting up part of the counter. "This is the drawbridge. Fear ye all who enter here!"

When Avery didn't smile, the secretary patted her arm. "It's a joke. You look as nervous as the kids. Listen, this isn't a big deal. He's not in too much trouble."

Avery walked through and waited by Principal Brisbo's door as the secretary knocked and peeked her head in. "It's Daniel's stepmom."

Stepmom? Avery almost turned to stare at the woman, taking in that word for the first time. How could she be that word or any word with *mom* in it in relation to Daniel? She felt so far away from him, it would take a plane, two ferries, and a bridge to reach her.

A large woman with spiky blond hair sat behind the desk and waved Avery in. "Thank you, Mrs. Panawek. Come in, Mrs. Tacconi."

Smiling quickly at Mrs. Panawek, Avery moved into the office and looked at the top of Daniel's head. He looked down at his shoes, avoiding her gaze. Avery winced as she bit down on her cheek, opening her mouth and sucking in a breath of air. She clutched her purse against her body.

"Have a seat, Mrs. Tacconi." Principal Brisbo motioned to a chair opposite her desk. Avery nodded and sat, crossing her legs and then uncrossing them and tucking them under the chair. She hadn't been in the principal's office since—well, since never. Loren was rustled into the office a couple of times because of fights with friends and then because in fifth grade she cheated on a spelling test by writing the words on her shoe. But Mara and Avery were good girls who stayed out of trouble. "Little princesses," her father would say at the dinner table as Loren glowered in her chair.

"What happened?" Avery asked, turning again to Daniel, who was now swinging his legs back and forth, the chair legs making a soft *rub-rub* noise on the linoleum tiles.

"I think it was a valiant attempt to avoid an in-class writing exercise, starting with a shirt-grabbing fight. His teacher didn't send him down here initially, so after recess Daniel here decided to hide for the rest of the afternoon in the sandbox. The yard duty supervisor found him just as she was leaving campus."

"Who did you fight?"

Daniel wouldn't look at her, and Avery closed her eyes and tried not to bite down on her cheek. *God, what a brat.*

She turned to Principal Brisbo. "Is the other kid okay?"

"Oh, fine. It wasn't a big fight."

"Jake Hsu is a jerk!" Daniel blurted out.

"Daniel!" Avery said loudly. "Stop it."

Principal Brisbo gave Daniel a quieting glance, but Avery could tell she wasn't taking any of this as seriously as she should. He was out of control. He was impossible. Somebody needed to do something now.

"I think," Principal Brisbo said, "that our main concern is to find out why Daniel hid in the sandbox."

"Why *did* you hide in the sandbox?" Avery asked. She looked at Daniel and waited. He swung his legs faster, faster. If he were her kid, she'd tell him to knock it off, to pay attention, to apologize. She'd ask him why he was hiding. She'd ask him what his problem was with writing. She'd hire a tutor. She'd call her mom.

"It was actually pretty smart, I told Daniel." Principal Brisbo folded her arms on her desk, her hands large and round, rings on each finger, even her thumbs. "But we need to find out what's bothering him in class besides this other boy. I know the transition to a new school can be difficult, and fifth grade is a hard year. What do you think, Daniel?"

"I don't know."

Avery rolled her eyes. "Daniel! Answer Mrs.— Is it Ms. . . ."

"Call me Anita. In this room only, I let everyone call me Anita. A big perk when it comes to being sent here." Anita smiled.

"Okay. Daniel, tell Anita what's wrong with the class."

Daniel looked up at Anita and then quickly at Avery. "I just want to go back home, that's all."

"So it isn't the class?" Anita asked. She sat back in her chair and pulled on one of her many hoop earrings.

"No." Daniel swung his legs.

"Well," Avery said, "this is school time. You have to be in school when it's in session. That's all there is to it." She stood up and adjusted her skirt. "Listen, Anita. I'll have my husband come and talk with you. He can deal with this. Daniel should go back to class."

"Oh, not today," Anita said. "He should go home. That's what this is all about."

Avery stared at her, her hand on her hip. Glancing up at the clock, she saw that there were at least fifty more minutes to the school day. Why should he go home now, when in less than an hour Flora would be here to pick him up? That way, Avery could go back to work and see what Brody and Lanny had cooked up. She could find out when she was going back to St. Louis. She could call Mischa on his cell phone. "But . . ."

"He's had a hard day. Go on, Daniel. Take your backpack. I'll see you tomorrow."

Daniel got up, grabbed his backpack, and slipped past Avery into the outer office, where Mrs. Panawek began telling him a story about a boy who played so long in the sandbox he turned into a sandworm. Avery sighed.

"Mrs. Tacconi?"

"Avery."

"This hasn't been a quick adjustment, has it, Avery? The transition into being a family."

"No. No, it hasn't."

"Are you seeing anyone to—to help smooth things out?" Anita stood up, revealing a pair of loose, rainbow-colored pants.

"Who aren't we seeing? We have two social workers and two psychologists, not to mention the calls from"—she waved her hand around the office—"the school. The court. The doctor. If I have to see anyone else, I'll lose my mind."

"It must be rough. But there's a little boy at stake. He's a good kid. He needs some help, sure, but in time . . ."

Avery put her hand on the doorknob, the brass cool on her palm. She glanced at Anita's desk and noticed that there weren't any photos of children or a husband. Just some older people—parents?—standing next to a house and one of a woman in a sailboat. So she didn't have any kids of her own, Avery thought, and here she was trying to give her advice. Like a man trying to tell a woman about abortion. How could Anita begin to know what the past few weeks had been like? How could she know what it felt like to see Daniel's loss every single morning? How could she know what it was like to need to ignore it?

"Really," Anita said. "There's the cliché, but it's true. Time—"

"I don't know how much time there will be. At least for me."

Anita opened her mouth and then said nothing.

"Okay. Well, good-bye." Avery pulled the door open and glanced back. The principal lifted her hands from the desk and raised her eyebrows in an expression that reminded Avery of one Brody would give her while on the phone with a caller who wasn't interested in their product. A look for lost causes.

Closing the door behind her, Avery walked into the outer office and watched Daniel laugh at Mrs. Panawek's story. He seemed like a different child. Kind of normal. One who didn't stare with big, bug eyes, tracking Avery's movements. A kid who might play with Sammy, Jaden, and Dakota at the next Fourth of July barbecue in the cul-de-sac, running with a ball or rolling on the lawn. Then he seemed to sense her, his body freezing, his face falling into its typical sullen stare. As they left the office and walked together down the long, empty hallway, all Avery wanted to know was how she could get as far away as possible.

Daniel sat in the backseat. She'd expected him to jump in beside her, but he'd opened the back, right-hand door and buckled himself in before she had even started the car.

"Do you want to sit up here?"

"No. I'm not supposed to."

Avery looked at him in the rearview mirror. "What do you mean?"

"The air bag. I'm supposed to be twelve before I can sit there. I'm only ten." His eyes were wide and serious, his hands raised up just like Anita's had been earlier. Avery shook her head and turned on the engine. She should have known that. Anticipating her own baby, she'd looked up the information on car and booster seats, read the latest recall information on air bags, and studied the new safety designs for cars. But with all that, she wouldn't have known how to protect Daniel. If they'd been in an accident—and she'd read somewhere that most car accidents occurred within five miles of home—he would have been crushed by the too-hard pulse of the expanding air bag. How would she have explained that to Dan and her mother and Valerie? No one would forgive her for that.

"Okay. Sorry."

"Can you turn on the radio to KLLC? I like that channel."

Avery rolled her eyes and pushed on his station. He sat back against the seat and stared out the window. Releasing the parking brake, she looked in the rearview and sideview mirrors a few times and then backed out slowly, looking for small children and pregnant mothers and yard duty supervisors. Even principals. Avery was dangerous, a lost cause.

At home, she poured Daniel a glass of milk and gave him two giant chocolate chip cookies before she picked up the phone.

"I'm supposed to have fruit. I'm not supposed to have sweets. The doctor and Flora said."

Avery held the phone to her chest. Daniel stared at the cookies with the same longing with which she'd looked at Mischa's knee. "Don't you like cookies?"

"Yeah, but—"

"Look, I won't tell. Flora won't be here for a half hour or so. Eat them up and do your homework. Whatever you have. You know."

Daniel bit his lip, touching the cookie gently with the tips of his fingers, and then picked it up and began eating, taking even bites, turning the cookie like a wheel in his mouth. After one spin of the wheel, he drank exactly a fourth of his milk. He didn't look up at Avery.

She shook her head and walked into the living room with the phone. She dialed Dan's cell number and held the phone away from her ear because of the scratchy static when he answered.

"Dan! Dan!"

"Avery! I can't hear you very well. I'm in Sac—"

"Where?"

"Sacramento. I went on a call. There's been some kind of jam on I-80. I think I'm going to go to my folks' for a while."

"What?"

"My *folks.*"

"I know. I heard you. I'm here with Daniel. But—"

"You're with Daniel? Okay."

"Yes. He's home. But I need to get back to the—"

The phone went dead, and she dialed again, gritting her teeth. He wouldn't be home for hours. His number rang six times, and then the automated answer came on, "I'm sorry, the PRQ customer you have called isn't available." Avery clicked off. There was no use talking with him anyway. She wouldn't even bother trying to call Bill or Marian. What was the point? All the alternative routes would be clogged with desperate drivers trying to get back to the Bay Area, and the only smart thing would be to wait it out.

It meant that Avery would be forced to come back home early and make dinner and get Daniel in his shower and read him a story, just as Dan did every night. Her stomach growled. Lunch had been so long ago.

She had started back toward the kitchen when she saw Flora walking down the sidewalk toward the house. Flora could stay late, while she went back to work. Avery could ask Flora to stay until Dan came home, and then everything would be fine.

When Flora walked up the front path, Avery pulled open the door. "Hi, Flora. I'm so glad you're here."

Flora broke into a wide smile and then almost seemed as if she would cry. "Mrs. Tacconi, you are here. Oh, *Dios mio,* I am so glad. I say to myself, God, help me today. I cannot work. Is no emergency, but I want to go home because of my daughter. Her baby coming today. Now, she in labor. My first grandchild. I have to go home, but I think of Daniel, and I don't know what to do. Your mother, she call me earlier, but I don't understand it all. Something about school, yes? I was talking to my son-in-law. *Pero,* now, I go home. The bus, it comes in ten minutes. I see you tomorrow. No problem, then. My youngest daughter, she will be here to help with the baby. I call Mr. Tacconi at his work. Yes?"

"But Flora!" Flora turned back to Avery, but at the sight of Flora's brown eyes full of tears and relief, Avery sighed. "Okay. That's— that's great. See you tomorrow."

Flora gave a little wave and walked quickly back up the street, her red-and-green-colored bag swinging. Avery would trade places with Flora right now. She'd take the bus to where?—Oakland, San Pablo, El Sobrante—and go to the hospital with Flora's daughter, hold her hand, whisper the same encouragement she had to Val. She would try not to care about yet another baby that wasn't hers slipping into the world. Anything would be better than being in the house with Daniel and his relentless stare.

Avery closed the door and walked into kitchen. The cookie plate was empty, and Daniel had turned on the television, a music video screaming across the screen.

"It's time for homework," Avery said. She put the plate in the dishwasher. "Daniel? Daniel! Turn off the television."

Daniel ignored her and turned up the volume.

"Daniel!" His small back hunched, but he still stared at the screen. She would never have disobeyed either Isabel or her father, turning off the television as soon as either of them said one word. If her father yelled, she and her sisters froze, waiting for the words that would come next, a promise of withheld privileges or threat of grounding. Isabel would give them the *stern* look, her eyes narrowed and dark, and they would all know they had gone too far. But this kid? Avery shook her head and walked over to the television.

"That's it," she said, flicking it off. "Homework."

"I didn't bring it home."

"What?"

"I didn't go back to the classroom, remember? I don't have it."

That damn Anita, Avery thought. She forgot or maybe she didn't. The principal probably believed Daniel needed a break from the usual three hours of homework a night that his teacher gave him. Every night, Dan said, "I don't remember having this much home-work until I was in college." He even went over to talk about it with Luís, who told him that parents wanted high test scores and college prep starting in elementary school, and homework was the evidence that some good results were in the offing. Later, Jared had said the same thing.

Tapping her foot, Avery looked out the window at the pool. The cover floated on top of the water like a giant blue lily pad. She was scared of the cover, its wet sopping stickiness, the idea of being trapped underneath it. Water—aside from the relief from summer heat—almost made her itch, the splash of chlorine-clean water re-minding her of relentless laps, one after the other. Sometimes at meets or at workouts, she'd lift her head, and there her father would be, sitting on the bleachers, smoking his pipe. He hadn't wanted to miss a stroke, bundling up in the winter months, wearing his sun hat and shorts in the summer.

Avery didn't want to deal with the pool cover now or Daniel's flail-ing arms as he struggled to learn freestyle. So what were they going to do for the three hours until dinner? And then what would they do after that? She turned the television back on, sat in the leather chair, and closed her eyes. This was why she'd gone back to work. To avoid hours like these—long, terrible hours of nothing with a kid she didn't know.

Letting the sounds of a TV song seep in, Avery thought about baby-sitting. Every weekend of her high school life, she'd had one, two, sometimes three jobs. After her father died, it was a way to get out of the house for a while, to avoid Isabel's droopy presence. Then she got used to the money, going on the weekends with her friends to Macy's or Nordstrom to buy outfits to wear during the week. How had she walked into strangers' houses and started up conversations with the parents and then the kids? She'd even gone to Hawaii with the Costellos, sleeping in a *cabaña* with the oldest girl and eating with the children every night at a restaurant while the parents went out to clubs. Maybe she'd been able to do it all because she knew what she was supposed to be. They knew exactly who she was—the baby-sitter.

"Who is this?" she asked Daniel, opening her eyes to angry, obscene lyrics, the exact, terrible noise that experts warned against in the "Adolescent" sections of parenting books. Dan would probably kill her for letting the boy watch this stuff.

"Eminem."

"Like the candies?"

"No, spelled like *E-m-i-n*—"

"I get it. What's so great about him?"

"I don't know."

"So why are you watching it?"

"Don't know."

"Who do you like?"

Daniel was silent.

"You can tell me. I don't know anything about music. Ask Dan. I listen to a news channel in my car."

Daniel turned to her, his eyes narrowed, and then back to the screen. "I like NSYNC. And Britney Spears."

"The soft drink one. The one with the blond hair?" He liked blondes. The actress on his mirror. The singer. After Midori's first call, Avery had thought about Dan's past for a couple of days before she'd made him show her pictures of Randi. He'd dug in a box she'd thought was full of college memorabilia and brought out stacks of photos that dated from high school. Avery had flipped through the stacks until she felt sick, even telling Dan to go to bed because she wasn't done. She'd learned a lot about her husband from the photos, but mostly she'd stared at Randi, his first, true love. The girl in the pictures was always smiling, leaning forward, her teeth crooked, white and big, her eyes crinkled. It was hard to find the drug addict under the laughter.

Randi had been dark and fair and skinny, nothing like these smooth, butter-brown blondes Daniel seemed to prefer.

"So are there girls at school you like?" Avery sat up and crossed her legs.

"No!" Daniel stared at the screen. "That's stupid."

"But if that actress were your age—"

"Only girls think like that. I just think she's pretty, that's all. When I'm older, maybe I'll have a girlfriend like that, okay?"

Avery was silent, watching the pale singer move his hands and yell into the camera. Daniel's picture on the mirror was like her list of perfect boyfriends. After Loren had left for college, Avery had written the list, hoping that maybe she'd find a different life, one unlike the strange, sad space she shared with her mom. Daniel had brought the actress with him from home, needing the same reassurance.

"So what do you like to do? Do you like that video game your dad got you?"

Daniel shrugged and didn't turn around.

"Have you ridden your bike around here much? It's pretty flat."

"No one rides bikes here. They all have skateboards."

"Oh."

A commercial for Neutrogena soap flashed on the screen, a flawlessly skinned actress splashing herself with water. Daniel stood up. "I'm still hungry."

"So do you have a skateboard?"

"No."

Daniel stood in front of her, a small ten-year-old boy with too-big jeans and a pale, drawn face. If she saw him on the news in a story about an abandoned child, she'd write a check to the account set up by the station. If she were at Sunvalley Mall, and he walked up to her and said he was lost, she'd hold his hand until they found a security guard. If he came to her door and said his cat was run over in the street, she'd hug him. What was wrong with her? Why had she let her feelings about Dan's huge lie step between her and this boy who needed so much?

Avery stood up and smiled. "Let's go get a skateboard. I know just the place. And we'll go get something to eat, too."

"What are all these people doing out here?" Avery asked as she circled the Fiesta Square parking lot for the third time. "Does everyone need to be out here at this exact minute?"

"Maybe they're buying dinner. When she wasn't sick, my mom sometimes took me out after school for dinner. I like KFC the best."

Avery looked at Daniel in the rearview mirror. He was staring out the window, his eyes searching for a space. "Is chicken your favorite food?"

"I guess."

"Did your mother ever cook it for you at home?" He was silent, and she looked back at him. "I had to learn to cook when I quit work. But it must seem like I don't make anything."

"Dan makes stuff. Isabel makes stuff, too. Loren makes cake. Valerie and Luís brought over something to barbecue. I liked that."

Avery stopped the Rover and let it idle, scanning the lot. Mothers and children walked back and forth, slipping into MacDonnell's department store, Starbucks, and Noah's. Couldn't one of them flipping go home? she thought. She was sitting here with this kid who didn't even know she could make the best pasta salad with pine nuts, kalamata olives, and currants. He didn't know about the epic dinners she made for Val and Luís and Isabel and Loren and her family. He probably didn't know what she did for work, either, and then she sighed. Of course he didn't. She'd never talked to him about it. Not once.

"There! There!" Daniel said, his hand waving. "A space!"

Avery put the car into drive and accelerated, just nipping into the parking spot before a Suburban made its eager, lumbering turn around the corner.

"Yes!" Avery said, smiling at Daniel through the mirror. "We did it! Good scouting!"

He smiled and took off his seat belt, scooting to the edge of the seat. "Where's the store? I can't see it. Will there be skateboards in the window?"

She felt her smile slip and fall, and she sighed, ashamed by how little it took to make him happy.

After they came home from The Grind, the skate shop in Lafayette, and Freddie's Pizza, Daniel took a shower. Dan still wasn't home, and Avery considered calling Bill and Marian but decided not to. Hearing her husband's voice always made her think of what he hadn't said, of all the stories he'd neglected to tell her. She'd pried more information from him after Midori's first call, but nothing seemed to satisfy her. What was she waiting for? Worse news than what she'd already been handed? Somehow, Avery imagined that there was one crucial piece of information that would make her stop asking questions. Even when they were speaking of dinner or the sprinkler system or the headlines in the news, she heard the other story, the one about Randi Gold. So, she changed into her nightgown and washed her face, and then knocked on Daniel's door.

"Yeah?"

"Can I come in?"

She could almost hear his shrug, and then he said, "Okay."

He was sitting on the bed, his hair stuck up in uncombed spikes, his new skateboard on his lap. The young man at The Grind had walked Avery and Daniel through every step of the purchase. At first, she'd been barely able to follow the conversation, caught up in his pierced tongue, eyebrow, nose, and ears. But then, as they walked with him through the store, she learned about boards, grip tape, trucks, and wheels. After two hours of discussion and then assembly, Daniel had a Shorty's skateboard with Spitfire wheels and Independent trucks.

"This is way cool, dude," the young man had said to Daniel. "This is a Chad Muska board!"

Avery had no idea who Chad Muska was, and she suspected Daniel didn't either, but he clutched his board and the issue of *Transworld-Skateboarding* magazine the kid gave him, smiling the whole way through his pepperoni pizza at Freddie's. He was still

smiling now, rubbing the shiny bottom of the board that was decorated with a Japanese rising sun.

"This design is what Chad Muska has on his board," Daniel said
to her as she walked toward him. "I read it in the magazine."

"Remember the guy at the store said it would get scratched. So
don't be upset."

"I know." Daniel kept his eyes on the board.

"Are you ready for bed?"

"It's only eight thirty."

"What time do you usually go to bed?" Avery realized she didn't
know. When she was home early, she was mostly in her room, locked
away from whatever Dan and Daniel were doing.

"Nine."

"Oh." She looked around and sighed. The whole afternoon and
evening had gone much better than she could ever have planned, but
now, standing in her nightgown in this boy's room, she felt exposed
and at a loss. "So . . ."

"I can read this magazine and then turn off the light myself,"
Daniel said. "I can do that myself."

He hunched over the magazine, his eyes hidden. It was as if the
skateboard and the pizza had never happened. She was indeed just a
strange woman in a nightgown standing in the middle of his room.

"Okay. Good night."

He nodded and lifted his hand, his eyes still on the glossy pictures.
Avery turned and closed the door softly behind her. Leaning back on
it, she wondered how many nights they would need to spend before
both of them felt near normal. And would either of them want that?
She closed her eyes and tipped her head onto the wood, and that's
when she heard it—little, ragged sobs. Opening her eyes, she jerked
her head up and turned around, grabbing the doorknob, ready to
rush in, knowing there were so many things upsetting him: his
mother, the incident today at school, Avery, even Dan. But before
turning the cold brushed-nickel knob, she stopped, her breath in her
throat, her heart pounding. How many nights had she cried in her
room after her father died? It became what she had to do, the darkness peeling away all the ways she faked herself out during the day,
school and friends and television keeping her from remembering.

When it was quiet and still and there were no voices around her, she could see his emptiness in the room, sitting in the chair next to her bed, not saying a word or making a sound.

Her crying was the sound she made to stay connected, to bring his absence closer, to wrap it around her shoulders so she would never forget.

Avery placed her palms on the door and listened until Daniel stopped crying and clicked off his light. She waited for the heavy thud of the skateboard magazine falling to the floor.

At ten o'clock, Dan still wasn't home. She turned the clock toward her. It was too late to call Bill and Marian now, not after their 9:30 P.M. bedtime. Jared once had said, "Fire. Flood. Gloom of night. Wouldn't matter. They'd be in bed during a tornado." But tonight was different, wasn't it? An emergency on the roads? Their almost estranged son over for a visit? Then the phone rang, and she grabbed it so the ringing wouldn't wake up Daniel.

"Dan?"

"No, it is not Dan," Mischa said. "And where is your husband?"

"What's up?" Avery picked a piece of lint off the bedspread.

"He is not home?"

"No. He's—he's at his parents'. What's going on?"

"Nothing," he said. "I was thinking about St. Louis. I was thinking about caviar and you."

This afternoon, Avery had wanted to push all the cutlery, dishes, and water glasses off the table at Andrés, throw Mischa down, and put her body on his. Their two bodies were like electrical currents, their combined power so strong. Now, she wished he would hang up and leave her alone.

"Look, I'll call you tomorrow from the office," she said.

"I don't know if I can wait that long."

Avery rolled her eyes. "You're going to have to. I'll talk to Brody first, and we can figure out what's next, okay? Got to go." She clicked off the phone and stared at the numbers. He was calling her at home, at ten at night, while she was in bed. Her stomach churned, lurching when the phone rang again.

"I told you I'd call you tomorrow," she said into the receiver.

There was silence on the other end.

"Are you there? Mischa?"

"This isn't Mish—whatever," said a strange voice.

Avery bit her lip. Why had she said Mischa? What if it had been Dan? "Sorry. Who is this?"

"Who is this?"

"This is the Tacconi residence."

"Good. That's what I thought. Is Dan there?"

"May I ask who's calling?"

"I think I want it to be a surprise. He hasn't seen me for a while."

Avery felt her stomach move again, nausea squeezing her esophagus. "He's busy right now. Can I tell him who called?"

"Sure. Tell him Galvin called. He'll remember me. We have a few dozen things to talk about."

"Galvin?" she asked.

"Yeah," he said. "That's right. Your hearing is one hundred percent. Gal-vin. Galvin Gold."

Ten

According to KCBS, there had been a ten-car pileup in Cordelia involving a tractor-trailer that was carrying pesticides and then a string of lookie-loo accidents, causing all I-80 traffic from Sacramento to Pinole to slow and stop. Dan had tried to take city streets, merging onto the freeway at Antelope, but despite his tricky maneuvers, all four freeway lanes looked like a parking lot. Sun glinted metallic off car hoods, traffic and police helicopters whirled in the air, and drivers opened their doors, stood on the hot pavement, and talked to one another, hands on hips.

Dan drove on the shoulder to the next exit and parked on the side of the street. He pulled out his phone, but service was sporadic, the lines on his phone rising and falling like a heart rate.

"Shit!" He threw his phone down on the passenger's seat and thought about Daniel. If he didn't get home by six, Flora wouldn't be happy, having told Dan when he hired her, "Mr. Luís tell me about this job, and I want it. But I have to be home for my family at night. This is okay? Six o'clock. I take the six ten bus. It all work out." He should never have told Steve he'd come out here to make the service call at Weymouth Industrial. But since his return from paternity leave, he could see Steve was watching him for further signs of weakness. Any misstep—a missed meeting, a lost account, a day off—would cost Dan something, respect or maybe even his job. Sure, Lacy or Bob or any member of the sales staff could have made the call today, but Dan had wanted to seem involved, concerned, interested. A good worker. But the truth was that since he had returned to work, all he saw as he sat behind his desk, flipping through company specs and pamphlets about new technology, was Daniel. His big eyes. His small pale hand. His hat pulled down almost to his nose.

Dan looked at his watch. With this traffic, there was no way he'd get back to Monte Veda in time. A stream of cars flowed off the freeway, drivers looking at GNDs in their cars or unfolding maps, trying to find alternative routes home. In an hour or two, every road would be bumper to bumper. He picked up his cell and dialed home, grateful when the phone actually rang and surprised when Avery answered. He managed to tell her what had happened and that he was thinking of going to his folks, and then the line went dead. Looking across the street, he saw a pay phone, but he didn't want to talk to her anymore. Her voice had sounded pinched and tight, paragraphs of complaint under her few words. At least she was home, early for some amazing reason. She hadn't said anything was wrong. She would just have to take care of Daniel. For once.

Leaning back in his seat, Dan closed his eyes. Right now in their house in Curtis Park, his mother was sitting in front of the television watching *Oprah* or the local station's afternoon show. She had a glass of iced tea in her hand, even though the air conditioner was on full blast. She wore a flowered dress and low, sensible pumps, her clean, white apron hanging on the kitchen door, ready for exactly four thirty, when she would tie it on and prepare macaroni and cheese or spaghetti with meatballs or chicken with some kind of sauce made with cream of mushroom soup. Or, if Bill had decided that it was "time for a night out" at either Español or Caballo Blanco—the restaurants his parents had taken them to once a month for years—Marian was looking in the powder room mirror, applying a bow of orange lipstick, the same color she'd worn for as long as Dan could remember. Even now, he could see her lips like two orange slices kissing him on his way to school or before bed, and later, whispering in tight, pinched, citrus hisses.

Either way, his father was outside in his work clothes—a pair of khaki shorts with pockets for tools and clippers and measuring tape, a white golfing hat, and well-worn Wolverine boots—hedging or pruning or mowing. Since their father had retired last year, Jared said the yard looked better than a park with a full-time caretaker, the entire half-acre blooming and totally green. Not one weed or sucker on the apple trees. Perfect.

Dan hadn't spoken to his parents since July Fourth. He'd taken Jared's advice, letting Daniel's existence and then homecoming stay a secret. Everyone—Isabel, Loren, Jared, and even Mara—knew about his son, but not Bill and Marian. In November, Dan knew he'd have to figure something out, because he and Avery were always invited for Thanksgiving dinner, even though it was always understood that they would not spend the night.

"The room's just a mess," his mother always said. "I haven't gotten around to redecorating. You and Avery shouldn't have to sleep in those silly twin beds."

Their first Thanksgiving together, Dan had shown Avery his old bedroom, and she had turned to him, confused. "It's fine. We can stay here, Dan. It's only one night. She doesn't need to go to any trouble for us."

He let Avery believe it was Marian's esthetics and house pride that kept them only day visitors, but the mess his mother was talking about was Dan. And she kept the room the way it had been when he was at home because she hadn't believed anything had changed, especially not him.

Bret Parish seemed to enjoy listening to stories about Dan's parents, nodding and writing down every word. And then one session, he'd looked up from his pad and said, "They'll never change. You'll either have to accept that or not. But you can tell them who you are. You can show them your life as it is now. And they can choose what to do or say or think. You can't control that. But you don't have to react."

"But what will they think?"

"What does it matter now, Dan?" Bret asked. "You're all grown up. You have a life of your own. You don't need them to like it."

"But . . ."

"You want them to?"

Dan nodded, ashamed. That's what he'd wanted before Randi and then after the drugs and stealing and lies.

"Of course. We all want our parents' approval. But some of us have to learn to live without it. Sometimes we have to learn to live without them at all."

Dan opened his eyes and sat up. Sweaty, red-faced people drove by him, their windows open as they talked to each other and yelled out the best advice they had. A highway patrol officer curved in and out of the traffic and merged onto the freeway shoulder. Dan looked at his watch again. There was time before dinner. There was time to tell them everything.

"Danny!" His mother stared at him and held on to the door, her mouth slack. "My word! What a—surprise."

He adjusted his tie a bit and put his hands in his pockets. "There was a terrible accident. I was here on business, and I decided to wait out the traffic. It's crazy out there."

Marian nodded, her hand still on the door. "I know it! The news crew has been reporting for an hour. Were you in that?"

From the backyard came the sound of a hedger or a lawn mover, the whirring engine going back and forth over something green. The front yard was just as Jared had said. The camellia bushes under the front windows were perfectly square, tiny green buds on every branch. The thick Bermuda grass fanned out to the road in orderly, mowed lines, and the sycamore was just beginning to yellow, one or two freshly fallen leaves on the lawn like fallen stars.

"Yard looks good, Mom."

She waved her hand, and the door drifted open. "Your father. He'll be pruning when the world ends."

Dan looked into the dark house. The local news circled around the living room and poured out to the porch on the cold, air-conditioned air. He caught some phrases: "I-80" and "haz-mat teams," "congestion," and "possibly talcum powder." Breathing in, he could smell something on the stove top—browning hamburger, tomato paste, chili powder. Marian was making goulash.

"I was wondering if I could—"

"Oh, come in. Yes. You don't want to drive home in that."

Dan walked in, and his mother turned down the television. On the screen was an aerial view of Cordelia. People in white protective suits stood on the freeway next to a pile of whitish powder that had poured out of the back of a trailer. The camera swung left and right, showing nothing but cars for miles.

"Have you called Avery? She must be worried sick."

Dan nodded and sat down on the plastic-covered couch. His mother almost winced at the sound, and he thought to get up. But Bret said he didn't have to react to *their* reactions. He didn't have to jump up and move to the recliner or the wooden desk chair. Since he'd left the house, he'd learned that couches were actually for sitting.

"Yeah, I called her. I'm sure she's been watching the news, too."

"So how are the treatments going?" his mother asked. "It's such a shame she has to go through all that."

Dan had hated telling his parents about the infertility treatments, knowing that they wouldn't really surprise them. He'd never been able to do anything right, and his inability to get Avery pregnant was only another example of his incompetence.

"Have you tried more on your own?" his father had asked last Thanksgiving as he made a bourbon and 7UP for Aunt Cleo. "I can't believe two young people . . ."

Bill had trailed off, stirring the drink, the ice clinking on the glass. "Anyway, it's a mystery to me why things get so complicated."

Dan had picked up a Corona, taking a sip and nodding. "I know," he'd said. "It's hard to believe."

Now, Dan tapped his fingers on the plastic armrest cover. "We've actually stopped the treatments for a while."

"Oh? Why?" Marian collected herself, smoothing the perfectly flat fabric on her knees. "It's none of my business. I'm sure there are good reasons. Can I get you something to drink, Danny? I've got to go and check on the meat."

"Water's fine," he said, starting to stand up.

"Oh, just sit. I'll be right back."

On the screen, the white-suited men seemed to be vacuuming up the powder, while groups of other officials stood off to one side, watching. Then they switched to a field reporter who pointed at a flashing clump of emergency vehicles and a long line of cars.

"Dan," his father said as he walked into the living room, drying his hands on a towel.

"Hi, Dad." Dan stood up and pushed his hair back. "I was in that."

Bill looked at the television screen. "Some trouble. They need to put more restrictions on truckers. I've always said that. Can I get you a drink?"

"Mom's getting me water."

Both of the men stood silently in front of the television as the reporter interviewed hot people stuck in their cars, until Marian came into the room and handed Dan a glass of ice water, the bottom wrapped in a green paper napkin. "Here you go. I think I can stretch the goulash. Would you like to stay? Or do you have to get back on the road?"

Dan sipped his water and almost coughed, struggling to keep the water in his mouth. "Thanks. I'd like to stay. Avery's home with— It'll be fine."

Bill didn't look at him, mesmerized by the action on the screen, the camera in the helicopter panning up, down, from side to side, taking in everything. Marian wiped her hands on her apron and went back into the kitchen. The glass was too cold in Dan's hand, but he couldn't put it down. Not a coaster in sight.

"So how is Avery?" Bill said, lumping a spoonful of goulash onto Dan's plate and handing it to him.

"Good." Dan took the bowl of corn from his mother without looking at her. As he spooned kernels next to the goulash, he knew this had been a mistake. He couldn't tell them about Randi and Daniel. Telling his mother about Avery's decision to stop trying for the baby hadn't been wise. He passed the bowl to his father and served himself some iceberg lettuce salad.

"How's it going with the treatments?" His father chewed and stared at him.

Dan breathed in and looked at his mother. She bent over her plate, moving macaroni noodles around. "We decided—for now—to stop. It's a very grueling regimen. I don't know how she did it for so long."

"It's natural," Bill said, nodding. "A woman wants a baby. Pure and simple. Can't blame her, though, for wanting a break. Doctors don't think about the patient as a person. Your mother has gone through hell with her sciatica."

Dan looked at his mother, but she raised her eyebrows and kept eating. Jared had never told him about the sciatica. Dan wasn't even sure what sciatica was.

"Are you okay, Mom?"

Marian nodded and waved her hand, as if she could make her sciatica and everything else disappear. "Oh, yes."

"So when will you start up the treatments again?" Bill leaned on his elbows. "When will we have that grandchild?"

Randi peeked in from the door to the living room, her hand covering her silent laughter. "I can't believe you're sitting there," she whispered, almost doubled over. "Oh, God! Your mom looks like she's swallowed shit!"

Marian was pale, her hair flat against her head as if she'd been nervously smoothing it as she cooked. What did she know? What did Midori Nolan say to her when she called looking for him? Maybe all his worry was for nothing. They knew but didn't want to talk about it, like always.

"I don't know," Dan said. "Maybe not for a long time. We've— we've been a bit preoccupied lately."

"You work hard, don't you, Dan?" His mother held the bowl of corn hopefully. He shook his head.

"I was on leave for a while. Six weeks."

Bill looked up and stopped chewing. "Leave? You weren't at work? For what?"

"Paternity. Paternity leave."

Both of his parents stared at him, unchewed food clenched in their mouths. The antique clock on the wall *click, clicked,* and outside, Dan could hear the spurt and flume of the sprinkler system turning on. He turned to Jared's usual seat, but his brother and his slight nod and support weren't there. Just Randi at the doorway, howling. "I'm sorry, Dan. I can't help it. Can you see them? They're going down for the count. You better get out of here before you kill them."

Bill put down his fork. "I don't understand. I thought you said Avery gave up the treatments."

"She did."

Marian shook her head, her hands on the table. "Oh, no. It was a miscarriage. Oh, how awful. What a tragedy."

"You know what they say," his father said, reaching a hand out toward Dan and then pulling it back. "That kind of thing can be a mercy. Nature's way and all that. Avery's time will come, mark my words."

The clock clicked through another minute, and his parents went back to eating. Dan stared at them. They'd already packed up the tragedy they'd imagined. Avery's miscarriage was already over, processed, put in storage. No one need talk about it any further.

"That's not what happened. There wasn't a miscarriage."

"Now you've done it," Randi said. "Now it's all over."

"So what is it, Dan?" His father wiped his mouth. "This is getting tiresome."

"Someone called you on the Fourth of July, right, Mom?" Dan asked.

Marian looked up and sighed. She folded her hands in her lap. "A social worker. From Modesto or somewhere. She just wanted your address. It was about Randi, wasn't it?"

Over by the door, Randi listened, her face still.

"Yeah. It was about Randi. She died."

Bill shook his head, and Dan wanted to jump on him, pounding away his father's smug, sanctimonious turn of neck. *You asshole!* he wanted to scream. *Leave her alone, she's dead. She's dead. Can't you let it go?* He was bigger and stronger than Bill now, younger, faster, and he could imagine how quickly it would end. How good it would feel to see the old man there on the hardwood floor, his hands covering his face, pleading, "Stop. Enough. You win." How wonderful to stand over him and see himself in the position he'd dreamed of being in all through childhood—dominant, powerful, able to give or deny mercy. And then, he could leave. For good. Dan could feel the outside air on his face as he slammed out the door, the hot sting of his car door handle in his hand as he got in and took off. He'd never come back. Never. But as he watched Bill, his heart pounding in his temples, he breathed in sharply. Randi grabbed him by the shoulder, digging in with her purple nails.

"Can't say I'm surprised by that news. Randi lived a hard life. Her parents . . ." Bill paused. "That father. But better to let it go and forget. She was bad news from day one."

"It's going to be hard to forget, Dad. She had a child. He's ten years old now."

From his mother's start and the quiver in her throat, Dan could see that she already understood, putting together Midori's phone call, the paternity leave, the ten-year span. But his father pushed his chair back and crossed his legs. "What a mess."

The food on Dan's plate began to swirl, his head filling with light and air. Randi squeezed him again, and he breathed in slowly and then exhaled. His mother held the table edge and looked down at her lap.

"It is a mess. But it's my mess. The boy is mine. His name is Daniel."

At first, Bill seemed not to hear the words, taking another bite of goulash. But then he slowed, looked up, stared. Swallowing his lump of food, he grabbed his iced tea and pressed tight, his fingers squeaking on the wet glass.

No one said a word. Dan nodded to himself and looked over at Randi, who shrugged and waved. Her eyes were full of tears, her face finally serious, her body quiet. He wanted to push away from the table and hold her, press her to him as he hadn't ten years ago. He wanted to stroke her dark, curly hair, whisper in her ear, and drive her to rehab. He wanted her to get better and to live. If she'd loved herself more, she might have called him and told him about the baby. She would have wanted more for herself.

And he knew that if he could go back and save her from her addiction, he would stay with her. Give up Avery and Cal and the house and his job. Stay with her and be a father from the start of Daniel's life. Live in the apartment and work at Macy's or in construction or for the telephone company.

Randi shook her head, turned, and walked out the front door, her thin legs flicking—white, shadow, white, shadow—in the afternoon sun. Then she was gone.

Dan didn't wait for his father or mother to say anything. "Daniel's living with us now. He's in school. He has some problems, but we're working on them."

Marian looked at Bill and crossed her arms across her chest. "How is Avery taking all this?"

His old habit of hiding grabbed him under the jaw and almost forced out the words, *Great. She's fine. She loves Daniel. It's working out better than I could ever have imagined.* Instead, he said, "Not well. It was a huge shock. I never told her about Randi. About that time."

Bill breathed out through his nose. "I'm not surprised about that. What a terrible load of news."

"Bill!" Marian said.

"It's true. What woman is going to want to be with a man who stole from his own parents, lived with a drug addict, and fathered an illegitimate child? And then stay and raise him? My God!"

"He didn't know about the child, Bill."

"But I did all the rest," Dan said. "And you've never let me forget it. Or redeem myself. Or even apologize. All these years, Dad, I've been waiting for you to forgive me. To trust me. I'm your son. I made some really stupid mistakes. But haven't I paid enough?"

Dan tried to keep the tears out of his eyes, but he couldn't. All of it was too much. Randi was dead. He'd never see her again, never have the chance to ask for *her* forgiveness. The only way he could make it up to her was to care for Daniel. Even if it meant his marriage was ruined. Even if his own parents wouldn't acknowledge their grandchild. He had to come clean, say what was necessary, and then move on. Like Bret Parish told him, he couldn't expect his parents to change. But Dan could change. He had to.

"Those were horrible years, Danny," his mother said softly. "We didn't know what we had done wrong."

"We did nothing wrong," Bill snapped. "We raised two boys the same way, and one stole and lied and ruined his life and the other didn't. It wasn't us."

"It doesn't matter who did what," Dan said. "We're left here, though, Dad. It's like you've wanted to keep living back when I was nineteen or twenty. You haven't noticed that I've changed my life. I didn't ruin it at all. I have a good life. I have a good job. I have Avery. You won't even let us sleep in your home. You still think I'm the same person I was back then."

Bill was silent, his arms tight around his chest. "You stole from us."

"Bill!"

"I know! I'm sorry. I was wrong!" Dan cried out. "My life was wrong, but out of it, I have a child. And I'm scared. He's hurt and scared, and I'm trying my best. But—but I need you. I need help." He put his head in his hands and wept.

"Oh," said Marian, standing up and then stopping as she looked at Bill. "Oh, Danny."

"Dan," Bill said. "Dan."

Choking on the river of salt and mucus in his throat, Dan scooted back in his chair and leaned over the table, pressing his face against the tablecloth, feeling the plastic lace against his cheek. Then there was his mother's soft hand on his hair and the sound he remembered from when he was very little, a soft low hum, letting him know she was there. "I'm sorry," he mumbled, feeling his mother's touch, listening as his father cleared his throat. Listening to his father's silence.

Before Dan left that night, the wreck cleared up, the traffic flowing through the arteries that fed into San Francisco, Dan went up to his old room. His parents were downstairs, watching the early local news, both silent and stiff in their chairs. After he had stopped crying, they'd all sat around the table, his mother still patting him on the head, the shoulder, finally resting her palm on his arm. No one said anything real after that, but the evening moved on without any further argument. Marian even said, "We'll come down on the weekend."

Dan pushed open his door and turned on the light. The two twin beds were crisply made, the bedspreads taut across their slim bodies, and the extra blankets he and Jared had used on winter nights folded neatly at the foot of each. The brown curtain on the big window between the beds was open, the Fitzgeralds' house lit up within the frame like a photograph. When he and Jared were very little, their bedtime was eight thirty. In the summer, it was still light when their mother closed the door softly behind her, the sky bright, then a grainy gray, and then barely dark because of the streetlights. Dan and his brother would climb out of bed, sit on the dresser under the window, and stare into the houses across the street, watching the awake life of everyone else.

"What are they doing?" Jared would ask, holding his skinny legs with his hands.

"The dad is leaving," Dan would tell him. "He's packing. He's going far away. He might never come back."

"How does Heather feel about that?" Jared would ask, worried about the Fitzgeralds' youngest daughter.

"She's happy. She's glad. Her mother is going to let her sleep in the big bed. She's going to let her play dress up with the dad's left-over clothes."

"Really?"

"Yeah. And then they're all going to go on vacation and forget about him."

"But won't he be lonely?" Jared squeezed his bony knees tighter.

"No. He has a lot of friends somewhere else. Away. Not here."

"Oh. What else?"

Dan would tell stories about all the neighbors, tales of fathers who were gone or at least happy. Children who ran away or were able to play games at night with eager dads. Stories of mothers handing out bags of candy and driving their kids to Disneyland. Tales with no school and all play. Days where the sun never set at all.

He sat on his bed and ran his hand along the grain of the red bedspread. Back then, he would never have imagined all that happened later: Randi, the stealing, the drugs, much less the miracle of college, Avery, and his job. And Daniel. He wouldn't have had the vocabulary to explain that to Jared or even to himself. All Dan knew then was that he was unhappy and couldn't work out a way to be otherwise. He wanted his father to change—he wanted his life to change, and he didn't know how to make any of that happen. When he was finally old enough to feel power in his body and voice, he yanked himself out of the riptide of this room, this house.

When he first moved in with Randi, he couldn't believe how good it felt to be away from Bill and Marian, free of their suspicious looks and disapproval. After a while, he saw it wasn't perfect, full of rent payments and late-night visitors who ended up barfing in the small bathroom, and tedious, part-time, minimum-wage jobs. But at least it had been different. At least he hadn't been sitting on the dresser, imagining life. He had lived it, all of it.

Dan stood up and walked to the dresser, feeling the thin layer of dust under his palm. When they were kids, Marian would never have tolerated a layer of dust—not even a speck. Early on, they'd both learned to use a rag and the can of Pledge. Before dusting, Jared would write his foamy name on the wood, the *J* melting as the *D* fizzed on the dresser.

Dan opened the top drawer on his side and sat back down on the bed. The T-shirts he'd left at home were still there, the dopey ones with logos on the backs, DISNEYLAND, TAHOE CITY, GUMBY. He stood up and opened the other drawers, all still full of his life. Briefs and tube socks and torn boxers. A leather belt. Two gum wrappers. A yo-yo.

Looking out at the Fitzgeralds', he knew that for the past fifteen years, his mother had been telling herself a story, one in which her oldest boy was a senior in high school, ready to move into his happy life. He could become anything, this boy: a doctor, a lawyer, a teacher. He may have a wild girlfriend, but he would meet someone else, a good girl. He would settle down. In these clothes, Dan's happy life was still possible. If these clothes still stayed folded in their drawers, waiting for his body, the future stayed unwritten.

Dan closed all the drawers. A comet of clean wood swooshed across the top of the dresser where he'd wiped it. By the time he'd worn the Disneyland shirt—senior year trip, Randi and he getting drunk on the Matterhorn and then booted off the Space Mountain ride—his mother's story of him was a cliché. By the last time she'd folded these shirts, he was in the apartment across town, rolling a joint and then sharing a double Whopper and fries with Randi.

Turning from the window and the neighborhood outside, Dan thought of the dresser that he, Luís, Isabel, and Val had put together and filled with Daniel's clothes, all new, crisp and clean and folded neatly. If they were lucky, maybe Daniel's story had time to change, to arc up and beyond its sad beginning, to curve down slowly into a happier ending.

It was late when he pulled up to the house, only a streetlight and the front lights Avery had left on illuminating Dias Dorados. Dan decided to park in the driveway, not wanting the rumble of the garage door to awaken Avery or Daniel. He closed the car door and stretched. It had taken more than two hours to get home. The freeways were still full of weary, hot, desperate commuters who'd also sat out the jam in bars or restaurants or with friends and family.

When he left his parents' house, both Marian and Bill had stood on their porch, Marian waving, Bill holding up a hand. It had been years since they had shown more than relief at his departure, but tonight, Dan had felt their sadness, the tears on his mother's fine, wrinkled cheeks, his father's Adam's apple moving up and down even though he wasn't saying a word. And they promised they'd come visit on the weekend. He told himself not to expect anything, but excitement radiated from his heart in waves. If his parents had listened, maybe Avery would, too.

The last of the summer crickets scratched their wings in the star jasmine. Soon all the leaves would fall, the sky would cloud and darken, and the season would turn. It had been almost a quarter year since his life changed. All their lives. Maybe by the time winter cracked into spring, this ugly story would have smoothed itself into memory, painful but harder to remember, the events not sensitive to touch.

He opened the front door, stepped in, and closed it quietly behind him. The house was dark save for the light over the stove Avery had left on, and he walked into the kitchen. On the counter was a bag from The Grind, the skate shop in Lafayette. He reached in and found the receipt: skateboard plus assembly, helmet, stickers, knee and elbow pads. Leaning on the counter, he closed his eyes, grateful for this gift from Avery and from whatever had made her treat Daniel with such kindness. Like a stepmom. Like a mom.

"Dan!" He swallowed and turned, still holding the receipt in his hand.

"Oh, Aves. This"—he moved his arm over the bag—"is so nice."

She ignored him and moved closer, her face pale. "Someone called. I think you need to call Midori or Vince. It was really weird."

Dan stood up straight. "Who?"

"He said his name was Galvin Gold. He hung up before I could ask him who he was. Who is he, Dan? What does he want? Is that Randi's dad? Daniel's grandfather? I thought he was dead."

Shaking his head and almost laughing, Dan wondered how he could have let himself feel happy. He should walk backwards out of the house, into his car, and sit in the driveway, listening to the crickets and remembering his parents' strangely apologetic faces. The empty bag that had been full of presents for Daniel would still be on the counter. He could still imagine that in a few months, he would have his family back in a way he'd never had them before. Parents. Wife. Child.

And even though Avery seemed disturbed by the call, Dan wondered if she envisioned Galvin Gold as a trapdoor through which they could shove Daniel so he would disappear and their lives could go back to normal. Galvin was Daniel's grandfather. Someone Daniel probably knew far better than he knew Dan and Avery. But Dan knew the truth about Galvin, could still see him on the couch with his Saturday six-pack of Olympia and a carton of Camels as he watched the Raider game. "What's up, lovebirds?" he would call out to them, laughing until he began to cough. "Going on a little datey?" They'd skirt the edge of the living room, shooting into Randi's room as fast as possible, slamming the door behind them. And Randi had told him just enough about the iron of Galvin's flat palm, the way it reached out for soft, smart-ass skin whenever possible, sending her sailing across the room. There was no way Galvin wanted Daniel—he hadn't had use for his own daughter—but he wanted something.

Dan moved past Avery and toward the bedroom, needing to call Midori right away. He crushed the receipt in his hand.

"Dan! Who is this man?"

He wanted to tell her about the way Galvin's slap looked hours later on Randi's cheek, a purple-red hand on her white skin. He wanted to tell her Galvin Gold was the reason Randi had left home, all her belongings stuffed in a sleeping bag. But Dan didn't know if he could risk telling her one more thing that might scare her even further away.

"No one," Dan said as he walked into the dark hall. "As far as I'm concerned, no one at all."

Eleven

As the plane took off, Avery held her stomach, thinking she might need to use the barf bag. As she was lifted up, up, she dug in the pocket in front of her, grabbing the white bag and opening it. She leaned back, closed her eyes, and tried her yoga breathing. In and out, one and two, soft and soft and soft. And as the plane slowly leveled off, the rush of hot acid slowly slid back down her esophagus, where it burbled in her stomach and then settled. Safe, for now.

When she opened her eyes, the man next to her smiled. "Rough takeoff?"

"Yeah. I shouldn't have had that cup of coffee at the airport." Avery folded the bag and stuffed it back into the pocket.

"Good advice for all airports. No food or drink." He turned back to his report, and Avery closed her eyes again, leaning into the leather of the business-class seat.

For the first time since she'd started back to work, Avery had not wanted to leave the house. Dan had been on the phone for over an hour with Midori two nights ago, and then he'd gone in late to work the next day so he could talk with Vince and then Anita Brisbo at the school. In almost an afterthought, Galvin Gold foremost in her mind, Avery had remembered to tell him about Daniel's fight and sandbox incident.

"He what?" Dan had said, sitting on the bed, cradling the phone in his hands.

"That's why I was home. Daniel fought with some boy and then hid in the sandbox so he didn't have to do some writing assignment. The person on yard duty found him on her way home."

Dan shook his head. "I'm doing such a great job as a dad. Daniel's just getting along splendidly, isn't he? No wonder my parents are so proud of me. By the way, they're coming over this weekend." He laughed strangely and then put a hand over his mouth.

Avery sat down on the corner of the bed. "I'm probably going to have to go to St. Louis."

"Great."

She looked up at the mirror and watched Dan. He swallowed back tears he wasn't showing her and then wiped his eyes. "I'm going to have to get the court involved if Galvin calls again," he said. "If you answer, you have to write down everything he says. Midori says I should get a tape recorder."

"What does he want?"

"I don't know."

Something in Avery's chest was hurting her, a pain deep under her breastbone. She rubbed at it with her fingers and wished she could cry for everything—her baby, Dan's lies, Daniel, Randi, tonight's strange call. But even though it would feel so good to comfort him, stroke his back, tell him it would be okay, something hard inside her held her back. That same thing made her say, "Fine," when Brody called her into his office the next day and told her that she indeed was heading back to St. Louis and Dirland Accounting and Mischa. The same thing helped her dress in her traveling suit and walked her to the United Airlines gate and sat her down in seat 8B.

Avery wanted to forget about Daniel and his bright, happy eyes as she handed him the skateboard, when she brought hot pizza to their booth, as he sat in the backseat looking at the skateboard magazine. She couldn't bear to think about Dan's reflection in the mirror, his huge sadness spread all over his body, every muscle sagging with too damn much. She couldn't even begin to imagine what had gone on at his parents' house if they had agreed to come down for a visit to meet Daniel. So she thought about Mischa Podorov, his scruffy blond hair, his blue eyes, the way he said her name as if she could fly.

*   *   *

Her assistant, Joel, had arranged an airport service to pick her up, so Avery was surprised to see Mischa standing in a group just past the security checkpoint. Heat spread through her body, and she flushed, hoping her response wasn't visible to the crowd around her, but all anyone would have to do is breathe in her body casting off scent and warmth in a pheromone advertisement. *Sick,* she thought. *You are sick.*

"A-vary," Mischa said as she approached, reaching out a hand to take her carry-on. "Aren't you surprised to see me? This is a surprise, I think."

She nodded, unable to talk, desire and nausea cutting off her voice. He was clean-shaved, and she smelled the shaving cream under his cologne. She clasped her hands, holding her fingers back from the line of his jaw, the long silhouette of his European nose, the lift of his hair over his forehead. Avery realized she knew him well enough to remember the tiny scar in his eyebrow, a parenthesis of flesh in the light curve of hair.

"I have called the service, and they will not be coming. So I will take you to the meeting, *krasaritsa.*"

Ignoring the new endearment, she thought of work. It was good to talk about work. She was glad he hadn't said anything about taking her to her hotel, where there was a room with a door and a bed that this particular hotel chain promised would be the best she'd ever slept on. She'd grab a cab after the meeting, and then she'd call Dan and find out if Galvin Gold had called again.

"So," she said, clearing her throat. "Your people are on board?"

"Oh, yes," Mischa said. "They will go where I navigate them."

As she followed him out the automatic doors and into the hot St. Louis air, he turned and smiled, his eyes like a reflection of the sky in a Florida puddle—a murky overlay of past and history and underneath, the pure blue. He reached out and took her hand, and she shut her eyes for a second, feeling his different hand, fuller and smaller than Dan's, holding her in another way. She pressed her skin against his, feeling guilt and sorrow and disgust under her flesh, and then pressed harder so she could have only this moment, now, now, now. Like her yoga teacher always said, "Stay in the present."

Responding to her squeeze, Mischa turned to look at her, and she imagined a future with him—a family with Mischa, not with Dan. A blond-haired, blue-eyed Georgian baby. A different baby. A different life.

They crossed over to the parking garage, still holding hands, the wheels of her carry-on *skid-scratch*ing on the asphalt. She tried to smile, and she held her stomach, pressing back the memories of Daniel carrying his skateboard, Dan in the kitchen reading the receipt, the crack of the phone when she hung up on Galvin Gold.

"That went well," Avery said, sliding into the cab, tucking her skirt carefully around her thighs. "I would never have thought it would go so easily."

"A-vary. What did I tell you? Once I said the word, they would agree. It was a matter of having us both in the room. By this time next week, we will be working on office system in Phoenix. I will take you to my favorite restaurant. Or better yet, I won't." He reached for her hand, and she let him take it.

Avery pushed a strand of hair behind her ear, trying to think about anything other than the pounding in her crotch. In a half hour, all her ache could be gone, Mischa and she in bed, making use of the heat and desire swirling through her body. And maybe she wouldn't ever have to go home, staying in the air at all times, every week off to another office, checking in by phone once a day, a week, a month, and then not at all. Daniel could grow up without her; Dan could remarry, find a wife to whom he'd tell the truth right away. And she could have Mischa, who wooed women at work, bringing over caviar, Stoli, the red wine he talked about all the time, and his sexy Georgian accent. She pulled her hand away and opened her purse, looking for anything.

"Tonight, though, I want to take you out, *ptichka*. You brought a celebration outfit, I hope?" Mischa dug in his pocket for his cell phone. "I will make reservations."

Outside, the business day went on, bicycle couriers flitting through traffic, pedestrians ignoring red lights and running across intersections, cabs honking at one another in a secret language. What was happening at home? she wondered. Had Galvin Gold come to take Daniel away? Maybe he wanted to steal him and then ask Dan for support. All Dan had told her was "He's a mean-hearted son of a bitch. He shouldn't be around kids. He shouldn't be around anyone."

Avery looked up as the cab slowed and stopped.

"Here you are," the cabbie said.

Mischa clicked off his phone and handed the man a twenty. "The change is for you."

Avery started to open her door, but stopped when Mischa smiled and shook his head, got out, and walked over to her side of the cab. "Please," he said, "let me."

As she began to slide out, her nylons slipping on the leather seat, she thought, *No. Don't go. Stay.* She imagined her hand on the door handle pulling the door closed. "Go," she could shout. "Airport." And the cabbie—always having waited for one of these moments after watching a hundred cabbie scenes in the movies and on TV— would accelerate through traffic, saying, "Lady, I knew this was going to be one hell of a fare."

At the airport, she would call Dan, tell him, "I'm coming home. I'll call you when I land." She would hang up and go to the bathroom, ignoring her wet underwear, the drumbeat in her womb and skin and breasts. All this feeling was as fleeting as a postcard she might hang on the refrigerator, throwing it away when the writing yellowed and the person who sent it was forgotten.

But Avery didn't say a word. She didn't pull the door closed. Instead, she took Mischa's hand and lifted her heels over and out of the door, standing up beside him, leaning into his body.

The bed was as promised, soft, luxurious, comforting. Mischa sat on it, watching her as she opened her carry-on, hanging up her other suit, smoothing out the wrinkles.

"Do you want a drink?" he asked. *What about morphine or heroin or nitrous oxide?* she thought, wanting the next minutes to take her into a coma.

"What does this bar have?" Avery turned back to her unpacking, putting her panties and bras into the dresser drawer, zipping up her bag and putting it in the closet.

"No Stoli, I am sure. Or caviar." Mischa winked, and she thought of the night he'd sat in a chair across from her, watching her, listening to her, not asking anything with words, although she'd felt his questions all the same. She'd felt his desire for her from the moment they'd met, the way their eyes connected when Ed in the St. Louis office asked stupid, repetitive questions about implementation, writing the same answer down at least twice on his yellow pad, his toupee shifting as he nodded.

Mischa and Avery both liked things to be perfect, neat, clean. But this wasn't clean or neat. She was married to a man she thought she still loved but maybe didn't like so much anymore. Mischa knew very little about Dan and nothing about Randi and Daniel, the drugs, and the stealing. She'd never mentioned a word about Isabel and her long depression or how her father died too young, before Avery knew all the things she wanted to say to him. He didn't know a thing about the IUIs and the exploratory surgeries or how she'd lain on exam table after exam table. And certainly, she didn't know a thing about Mischa except what he'd told her between meetings and on short, choppy phone calls. He was from Georgia, where they drank strong red wine and the summers were hot and lazy. Not the peaches-and-cream Georgia. The original. He was a computer genius. He was beautiful. It was possible he had as many secret stories as Dan did—a family in Europe, wife, kids, parents, siblings, all waiting for him to come home. Maybe worse. Maybe desperate stories, sad stories, crime or jail or sex stories. She didn't know anymore what people could hold inside and live with.

Mischa handed her a drink, clinking her glass with his. The glass was cold, ice-filled, and she shivered. "Here's to you, A-vary."

She took a sip and swallowed, feeling as if the liquid were going nowhere, her body weightless, the drumbeats stopped, everything below her neck in another dimension. With her eyes, she saw him put his drink down on the table and take off his jacket and move toward her, his hand setting her drink next to his. She felt his touch on her elbows, his hands gliding up her arms, pulling her even closer as he held her shoulders, her back. She shut her eyes because if she couldn't feel anything and now couldn't see, none of this would be happening. But then the drumbeats started up again, her skin feeling the pressure of his embrace, her nose remembering his smells, the still-present layer of shaving cream and cologne, her tongue taking in the taste of his mouth—gin, tonic, warmth—her heart pounding as it hadn't in months, not since Daniel had slipped into their house through the phone lines. Not since everything became a lie.

She let herself kiss him and then forgot she was letting him do anything, kissing him back with lips and tongue and teeth and hands. She pressed against his body, which was leaner than Dan's—*forget, forget*—and tighter, her hands at the small of his back, the muscles flaring away from his spine in hard, beautiful arcs. Pushing at him with her hips, she felt his erection through their business clothes. She hadn't had sex with Dan since that night they did it in their sleep, remembering the rhythms from before their lives cracked open, and now her body felt full and ripe and ready.

"You are so beautiful," he said, kissing her temples, hair, cheeks. "Perfect." He grabbed her hair in his hands, strands between his fingers, and whispered, *"Lubov moia, sladkaya."* Closing her eyes, she hoped the words were kind. They sounded kind, gentle, his voice holding them softly, giving them to her with his mouth and hands and body. But she didn't know, and she couldn't ask, her breath too high in her throat for words.

She leaned against his shoulder, rubbing his back through his shirt. He yanked at his tie, pulling it off, holding her tight as silk slid across silk, his hand steady on her back. He began to push down her jacket top, and she pulled away, still feeling his body on hers, her skin a map of heats, red where his legs had pressed, rose where his hand had stroked, vermillion where his lips had touched.

"Let me . . . ," she said, lifting her hand toward the bathroom.

He nodded, untucked his shirt, unbuttoning, undressing. She turned and walked into the bathroom, closing the door behind her, leaning against the wood. Squinting against the bright lights that flickered off glass and marble and brushed nickel faucets and towel racks, she lifted her hands and watched them shake. Gripping them together for a moment, she closed her eyes, imagining her yoga teacher, the breathing, the body open and empty and pure, full of nothing and then nothing again. The moment. This moment.

She opened her eyes and brought her hands toward her chest, rubbing the palms together, both so cold, like everything in this bathroom. Breathing out, she slowly began to unbutton her jacket, one brass button, and then another. She hung the jacket on one of the padded satin hangers on the back of the door, then slipped off her skirt, and laid it flat on the counter.

Turning on the water, she stuck her hands under the faucet but then didn't know what to do except watch the water run over her hands and splash onto the marble. The minute after she picked up the soap, rinsed, and wiped her hands, she'd have to go back into the bedroom. It had been so long since she'd slept with anyone other than Dan, who knew and liked her smells. *Don't. Stop.* Should she clean herself as she used to do in college, ashamed of the smells that feminine hygiene sprays promised to eliminate? She'd been on the plane and in a long meeting; no deodorant was that good. Holding up her arm, Avery bent her head and began to sniff, when she caught her reflection in the mirror. There she was, her arm raised over her head, her armpit darkened with a slight stubble, and yes, she did· smell. She needed a shower. Her hair was hanging lank on her shoulders. She put down her arm and stared at herself, her skin slightly green in the mirror, her body different from when she was at home, sort of lumpy. Her hips and thighs and stomach were lumpy. Her face looked mottled, her mascara smudged, her toes slightly purple from cold.

There was a thump from the bedroom outside the door, and Avery pulled away from the sink and grabbed a towel, holding it to her chest, feeling her heart pulse hard until she remembered what she was doing. Mischa was waiting, wanting her, even though she looked like this? But he hadn't seen her like this. He didn't know her at all. It was Dan who knew her, who wanted her even if she couldn't have a baby. Even though she had turned from him since July, ignoring everything, even his son.

Avery shut off the water and stared at herself, bending close, looking at her eyes, the way the blue was speckled with darkness, browns and even blacks. Dan had made mistakes, forgetting they were mistakes, thinking that what he was doing was right. And then, years later, he'd figured out what he wanted and hid the past, scared that Avery would see him like she was seeing herself right now. Sitting down on the toilet, her elbows on her knees, she could see how easy it was to fall into what wasn't right, to stay because mistakes often felt good before you realized the error. They felt like Mischa's hands and lips. They felt like his erection under his pants. They felt like her mother's long naps, her hazy grief, the worn, slightly dirty sheets that almost smelled like her husband. They felt like delirious nights and days on an apartment couch, Randi's reality softened by whatever drugs she could get. They felt like the sun on Daniel's neck as he crouched in the sandbox, the minutes slipping into the grains of sand on his cheek, the up and down of his breath, the noise of school echoing far away.

Avery stood up, turned, and stared at herself again, her long arms and legs, her stomach slightly pouched out because she had missed so many days at the gym due to work. Mischa was wrong. She wasn't perfect. She wasn't even good. The soft Russian words were not meant for her at all.

Grabbing a white cotton robe off a hook behind the door, she put it on, tying the belt tight, knowing that she would go into the bedroom and embarrass herself and humiliate Mischa by saying no. She would probably lose a client and the entire Dirland account. Later, Brody might even want to fire her. In her other life, the one before Daniel, everything she was deciding now would have seemed like a terrible mistake. "What will people think?" she'd have asked herself, worried about the stares from people in the office, Lanny's sarcastic laugh, Brody's raised eyebrow, Mischa's glare from across the dark hotel room. But by making this choice, she was finally right.

Of course, by the time she'd turned off the bathroom light and opened the door, Mischa was under the covers, naked, his clothes laid out neatly on a chair. Belt, pants, underwear, socks, shirt. He'd prepared carefully—two condoms were tucked into the corner of the bedstand, their dark purple wrappers shining in the flickering light from the candles he'd lit. She looked away.

"Mischa," she began.

"A-vary," he said, pulling back the blankets. There was his thigh, smooth and almost hairless, his hip, chest, shoulders. "Come to bed."

"Mischa."

"You have already said that."

"I know." She sat on the desk chair, holding the robe so her knees didn't show. "I've made a mistake. I'm sorry."

He blinked a few times, his blue eyes there, gone, there, gone, and then he pulled himself up to a sitting position, his mouth tight. She felt goose bumps scurry up her skin, the hair at the back of her neck rising. The Mischa of minutes ago was gone. He could be crazy. He could force her to have sex, rape her, hurt her. She'd led him on, he'd say, and it would be partly true. She hadn't let go of his hand at the airport until they'd reached the car. She'd leaned into his body, opened her mouth to his, felt his skin under her palms. She hadn't said no until they'd both taken off their clothes. Avery swallowed and tried to find her voice.

"I—I'm not ready for this. I thought I was. Really. I'm very attracted to you, but I think I'm doing it for the wrong reasons."

"What could be more reason than this?" He brought a hand to his heart. "I am not understanding you at all."

"My husband," she said.

"Oh, this. Always this American guilt. Always this husband at home who suddenly is important. I ask you, where was he before?"

She had to be soft and reasonable, and he had to leave, now, without hurting her. "We've had some trouble. My husband—he found out he had a son from another relationship. A ten-year-old boy. He's living with us now, Mischa. The boy's mother died. I didn't . . . I don't know how to deal with it. That's what I was doing here, and I'm sorry. Really."

Mischa stared at her, and she held his gaze as long as she could. Just as she was sure she needed to bolt to the door and run into the hall in her robe—his face had flushed, become hard and angry—he cocked his head, nodded, and sighed. "This must be difficult."

"Yes. That's why I wanted to do all the traveling." She was almost panting with relief. "I haven't figured out how to, well, how to be."

"So," he said, sliding out of bed and grabbing his pants and underwear. "I will go."

He kept his back to her, slipped on his shirt and tie and jacket, and turned to her. She stood up and crossed her arms. "I really don't know how to—"

"Never mind that. I think I will go back to the office and try to make some more money for the company and go out for a few drinks. This, I can do." He sat down on the chair and tied his shoes, his hair hanging over his eyes. He pushed it back with one hand and almost smiled.

Grateful, she moved toward him, but he waved her off. "No more. That's enough. And Avery? I hope that maybe your company can send someone else on the trips for a while. What about that terrible Lanny person? He, I don't want to look at. It is good, yes?"

"Yes," she said, opening the door and letting him pass, a yard of air between them. "It's good."

Avery went into Dirland in the morning and gave the presentation to the company's representatives from other offices, passing out the implementation calendar, handing out Lanny's card to everyone. "I've got a family crisis," she said. "Lanny will take care of everything."

As the day went on, she swallowed the anxiety that burned in her throat, smiling at the right times and clicking her PowerPoint presentation at just the right tempo, the audience murmuring its appreciation for her organized lecture, clear demonstration, the sharp blues and greens and lively fonts on the projection screen. Mischa was nowhere to be found, and she silently thanked him for the way he had left the night before and the way he had left now, letting her clean up and get out.

Back home at the Oakland airport, Avery hailed a cab and was silent for the entire twelve miles to her house, ignoring the cabbie's comments about the state's budget problems, the lack of significant rainfall, and the Raiders' prospects for the football season. When they pulled up in front of her house, she paid him and stepped out, breathing, it seemed, for the first time since last night. She closed her eyes and listened to her street, to the whine of lawn mowers, the cabbie turning into a driveway, backing up, accelerating, Steller's jays squawking in the bay laurels and oaks.

"Avery?"

She jerked her eyes open and turned. Val was standing in front of her, with Tomás in his brand-new backpack. "Val. Hi." Avery let go of her carry-on handle and looked at her friend. Valerie was tired, with circles under her eyes, her shirt stained by carrots or sweet potatoes, a swirl of orange on her sleeve. Her Keds were fraying and spotted with dark drops—garden dirt, beet juice, pureed green beans. Her pants weren't ironed, and neither were they entirely zipped, Val's waist not having gone back to her prepregnancy form yet. Maybe it never would. Maybe this was what Valerie would look like from now on.

Tomás crowed, waving his hands, a smile on his face, and Avery felt her insides melt and fall, leaving nothing but her heart—beating, beating. She wished she weren't in her suit or even in clothes at all, wanting the fall air to wrap around her. She wouldn't even care if Ralph Chatagnier or Frank Chow saw her lumpy thighs and greenish skin. She wouldn't care about anything.

Avery walked over to Val and smiled, putting her arms around her friend and the backpack, hugging tightly. Tomás squealed and patted Avery's head, saying, "Maaa!"

"What is it?" Val asked, her voice muffled in Avery's shoulder. "You're home early. Are you okay?"

"Maybe," Avery answered. "Maybe I am."

"What happened? Is it something with Dan?"

She pulled away from Val and looked up into Tomás's face, his little head like a smiling happy pumpkin. Since her father had died, she'd made it a point always to know what she was going to do. That's why she'd gone back to work. That's why she'd cancelled her appointments with Dr. Browne. If she could plan, if she could make the decisions, then she was in control, wasn't she?

She sighed and looked down at Val's splotched Keds. If she were Dan and had to hear what she held inside, she'd pack her bags and suitcases and kick herself out of the house. She'd slam the door and then go to the yellow pages to find a locksmith. She'd learn to live without herself, learn to forget she'd ever existed.

"Aves, what is it?"

Avery shook her head and reached out for Tomás, letting him curl his hand around her index finger. "Nothing. I hope. I really do."

The house was quiet. In the kitchen, the dishes were rinsed and stacked in the sink, one lone marshmallow Lucky Charm on the counter. Avery wet her finger and pressed it on the blue star and brought it to her mouth, the piece dissolving into sugar between her teeth. Outside, Dan had covered the pool, and leaves skittered across the plastic top in circles. Two slightly deflated blow-up balls lay on the glass table.

Avery put her briefcase on the counter and pulled off her jacket. All she wanted was to take a shower, wash away all of St. Louis, work, and Mischa. Then she would call Brody, even though she didn't know what she was going to say to him. Already, she'd ignored his three messages on her cell phone, each one starting with, "Hey, Avery! What's going on?"

As she turned to go down the hall, the phone rang. She stopped, listening, thinking it could be Brody, but he called her cell only. Maybe it was that Anita, needing someone to come pick up Daniel because he'd gotten in trouble again. Avery turned, moved to the phone, and picked it up. Maybe it was Dan.

"Hello?"

"You again."

Avery drew in air and felt her knees lock. "What do you want? I know who you are."

"So you know the whole story, huh? You know about your hubby and my daughter? Those two bums. Then he takes off and leaves her with a kid. Nice guy, huh?"

Holding the phone tight to her face, she was silent, listening to his breathing. "What do you want?"

"That's my grandson you've got there. I think little Daniel needs to get reacquainted with me. Then he and I can take some nice trips—maybe Florida. I've always wanted to go to that Key West. That Hemingway place. Those fish—what are they? The ones with those spiky noses. I don't know. Hawaii's nice, too. Maui, I've heard. But I think that Dan could front us a little bonding time. Won't be a thing to him now, big Cal man with the high-tech job. Not a thing at all."

Avery shook her head. "That boy doesn't need anything but his father," she began, suddenly remembering she was supposed to tape the phone calls. She glanced around the kitchen for Dan's tape recorder, but she couldn't find it. Instead, she grabbed a pen and a notepad and started writing down what Galvin had said. "And you didn't seem to need him while your daughter was alive. We are going to take care of Daniel. We are going to give him a home. We're going to bond with him. Not you. So stop calling here, or we are going to have to get the authorities involved."

She slammed down the phone and breathed out, dropping the pencil on her scratchy handwriting: *bums, takes off and leaves her, high-tech job, Key West, won't be a thing to him now.* She didn't even know this man, and she wanted to kill him, hating his raspy voice, his calm extortion, his greed. She shook her head and then looked up to see Flora and Daniel in the kitchen door, both wide-eyed and silent, Daniel staring at her so hard, she wanted to turn away.

"Who was that?" Daniel asked.

Flora squeezed his shoulder. *"Mi'jo,"* she said. "Let's get your snack."

"Who was it?" he whined. His face was pale, his eyes still on Avery.

Rubbing her forehead with the tips of her fingers, she didn't know what to do. Wait for Dan to come home to explain everything slowly and thoughtfully to his son? Lie? Tell Daniel the caller was a salesman or the Barnetts wanting him back in their foster care? Or a prank call? Avery wished she could just disappear like smoke in a breeze and materialize hours later, but this was what she'd been running away from for months. This avoidance was what had made her take Mischa's hand and bring him up to her hotel room, kiss him and push up against his body. Galvin's phone call had been ugly, but so were secrets.

"It was your grandfather."

Daniel paused and looked up at Flora, whose lips were pressed in a tight line. *I did it wrong,* Avery thought. *Flora knows how to do this better than I do.* Turning back to Avery, Daniel stared at her, but this time, it didn't bother her. He wasn't trying to annoy her or bother her, he just wanted to know what was going on in the house—in his house. Avery's heart bumped in her chest, and she imagined what it would feel like to hug this little boy.

"Which one?" Daniel asked. "The one that will be here this weekend?"

Avery started—she'd forgotten that tomorrow Bill and Marian

were coming. She would be home after all. "No. Not Dan's dad. Your mom's dad. Galvin Gold."

"What did he want?"

"I'm not really sure," Avery said. Flora shook her head, and Avery closed her eyes and breathed out. "Well, he seems to want to see you. But he's not asking in the right way. Do you know him well?"

"Kind of."

"Would you want to see him?"

"Why do you care?" Daniel asked, letting his backpack slip to the floor. "You haven't cared before. You don't even like me."

"Mi'jo," Flora said, but Avery glanced at her and raised her eyebrows, wanting his words.

"You're right. I haven't been around. I haven't helped you enough." She walked over and bent down, putting her hand on his arm. "I'm sorry. I just— I was jealous. Dan had a child and I didn't. I didn't know how to make you my child. I still don't. But I want to try."

She tried to keep her tears in the corners of her eyes, but they spilled over, and then she was leaning against the cabinets, her hands on her face, sobbing. Crying for the Dan she never knew. For all his pain. For his parents. For her father. Isabel. The baby, who didn't have a room anymore. Daniel without a mother. Randi. Randi having to live with Galvin Gold. Herself in the hotel bathroom, lumpy and green and adulterous. Everything inside her body, even organs she didn't really understand—pancreas, spleen, appendix, duodenum— seemed to pulse and burn. Behind her eyelids, blotches of red and yellow hovered and faded, until everything was black. All this feeling and memory and pain came at once, in the kitchen, Flora clucking over her, and then a soft, small hand fell on her shoulder, patting her, saying words he must have learned from Randi, "It'll be okay. There. There."

Twelve

When Dan came home from work, Avery opened the door, her eyes runny and bloodshot. She didn't give him enough time to ask her why she was home, instead handing him the yellow notepad, her hand shaking. "He called again. He wants money. He's using Daniel."

Dan looked at the scratchy writing on the pad, unable to focus on the words. Why was she home? And why did she look so awful? He stepped inside and put down his briefcase, remembering the phone conversation they'd had back in July, the quiet noise behind her in the St. Louis hotel room and her insistence that she was alone. So there really was someone else, and she was going to tell him. She'd come home to pack. To tell him that it was over. To leave.

"Dan! You've got to call the police. He can't harass us like this. He's a bad man. He'd hurt Daniel."

Us, Dan thought. *Daniel.*

"I know. You're right. Where's Daniel?"

Avery looked over her shoulder. She was still in her travel suit, the collar unbuttoned, her part (usually a straight strip of white scalp) crooked, her hair almost knotted in the back. "He's finishing his homework. I sent Flora home. She has a new granddaughter, you know."

Dan swallowed and looked down at the floor, wondering if he and Avery were really having this conversation. Already, it had gone on longer than most of the talks they'd had in the past months, and he couldn't move away, even if he was supposed to call the police and Midori and Vince. He didn't want the conversation to stop.

"Did Daniel hear the phone call?"

"Yes." Avery motioned him to come closer. "He asked me what he wanted. We talked about Galvin."

She smelled like airplane food and silk and herself. Not the self usually covered with Estée Lauder or one of those smooth, milky lotions on the bathroom counter. Not her work body, perfumed and deodorized and powdered. She smelled like Avery in the morning after a night of sleep . . . like Avery after sex, the warm, tan smell of her skin salty, slightly oily.

"What did you tell him?"

She rubbed one eye with two fingers and sniffed. "I don't know. It probably didn't make sense. He knows something's wrong."

"What do you mean?"

She dropped her hand from her face and looked at him, her blue eyes glassy and exhausted, her mouth twitching with tears. "I kind of— I was upset, that's all. You better talk to him, okay? And then call the police. I'm so tired. I've got to take a shower." Avery reached out and grabbed his arm, and Dan put his hand on hers, holding it there, not wanting her to leave. Because he knew that's what she was going to do. She was being nice and concerned because she felt guilty.

And then she leaned in, closer, and rested her head on his shoulder. He looked down at her messy hair and brought a hand up to hold her, to let her rest, to try to bring her back to him.

"Dad?" Daniel stood in the doorway, staring at them. Avery jerked away and walked down the hall toward the bedroom.

"Hi, kiddo. How are you?"

"Avery's upset," Daniel said. "There was this phone call from my other grandpa."

Dan watched her walk down the hallway until she turned into the bedroom and closed the door behind her. Something was so different, her body dense and scared and heavy, her eye makeup smeared, her nylons snagged, a long, thin run up the back of her left calf. She'd been crying and she'd needed him, leaning against him as she used to. But why now? What did she want? What was she going to do?

Daniel hit the toe of his shoe against a floor tile and pulled on the lock of hair behind his ear. Breathing in and turning away from the hallway, Dan walked over to his son and picked him up, even though he was ten years old and struggled against the embrace.

"I'm too big!" he said, his body stiff. "This is baby stuff."

But Dan didn't listen, pressing Daniel's skinny body against his chest, feeling the rapid beat of his boy's heart against his own ribs. And then Daniel's head was on his shoulder, just as Avery's had been, allowing the embrace, holding his father around the neck, accepting Dan's tears.

"So what are we going to do?" Dan asked Vince on the phone. "If we can't get a restraining order, then what?"

"It's hard to restrain someone who is only calling on the phone. It's harassment, but my advice is to change your phone number. If he starts coming by the house, that's another story. If he starts calling your work, as well, then we can move on it. But it's only been a few phone calls at this point. I don't think any judge is going to do much with that."

Dan paced the patio out by the pool. Daniel was watching a television show while he heated up the goulash from earlier in the week. Marian's recipe. "But what am I supposed to tell Daniel? He's already asked Avery what the call meant. This can't be good for him. We were just starting to get into some kind of groove here."

"You're right. It's not good for him at all. But you can only do what you can do—and then, when we have to, we'll get the law involved. It's not like we can control Daniel's entire environment. You can't do everything."

Dan nodded at Vince's words, but he didn't like them. He hadn't ever had control of Daniel's environment until now. And then what had he been able to give him? A house where the husband and wife were barely speaking? Where a long-missing grandfather wanted to whisk the child away to a drinking vacation in some sleazy Florida hotel? Where the other set of grandparents hadn't even met him? "Okay," he said slowly. "Fine. But Vince?"

"What?"

Dan breathed out, thinking of his father. When Dan first didn't obey Bill, he'd lost his toys and then his playtime outside after dinner. Jared and all his friends would be running around the street as Dan sat looking out his bedroom window. Later, he lost nights out at the movies or the television. Finally, he lost the family altogether, the police escorting him away from the front door. The sergeant had said, "Kid, don't come back for a while. Things have a way of working themselves out. Understand?" But things were still as bad for Dan as they'd ever been, worse even, with both Avery and Daniel barely here at all.

"Galvin can't take him, can he? I know I've asked this before, but there isn't some legal precedent I don't know about, right?"

Vince breathed a pause into the phone, and Dan felt the veins in his neck pulse under his ears. *Say no,* he thought. *Please.*

"He could take you to court to sue for custody. Stranger things have happened. But with his background, it's unlikely. From what you've told me, I'm sure he's not interested in bringing up the past."

"He doesn't have the right to Daniel or anything, does he? I am the father."

"Oh, God, no," Vince said. "You're the father. Everyone who is important—the court, the doctors, Social Services—acknowledges that. Don't even think about that."

"You don't think he's going to snatch him, do you?"

Vince was silent for a moment, and Dan thought of all the children who disappeared each year, taken mostly by strangers who did terrible things to them, but sometimes by estranged mothers or fathers or righteous, insane, or confused grandparents. He would have to teach his son to be careful. He would have to alert Flora—maybe he could dig up an old photo of Randi and her family and point Galvin out. *"Peligro,"* Dan would warn her in his high school Spanish. *"Este hombre es muy peligroso."*

"He wants what he can get out of you, but Daniel would probably be an annoyance to him," Vince said. "From what you've told me, he wasn't such a great father to Randi. Maybe he thinks you'll pay him off to leave you alone. But don't be tempted. People like that always come back for more."

"All right."

"Just keep taking notes if he calls before your number gets changed. Same thing at work. Hopefully, he'll give up."

Dan closed his eyes and heard the sound of a beer can hitting Randi's closed bedroom door, a cackle of laughter, the television blaring, and then lumbering steps to the kitchen and the slamming of cupboards. When Galvin was around, he was all there, loud and annoying—but, he'd disappeared, too, leaving Randi to waste away on her own. To die. Maybe he would go away again.

"Thanks, Vince," Dan said, looking into the house. Daniel stood at the French doors, watching him. "I've got to go get Daniel dinner."

"Right," said Vince. "That's exactly what you should do."

"So my parents are coming to visit tomorrow," Dan said as he waited for his plate to cool a bit, the noodles, meat, and sauce steaming. "They want to meet you."

"What are their names again?" Daniel asked. He picked a baby carrot out of his salad and popped it in his mouth. Dan had discovered that the only vegetables his son liked were raw carrots, iceberg lettuce, and cucumbers drenched in Good Seasons dressing, so they had all three in a tossed salad almost every evening.

"Well," Dan said. "Their names are Bill and Marian. You can call them Grandma and Grandpa, though."

"I don't even know them." Daniel blew on a forkful of goulash. "They don't even know me."

"You're right. What do you want to call them?" He began to eat, crunching the noodles that had begun to crisp and brown while he talked with Vince. Daniel seemed to think about what names to call them, and Dan thought that his son had the right to yell out, *jerks* or *losers* or maybe something more Randi-like, such as *dipshits* as Marian and Bill walked up to the front door.

That would get them all out of this visit, his parents turning in a huff and driving home at fifty-five miles per hour even though the speed limit had changed to sixty-five during the Clinton era. But he had no idea how his parents would act, especially if Daniel came at them with the potentially worse Grandma and Grandpa. Calling them Bill and Marian or Mr. and Mrs. Tacconi was probably the way to go. But he didn't care at this point how they felt about Daniel or the name he called them. Dan was worried about Avery in the bedroom, sleeping so heavily, he could hear her breathing from the hallway. He was worried about Galvin Gold out in the world, hatching an evil plan; and he worried about his boy, in front of him, feared that someone else would take him away.

"What do you think?" Dan wiped his mouth.

"I'll just call them their names. Like Avery."

"Sounds like a plan. So, what about this phone call?" Dan began, putting his fork down. "Tell me about it."

Daniel nodded. "Avery got really mad."

"What do you mean?"

"She was like hecka yelling at him and told him that I needed to stay here, with you. She said that I live here, with you guys." Daniel put down his fork and pulled on the lock of hair behind his ear. "And then she hung up the phone and started crying. She said he was asking for things in the wrong way."

"And how did you feel about that?" Dan said, feeling the shadow of Bret Parish behind him.

"I don't know." Daniel let go of his hair and looked down at his plate.

"I mean, it must have been weird to hear that and then see Avery crying." Dan was leaning forward, almost touching his plate with his chest. He caught himself and pushed back, trying to look unconcerned.

"It was weird when she sat on the floor, but then Flora got me my snack."

"The floor?"

"I told you. She was hecka mad. Can I have some more cucumbers? Cucumbers only?"

Dan served him some more cucumbers—sneaking in one carrot—and then let Daniel eat in silence, the sound of his crunching echoing in the dining room. Nothing about Avery was making sense today, not her early return in time for his parents' visit or her reaction to Galvin Gold, to him, to Daniel. If she was preparing to leave him, she was doing it in a strange way, killing them all with concern before she picked up her bags, jumped in the BayPorter, and rode out of their lives.

"Dad!" Daniel was looking at him. His plate was empty.

"What?"

"I'm done. I know I have to say 'Can I be excused?' So, like, can I?"

"Yeah, sure. Clear up."

Daniel looked at him with a 'Duh!' expression, picked up his plate, and took it into the kitchen. There was the sound of running water, the clink of plate against dishwasher rungs, and then footsteps down the hall.

Dan looked around the house for things he needed to do for the get-together tomorrow. But the housecleaner had been here the day before, and the furniture shone, the carpets still had vacuum marks, and aside from tonight's dinner dishes, the kitchen sink and tile were spotless. Outside, Ramón—rehired and making up for what he saw as Dan's lazy pruning—had hedged to within an inch of every crape myrtle's, redbud's, and rose's life. The lawn was an immaculate green thatch of growth, red and gold leaves swirling across it. Loren was bringing appetizers. Valerie and Luís had promised to be in charge of the barbecue, and would be bringing over *carne asada* and *pollo preparado*. Isabel was bringing her famous green Jell-O salad, and Jared was in charge of dessert. There was nothing left for Dan to do but go into his bedroom, wake up his wife, and ask her the questions he needed to ask.

The bedroom was stuffy, the warm afternoon stuck between the walls, pulsing. Avery slept on her side, a hand on the pillow, her mouth open. Her skirt and jacket top were on the floor, her nylons wadded in a ball, her pumps kicked off into the corner. Dan walked slowly into the room and stopped, staring at her purse. The answers to his question were probably inside the black leather. All he'd have to do is reach in and pull out her cell phone, Palm, receipts. Out in the living room, he could listen to her messages, find out the secrets she'd been keeping from him, uncover where she'd really been and whom she'd been with. Then he'd have her over a barrel, just as she'd had him. "You lied to me!" she'd cried. "You didn't tell me anything!"

Now, with all the evidence Dan was sure he'd discover, they'd be even. But it was probably too late. She had someone else without the baggage of lies and a child and a past. Dan closed his eyes, wanting to turn and leave. He'd wait until after this weekend to confront her, after his parents left. How would he possibly get through tomorrow, though, with Avery on a plane heading toward another man? It would be easier, as it had always been, to run away, as he'd done before.

Avery breathed out and turned onto her back, lightly snoring. Dan opened his eyes and almost laughed. "I do not snore," she'd insisted on their honeymoon. "I have never snored in my entire life. Once I stayed awake to listen to myself, and I don't."

"What?"

Avery had blushed and covered her face in her pillow. "I've never heard it," she said, her voice muffled.

"I'm going to tape it for you. Wait, I'll give you an example." Dan had breathed in hard, exhaling with a puff. "A lady snore. Not too bad. Not like the guys in the frat."

"Oh!" She had punched him in the shoulder, and they both laughed, holding each other, not caring about snoring or anything but each other's lips and hands and bodies.

Sighing, Dan walked toward the bed and sat, looking at Avery. It had to be now. Whatever she needed to do should happen tonight. He'd call Isabel or Loren to watch Daniel, and then he'd drive her to the airport. He'd pack up her clothes in boxes and drop them off at eight a.m. at UPS. The first thing he'd tell Daniel, Jared, Val and Luís, and his parents would be the truth. Right away. And then he'd go on.

"Dan?" Avery looked over at him and yawned. "What time is it?"

"Almost eight. You've been sleeping for hours."

She sat up and pushed her hair back. Half-moons of mascara hung under her eyes. "I'm exhausted."

"Hard trip?"

"Did you call?" she asked suddenly. "Did you find out what we can do about that asshole?" Avery licked her lips; her eyes focused.

"Vince wants us to keep a log of his calls and change our phone number as soon as possible. We have to be aware of who drives by. That kind of thing. I've got to talk with Flora about this. But we can't give in to anything Galvin says. He has no claim at all."

"Of course he doesn't! You're the father, for Christ's sake." Avery folded her arms and yet looked like she could weep. "That poor boy."

"Daniel?"

She nodded and wiped her eyes. "God."

"Aves. Aves?"

She shook her head and breathed in. "I'm okay."

"Are you?"

"What do you mean?"

Dan scooted closer to her, his hip next to her thigh. "Something's happened. You're home. You weren't supposed to be. Brody called earlier and said that he'd been trying to reach you for hours. He wouldn't leave a message. What's going on?"

She looked down, biting her cheek in the way she always did. Once he'd made a point of feeling the inside of her cheek with his tongue, running it over the bitten sides as she laughed and then pushed him away. "You're finding out all my quirks," she'd said.

He'd tried to find them those first months of knowing her, wanting to make sure she was flawed—flawed enough to want him.

"Aves."

"I—I don't know." She wouldn't meet his eyes.

"You can tell me," he said.

Dan put his hand on her thigh, and she glanced up, her eyes full again. "I'm sorry."

"For what?"

"For everything since July."

"It's not your fault," he said, scooting even closer.

"But it is. You don't know— I've been so gone, Dan. I didn't know how to deal with the stories you told me. I felt like Randi had moved into our house and was changing everything. It was like she was here, even before Daniel came. I could almost see her. But I was wrong. And now it's too late."

Dan stared at his hand on her thigh, his skin almost gray in the bedroom darkness. He'd been right. She was going; she was being nice because in some way she still loved him and didn't want to crush him. As she'd been crushed by the news of Randi, Daniel, and his other life.

"No, it's not," he blurted out. "It's not too late at all. It will get better. It is getting better. Can't you tell? You bought him the skate-board!"

She leaned forward and grabbed his shoulders. "It's not you, Dan. It's not even Daniel. It's me. I've screwed up. I made some mistakes, and I don't know how to be anymore. I can't *be* at work. I can't *be* here. I don't know how to fit into anything anymore."

"What mistakes?" he asked, closing his eyes, feeling her grip on his shoulders.

She let go and sat back against the headboard. "I screwed up."

"How?"

"Oh, Dan. I don't know how you could want me for a wife. Or even around Daniel."

"What did you do?" he asked. His stomach broke apart into a hundred fires, and he tried to keep his mouth from trembling.

Avery nodded. "I—I almost did something stupid."

Almost. Almost. Dan was silent, listening to the word in his head.

She sniffed. "I started to—to get involved with a man I met in St. Louis."

"The man in the room that night." Dan felt the words on his tongue like rotten fruit. He pinched his lips, hearing the man's breaths as he sat behind Avery on the bed, seeing the man's laughter as Avery waved him into silence as she talked.

"Yes," she said, nodding. "But nothing happened. Nothing im-portant."

"What would be important?"

"Having an affair. Having sex. Sleeping together. It didn't happen."

"What happened?" Dan asked, letting his mouth go slack, feeling his tears in his cheeks and throat. He wanted to bolt out of the room, and he wanted to hear. It was how it felt when he watched *Nightmare on Elm Street* when he was little, covering his eyes with his hands but leaving space to see through his fingers. Even though it was horrible, he had to know.

"We kissed. He wanted to—maybe I did, too," she said, almost gasping. "I wanted not to be home, in this mess, trying to figure out this life. I wanted a new life. Something to make me feel not me. Not this. And he was there. It wasn't about him, really. I was running away. That's all."

"What's his name?"

"Dan, don't ask. It doesn't matter, does it?"

"What's his name?"

"Mischa."

"Did you love him? This Mischa?"

She shook her head. "No. But I wanted to. I wanted to have an excuse to leave, but when it came down to it, I thought about us. You. Daniel. How we—how we're a family. Even if it's messy and ridiculous and not the way I wanted it at all. That's why I came home, Dan. That's why I'm here now. That's why I'll stay, if you want me to."

Dan took his hand off her thigh and stared blankly, feeling everything as if from a distance. Tears cooled on his cheeks. This was what he'd wanted, wasn't it? She wanted to stay with him. He wouldn't have that strange life he'd imagined, the house run by Flora, Ramón, and a housecleaner—Irma? Edna?—he didn't even know by sight. He'd already pictured the vacations he and Daniel would take to Disneyland and Hawaii, the two of them a sad, uneven couple on the roller coaster or on the beach. The dinners out at Sizzler and Applebee's, the cartoon or action movie matinees. Back-to-school night, class Christmas parties, open house. Softball games, swim lessons, shopping trips at Macy's. "Where's the wife?" people would say as he walked by. "What's wrong with him?"

Dan swallowed. "Why?" he asked, knowing the answer.

"I don't know. I know, but I don't."

"I don't understand. You were mad at me for keeping Randi a secret."

"Yeah."

He thought of that song from years back, the one about irony, the rain on a wedding day, the no-smoking sign on a cigarette break. He'd finally understood irony when he heard the song, and when he found out about Daniel, he felt it. Could he add this scene to the lyric, getting your wife back after she's tried out another man? Was this irony?

"Dan?"

He wanted to get up and throw something. He clenched his hands, feeling the sledgehammer heavy in his palms, hearing the crack and split of the crib. But everything was already broken. That was the real irony. His life had come back together in pieces. He'd worked so hard to fix it since Daniel came into his life, but he hadn't been able to do so. Not without Avery. And she wanted to stay. With him. With both of them. He breathed that idea in and out, and let it sit in his chest, along with the facts of his and Randi's and Daniel's story, Avery's running away and coming back, her arms around another man's shoulders, and everything they'd both done since July.

It was hard to see his wife in the dark, so he leaned over and turned on the nightstand light. They both blinked and then looked at each other. The room was warm in the light, the mess of the rumbled bed and the tossed clothes somehow comforting, as if nothing had changed. But everything had changed. For one thing, Avery and Dan hadn't had a conversation this long since before the Fourth. Dan stared at her, her hair ratted from the pillow, her eyes weepy with dark circles, her lips pale and slightly cracked. Breathing in, he smelled her in a way he hadn't before, something disgusting pricking his nose, the smell of her arms holding another man, her lips—those dry lips—pressing against another's neck, face, forehead. What else was different? What had happened to her breasts and to her vagina, lust and desire changing the very cells that were geared for him, hormonally stimulated for him! All that work of making their two bodies function together, and she had touched someone else.

Dan grimaced, acid in his throat. He hardly recognized her. "What do we do?" he asked.

She reached out a hand, but he wasn't sure if he could touch her. She'd held this Mischa in the way she'd held him, and he bit down hard until he felt his jaw ache. She'd been confused, upset—but so what! "Avery," he said, shaking his head. "Oh, God."

"Dan?" Her eyes were wide, her hand still outstretched.

He took her hand and closed his eyes. Even though she looked and smelled like a different woman, at her touch he remembered everything—their wedding, the way her smooth hand fit into his, her touch at night while they were asleep or making love, the way she waved her hands when she told him to fix the sink faucet or take out the trash. It was she. Avery. She was still here. She was still herself, just as Randi had been herself even while addicted to drugs.

"Let's just figure it out as we go on, okay? I don't know what to do about it all now."

Avery looked at him as if she had something else to say, but she sighed and nodded. "Okay."

"It's going to take a while. For everything. For us."

"I know."

"I can't believe you—"

"Neither can I," she said, and he looked at her eyes, blue and wet. "I can't believe anything."

She turned off the light with her free hand, and they sat there in the dark, the sound of Daniel's TV show slipping under the door, the long Friday shutting down.

Thirteen

Despite the ache in her body from the plane ride yesterday and the constant acid wooze in her stomach, Avery got out of bed as she had for all the months and years before the Fourth of July. There were things to do.

Dan was still asleep. Last night, they'd sat up for a half hour in the silent darkness before Daniel had knocked on their door, and then Dan stood up and left the room. Avery had leaned back against the pillows, listening to the sounds of bedtime—running water, laughter, the steady sound of Dan's voice reading a story—and then it was morning, Saturday morning. The day Dan's parents were coming to meet Daniel for the first time. The day Avery was back home, feeling like she'd been gone forever.

In the kitchen, she opened the fridge, looking to see what Dan had planned. There were green salad makings, but not much else. He must have farmed out the rest of the food, she thought, realizing that this would probably be a party that included the whole clan, even Val and Luís. She picked up the phone.

"Hello," Valerie said. Tomás was gurgling in the background. Avery imagined him on Val's hip, his eyes huge as she bounced him up and down.

"It's me."

"How are you?"

"I'm sorry, Val. I'm so sorry."

Tomás squealed as Val passed him to Luís, and then there was the rustle of fabric and the sound of footsteps as Luís carried the baby away. "For what?"

"For everything. For being a shit. For being jealous and mean and thoughtless. Whatever else there is. Whatever else I was. Am."

"Oh, Aves. You've been in the weirdest situation. I know that so much of it was the news about Daniel."

Avery shook her head and sat at the kitchen table. "No. It was before. I couldn't bear your good news. I couldn't stand that you got what I wanted first."

Val was silent. Avery wanted to put down the phone and run next door and make amends with her whole body, not just with words. If she could hold Val's hand and look at her and touch her shoulder, maybe her friend would forgive her and they could go on like before. Avery knew that when she told Val the truth about her dark ugly feelings, Val might not want to see her ever again. But she had to say it all.

Val sighed into the phone. "I would have felt the same way."

"What?"

"I know I would have. When you went for all your tests, I kept thinking, thank God it's not me. I did. Once I was pregnant, I knew I could never not have been pregnant. I knew I couldn't have waited for Tomás."

Avery's eyes pricked with tears and anger and sorrow. She thought she had shared those months of tests and pills and shots and office visits with Valerie, and all along, her friend had been secretly chanting, *It's not me; it's not me.* It had been the same at the party after her father's funeral, all Isabel's friends hugging her, holding her hand, promising assistance, help, and kindnesses, when Avery had seen them thinking, *My husband's at home alive. My husband isn't dead. It's not us. Not me.*

And then after the first busy weeks—casseroles and cookies and phone calls arriving at all times of the day—there was silence and distance, as if Isabel and her children were under quarantine, with death on the doorknobs and sink faucets, in the entryway air. No wonder Isabel took to her bed. Under the covers, her mother couldn't hear the empty house and the dead phone.

But who in their right mind would want what Avery had gotten? Who wanted infertility and a husband with a secret life and a ten-year-old boy? Who wouldn't want to run away from such bad news? Look at what she'd done when Dan told her about Randi, skipping out of town the minute Daniel showed up. She was the same as Isabel's friends and Val. No one had to ask her forgiveness for anything.

"Oh, Val. I know. We both wanted a baby. Why would you wish your own happiness away?"

"Aves," Val said. "I wish it could go back the way it was before. I miss you."

"It can't go back. It's going to be different. For all of us." Avery breathed in, putting her hand on her stomach. "It's going to be new."

Val sniffed into the phone, and Avery wiped her eyes. "Listen," she said after a moment. "I didn't call for this great apology scene. I really need to know what in the hell we're all eating today."

They both laughed. Relief and sadness and joy beat in Avery's chest. She felt lighter, as light as her voice reaching up into the telephone wire, floating in the electric air.

"Avery," Marian said, walking up to the front doorway. "You look . . ." Her mother-in-law searched for a word that wouldn't offend. Avery wondered what Marian really wanted to say—different, tired, fat, ugly, maybe just bad. She was sure that the day in the hotel room with Mischa glowed purple on her skin and her constant avoidance of Daniel was tattooed on her shoulder like a black flower. But she was surprised when Marian said, "Radiant."

"Really? Thanks." Avery folded Dan's mother into her arms, surprised again by how strong Marian was, her bones long, her body solid. For some reason, Avery always thought of her as more like Isabel, thin and wispy, light as dried flowers.

"Is he here?" Marian pulled away and looked over Avery's shoulder. "The boy?"

"He lives here, Marian. Of course Daniel's here."

"Yes, right."

Bill locked the car door and walked slowly up the path, stopping to examine the chrysanthemums that had just opened in wide, bronze flowers, and the last of the Mexican sage. Finally, he came up behind his wife and placed a hand on Avery's arm. "Good to see you, Avery."

She smiled and wished she could close the door. If she thought about it, she could recount each of the short visits they'd made to this house, stiff hour-long sits in the living room, Marian asking, "Did you make that? Did you find that fabric on your own?" And Bill wanted to know the exact fertilizer Dan used on the lawn or the specific week in January he thought he'd trim the plum trees. She used to laugh when they left, mimicking Marian, saying, "I whipped it up in a jiffy on the Singer," not knowing then how important those cold, strange visits with Dan's parents were to him.

"Come on in. Everyone's in the backyard," she said.

"Everyone?" Marian asked, following Avery down the hall.

"Oh, my mom and my sister and her whole family. Luís and Val. You remember them from next door. And Jared, of course. He brought an amazing chocolate cake. And my mom brought her famous green Jell-O salad. You missed it on the Fourth."

Neither Bill nor Marian said a word, and they all walked through the house and then out onto the back patio. Dan had pulled back the pool cover, and he, Daniel, Tomás, and Luís were in the water. Tomás floated in a plastic baby tube, and Luís, Dan, and Daniel stood next to him, spinning it and laughing. Jaden, Sammy, and Dakota were sitting on patio furniture as Loren tugged swim fins and goggles onto them. Jared and Loren's husband, Russell, stood over the gas grill, discussing the optimal temperature, and Val and Isabel sat on the picnic table bench, talking.

"Dan," Avery said. "Your parents are here."

Dan turned and smiled, walking to the side and pulling himself out of the pool. He grabbed his towel and dried off quickly. Even though he was still smiling, Avery could tell he was nervous. "Hi, Mom. Dad," he said, gesturing to his damp state and holding out his hand, shaking his father's hand and squeezing his mother's.

The talking and noise had stopped, all eyes on Bill and Marian. Avery wanted to run inside and close herself in the bedroom and wait for the awkwardness to pass. Why had Dan invited so many people? she wondered, slowly moving forward, leading Bill and Marian to Isabel and Valerie, who had stood up. But as Isabel began to say hello,

Avery looked at Dan and saw why he needed the crowd. He was scared. For himself and his boy.

"It's so nice to see you," Isabel was saying, shaking Bill's hand. "Oh, my. It's been a long time. And this boy." She motioned toward the pool. "What a sweetheart."

As they looked toward the pool, Isabel held her hand out to Avery, and Avery took it, pressing tight, saying what she could with her squeeze. *Thanks. Thank you. I'm sorry.*

Bill gave Isabel a flat smile, but Marian turned to watch Daniel, her eyes on him as he dived under the water and shot up next to Tomás, like a slick, wet seal. "Boo!" he said gently, and Tomás squealed.

Jared put down the thick steel barbecue tongs and spatula and came over to his parents. He moved smoothly, hugging his father and mother easily, their bodies accustomed to each other, the shifts of arms and chests practiced and routine.

"Dan." Bill was businesslike. "Nice day you've got here. The garden looks good."

"Lovely," Marian agreed.

"Please sit down," Avery said.

Dan stood silent, pale, and then he nodded. "Yes. Can I get you both a drink?"

"Soda for us both. Too early to get anything else going," Bill said.

Dan went to the cooler, and Avery motioned to Valerie, and then to Luís, who was still in the pool. "You remember our neighbors the Delgados. Val and Luís have been a big help to us with—with our new situation. And you've met my sister Loren and her husband, Russell, and my nephews."

Luís waved from the pool, and Valerie shook the Tacconis' hands. Avery could see Val searching for something to say, her mouth open slightly, the tip of her tongue touching her front teeth. But nothing came out, and she simply nodded and smiled. Loren and Russell both nodded and smiled, too. Avery knew that given the chance, everyone else here would rather be at home.

"Here you go." Dan handed them both glasses of Coke. "Daniel, please get out of the pool and dry off. There are people I want you to meet."

Daniel swam to the edge, his skinny arms twirling in the water. Avery remembered what she heard her swim coach say once: "It was like a manikin factory—arms and legs everywhere." Next summer, she'd take Daniel to the club and enroll him in lessons, practicing with him afterwards. She'd show him how to keep his head down and pull his arms past his hips. After a few weeks, his arms would glide into the water as if he'd been swimming all along. Maybe later, she'd take him to Isabel's and show him her medals, trophies, and newspaper clippings.

All the adults watching him, Daniel pushed out of the water and grabbed his towel and walked toward them, dripping, with his hair slick against his face. Avery wanted to hold up a towel, cover him, and push him into the house, promising him anything—ice cream, computer games, television—just so Bill and Marian wouldn't see what she saw now: Randi from the photos, dark haired, freckled, smiling, all elbows and knees and ankles.

Dan saw it, too, and almost seemed to be nodding, as if Randi were standing behind Daniel, her shellacked nails resting like exotic shells on his shoulders, as if she were saying, "He's my boy. Look at him! One hundred percent mine-oh-mine."

Unable to swallow, Avery stepped closer, reaching out for Daniel until Dan stopped her, pulled her close from behind and pressed her to his chest, his hands holding her upper arms. She felt his wet trunks seep against her shorts, but she didn't move.

"Mom, Dad. This is Daniel. Daniel Tacconi."

And then, as the afternoon stilled into fall heat—the pool a silent wash of blue in the background, Dan's body warm behind her, her mother, her sister and her family, best friends, and brother-in-law near her—Avery watched Bill and Marian smile slightly, shake Daniel's hand, ask him about school and his friends and his bedroom. Nothing cracked open; no one cried or shook or blew away with the leaves dropping from the Delgados' sycamore tree. Now, they all knew the truth about everything, except for one small thing.

She hadn't been able to tell Dan about the test she'd done in the bathroom before her nap yesterday afternoon, peeing on the wand she'd bought at the drugstore in the airport. The flight home from St. Louis had scared her; her stomach was churning, her head pounding, her body bloated. *Food poisoning,* she thought. *Or worse, brain tumor. Stroke.* Stomach cancer, just like her father. This was how it had started, after all—the terrible indigestion and fatigue. But somewhere over Nevada, she thought back through the months since July. For a couple of cycles, she'd imagined her body was reeling from Clomid, lurching back to normal by shutting down and recalibrating. Then she'd forgotten altogether, what with Daniel and work and Mischa.

As she'd wheeled her bag out of the terminal, she spotted the Pay Rite and bought the test, almost shaking her head as the clerk rang it up. Right. One night of sex, the time she didn't even think Dan remembered, both of them half-asleep, drugged with dreams. After the surgeries and tests and shots she'd been through, she'd be crazy to think that one night would do it. It was a waste of money, but if she wasn't pregnant, she was dying. Either way, she had to get home to Dan and make him forgive her.

And then, through a fog of sleepiness making her clumsy and slow, she stared as the wand changed color. Blinking her eyes and staring at it, she sat back on the toilet and watched the bathroom wall stay the same yellow. Her whole body was pulsing. She wanted to scream and cry out, not for the baby, but for her and Dan, for what they could have. But she wasn't sure how Dan would react. He might tell her it was too damn late. He might not want this baby at all.

She'd pulled off her nylons and gotten off the toilet, walking to the bed, dropping her clothes as she did. Five minutes. She'd sleep for five minutes and then go find Dan and tell him the whole story.

But even though he held her now as Daniel smiled up at Bill and Marian, Dan was too raw for the grand, ironic finale. She'd wait until he could hear what she had to say; she'd wait for Daniel to feel more at home with all of them, his grandparents and neighbors, family and parents.

The air crackled with a gust of cooler air and leaves, and then the moment was over. Daniel rushed back into the pool, Luís spun Tomás in the tube, and Bill and Marian settled next to Isabel, Valerie, and Loren around the picnic table. Jared and Russell returned to the barbecue. Dan still held on to her arms and she let herself lean into him, her husband she'd returned to.

"Aves," he whispered into her ear, "I think it will be okay."

He kissed her over the ear and went back into the pool, splashing Daniel and laughing, picking up his son and throwing him high as everyone watched.

Avery wished she could say "Yes, it will be okay" so loud that everyone could hear, but somehow Mischa Podorov and Randi Gold had slipped in and gotten comfortable on the lawn chairs. She knew she wasn't ready. It would take a while for that sexy Georgian ghost to slink away, turning the corner with his jars of caviar and Stoli and dark red wine. Randi would be with them as long as Daniel was, but she wouldn't always be standing before them, clicking her long nails.

And Galvin Gold lurked somewhere, ready to leak out like more bad news. But Avery knew how to deal with that, didn't she? She'd finally learned something.

She closed her eyes. She would never have planned for this life, listing it on scraps of paper, organizing minutes and hours into this exact day to create the scene out by the pool. Slowly letting out air she seemed to have gulped in the moment all those months ago, when she first heard Midori Nolan on the phone, she listened to the long-ago voice of her yoga teacher, finding the moment in the light fall air of her backyard, feeling the rightness in all of it. Dan and her. Daniel, Isabel, Loren and Russell and their children, Marian, Bill, Jared. Luís and Valerie and Tomás. The fullness in the center of her belly.

The sun flickered in white flashes on the water. Avery blinked. The moment was over, and she found the next moment and the next, turning to go sit with her mother and sister and best friend, feeling the fullness expand from her belly to her heart, until she felt it everywhere.

ACKNOWLEDGMENTS

As usual, without the help of my tribe, this novel would have been impossible to write. Thanks to Jill Christofferson, Donna Downing, and Sue Graziano Adams for sharing their fertile experiences. My writing group—Gail Offen-Brown, Marcia Goodman, Julie Roemer, Keri Mitchell, and Joan Kresich—read it all and gave me the tools to make it work. Susan Browne held me up through the planning stages and then the hard writing, commenting on every idea and character. Without her help and enthusiasm, I wouldn't have gotten through the first draft. Cody Cummings shared his experiences with me honestly and thoughtfully. My uncle Brad Randall gave me information that didn't make it to this draft, but I thank him all the same. Kris Whorton, Lisa Wingate, and Carole Barksdale read portions via e-mail, and I always think that deserves a medal (or a back brace). Tom Barber helped me out with geography. Dina Krayzbukh helped with language. Mel Berger, my agent, was there to counsel me through the rough times, and my editor, Ellen Edwards, again, pushed me to a better story—again, I appreciate you both so much. Thanks to Serena Jones and Julia Fleischaker at NAL. Finally, my family—Mitchell, Julien, Jesse, Carole, and Bill. Thanks for it all.

JESSICA BARKSDALE INCLÁN

One Small Thing

This Conversation Guide is intended to enrich the
individual reading experience, as well as encourage us
to explore these topics together—because books,
and life, are meant for sharing.

A CONVERSATION WITH JESSICA BARKSDALE INCLÁN

Q. Infertility is a subject that's frequently explored in fiction. Why did you particularly want to write about it in One Small Thing?

A. One of the big issues for me as I contemplated this book is how we are driven—no matter who we are or what our socioeconomic status, race, or culture—to reproduce. So often in papers and magazines, I read about couples who have "everything" yet are trying to have babies, going through months and years of tests and procedures. Friends of mine have taken fertility drugs, injecting themselves daily. They've gone for ultrasound after ultrasound and basically worried themselves sick over the process. Some people I know have then— when Nature failed—taken trips to dangerous locales to pick up their adopted children.

I can't imagine how demoralizing trying to have a baby must be when it doesn't work. I was "lucky" to get pregnant without trying. (Maybe we were just a bit surprised.) But my experience as a mother tells me that the bond between parent and child is ancient, archetypal, fundamental—in our bones. Many of us—men and women— feel we have to reproduce as part of the human experience. And when we can't, we feel as if we have not lived up to our potential, as if we haven't fulfilled our earthly promise.

Of course, not all people feel this way. Not at all. And I don't think that having a child necessarily makes you a better person or a more enriched person or a happier person—in fact, some of my most painful moments on this planet have been because of being a mother. But so many women do feel this biological urge, and so many women—like Avery—go through the intense, often embarrassing and humiliating process of trying to get pregnant.

Q. Are pregnancy, childbirth, and raising children important themes for you?

A. Yes! In fact, I cover different but similar ground in each of my novels. The most important thing I've ever done in my life is have my two boys—nothing else has come close; nothing else matters as much, not teaching or writing—and I am always exploring those powerful emotions in my stories.

Q. What other themes occupied you while writing One Small Thing?

A. I thought a great deal about the past—how we really can't hide from it. How we have to acknowledge it to ourselves and to those we love. No matter what, the past creeps into the present. Lying never works. Hiding never works. Avery hides from her past—not wanting to talk about her father or deal with her mother's depression—and Dan lies about his life with Randi and his years of drug use. Daniel is a living symbol of Dan's past, and there is no place Dan can go to avoid the consequences of his actions. Not that he wants to avoid Daniel. But he wants to avoid what Daniel's existence actually means—that he lived the life he did with Randi.

Of course, facing the truth about the shameful things we've done, or about the painful experiences we've endured, is hard. Flat-out hard. And that's why we avoid it. But sometimes—as with Dan—circumstances force us to either confront the past or run from it. In Dan, I wanted to show a character who has developed enough maturity—and perhaps security—to stop running.

Q. Avery is a prickly woman, and it's not always easy to like her. What drew you to her and made you want to not only explore her but also place her at the very center of your novel?

A. In some ways, I am like Avery. I have control issues—I want to keep tabs on my life, my career, my family. It's one of the things I try to keep in check. But in other ways, I'm not like Avery at all. She's curt, quick, able to compartmentalize. As I was starting this novel, I wanted to write about someone who has not kept her control issues in check and now wants what she wants immediately—although she is willing to work hard for it. As Avery developed as a character, she became more different from me, and I realized it was enjoyable to write about someone who is not nice, who does not follow the "traditional" female role in some ways. Her transformation during the novel—though she is still holding the cards at the end—was also gratifying to watch. And it was reassuring, too. People can change if they want to.

By planning everything to the nth degree, Avery has the false conviction that she's got a handle on her life. She thinks she can force her life into a perfect box and orchestrate every important moment of her career, marriage, and children. But the irony of trying to control things is that no matter how tightly you hold on to all the loose ends, one, two, three always fly away from your hand. And when you get ahold of those, others slip free. We can't control a thing. We can pay attention, be prepared, and learn how to react when the unexpected occurs, but we can't control events or stop people from behaving according to who they are. No matter how much Avery pretends otherwise, Dan's past is there, a part of him, and no amount of ignoring him or Daniel can change that. I think the biggest part of Avery's growth comes when she realizes that she can't make the whole mess disappear.

Q. Dan's ex-girlfriend Randi is a colorful character. Can you describe how she came into being?

A. As I was writing, I realized there was another voice trying to speak to me. It was Randi. And though she was not really a "good" person in terms of behavior and background, she was a live wire, a creature of spontaneity, a polar opposite of Avery. In a way, I think Avery had to take on some of Randi's qualities in order for her life with Dan to go on. She had to see the good part of Randi and Dan's relationship—which includes Daniel—and then accept it. I also felt sorry for Randi. She was a product of her parenting, and while I don't like the choices she made, her "ghost" voice helped Dan figure out how to be a parent to Daniel.

Q. Who is your favorite character in the novel?

A. I have been accused of writing "not so nice" male characters, but I must say that Dan is my favorite character and the one I feel closest to. Avery and I are not very similar, but Dan with his tender heart, his guilt, his desire to hide is more familiar. He needs the sense of control that Avery projects; he needs something different from the loose, crazy life he and Randi had. I also admire how he chooses Daniel over Avery—how he plans to go on and be a good father regardless of what Avery chooses.

Q. Did you approach writing One Small Thing *any differently from the way you wrote your previous novels?*

A. Two summers ago, a friend who wanted to write a novel asked for some help plotting her story. As we shared our thoughts, I decided that it would be fun to work on our novels together. So we brainstormed ideas for what became *One Small Thing,* and then we met every week or so, reading bits aloud and swapping written portions. I have always had a writing group—and they read this novel as well—

but it was fun to work with a close friend, both of us engaged in the "same" project at the same time.

With this novel, I also kept a novel journal. Before each day's work, I would write down what I imagined would happen to the characters, but I did not hold myself to anything. At the end of the day's writing, I would write down what I imagined would come next in terms of plot, character development, and themes. With all these notes, I laid some great groundwork. A novel journal is also a great place to write down the inspirations that come at odd moments—like at dinner or in the middle of the night.

QUESTIONS FOR DISCUSSION

1. Avery desperately wants a child of her own. Do you, or have you, felt a similar desire, or do you know other women who have felt this desire? Why do you think some women feel it so strongly while others don't? Do some men feel it equally strongly?

2. Today, women seek out expensive, uncomfortable, and complicated fertility therapies in their quest to have children. In your opinion, how far should couples go in trying to have a child? What therapies do you consider unethical, and why? Where should we as a society draw the line?

3. Avery seeks perfection in every aspect of her life. Do you know other women like her? Is her perfectionism typical of upper-middle-class suburban women, and if so, why do you think that is? What personal, social, and perhaps even professional pressures might be pushing them toward such perfectionism? What might be some positive and negative aspects of such perfectionism, in individual lives and in society as a whole?

4. How would you feel if your husband or boyfriend brought home a child you knew nothing about? Given your unique set of circumstances, do you think that, like Avery, you could ultimately accept the child into your home, or would such acceptance be impossible?

5. Do you sympathize with Avery's shock upon learning that her husband had a "secret life" that she knew nothing about? How would

you feel and react if you learned that someone close to you—especially the man in your life—had a sordid past that he had deliberately kept hidden? Do you think it's common for women to fear that they're married to men they don't really know?

6. Avery almost has an affair with another man. Why do you think she's tempted to break her marriage vows at this particular time in her life? Do you understand and sympathize with her reasons for almost giving in, and for her reasons for ultimately remaining faithful to Dan? Would your feelings for her have changed if she'd succumbed to temptation?

7. Who's your favorite character in the book? Your least favorite? Why do you like or dislike them?

8. There are many mothers in *One Small Thing*—Randi, Isabel, Marian, Valerie, and in the end, Avery. Discuss how each woman is a "good" and/or "bad" mother. Can you begin to identify some of the qualities and behavior that, in your opinion, make a good mother? Do the same qualities and behavior make a good father?

9. When Avery's father died, her mother, Isabel, withdrew into depression, which had a deep effect on Avery and the way she coped with the world. Would you feel comfortable sharing moments in your life when, like Isabel, you weren't able to "be there" for your children or when your parents weren't there for you?

10. Daniel comes to Dan and Avery as a ten-year-old who has endured an unstable childhood and the trauma of having been abandoned when his mother died. Do you find Jessica Barksdale Inclán's portrait of Daniel believable? Touching? Do you think Daniel will suffer long-lasting effects from his troubled early start, and if so, what might they be? Is there evidence in the novel that he's resilient enough to overcome his past and grow into a secure and happy child?